I0653866

THE MERMAID KILLER

WRITTEN BY:
JOSEPH MIGUEL

ALSO BY
JOSEPH MIGUEL

TRIANGLE BLACK:
A NOVEL

THE MERMAID KILLER
By Joseph Miguel

First Edition

© 2024 JOSEPH MIGUEL

Publisher: Scorched Pages

This is a work of fiction. Names, characters, places, and incidents either are the products of the author's imagination or are used fictitiously. Any resemblance to actual persons, living or dead, businesses, companies, events, or locales is entirely coincidental.

All rights reserved. No part of this publication may be reproduced, stored in a retrieval system, or transmitted, in any form or in any means – by electronic, mechanical, photocopying, recording or otherwise – without prior written permission, except as permitted by U.S. copyright law.

Visit the author's website at: www.JosephMiguelArt.net

For permissions contact:
J.Mig1982@gmail.com

ISBN-13: 978-1-7359926-2-4 (E-book)
ISBN-13: 978-1-7359926-3-1 (Hardback)
ISBN-13: 978-1-7359926-4-8 (Paperback)
ISBN-13: 978-1-7359926-5-5 (Audiobook)

"Hell is empty and all the devils are here."

— WILLIAM SHAKESPEARE

1

‘1998’

I'll start the only way I know how—I'm a *killer*.

A murderer, fiend, psycho bitch. The intellects may even call me degenerate. It's all fine by me. I wasn't always like this, you see. At least not to such a degree. Then again, I wouldn't want you running to grab your tissue box at my expense.

Don't bother.

Does it matter, though? In the grand scheme of the plunders of humanity? The art of stealing life or strictly fantasizing about it? It's not easy being the monster under your bed, you know. The cold shadow that slithers through your streets at night.

Waiting . . . for that perfect moment.

But that's what I am, and there's nothing you can do about it.

I can conceptualize what you must think of me. You probably want to shut your eyes and quit reading. Or throw this manifesto of jumbled chicken scratch across your cozy bedroom. Or maybe chuck the little bastard in the fireplace.

I understand.

I do.

I'm not *all* bad, you see. I have feelings and dreams and desires, like you. I like animals and play the guitar. Well, I used to. Those trivialities seem all for naught now. Even writing on these dirty floorboards sitting cross-legged feels insignificant.

Is there a point to my telling? Will someone get the chance to digest or understand my gory plight? I can hope, but I doubt it will change a thing.

I'm on the cool floor in my underwear. It's an unusually hot one in my Golden State. My apartment has become my tomb, a personal playpen for my deepest and darkest desires. It's nice to be free, to be out of that prison after so many years.

This fan I boosted from a drug store off Fickle Street isn't doing the trick with the heat, but it does feel nice to be in my own little world.

I've never had that, you see.

Had what, love?

"Not now—I'm trying to write."

Answer me.

"You already know."

I want you to say it.

"Freedom."

～∞～

It's different when she's awake. The world seems to breathe when I breathe. The plants pulsate and speak, the skies move and sway, like a musical coursing through me. The cityscape tilts and shifts like a game of wacky Jenga. Entire city blocks become pieces in the wooden game, ready to be plucked away until everything comes crashing down. Colors are never black and white, brown or blue.

They never are in my world.

Especially when I'm around.

There are different variations when she takes over—such rich vibrance and colorful saturations. We can study a gaping knife wound or a severed head for hours, becoming lost in the sinews that make everything imperfectly human. She can break down a tree in the middle of Golden Gate Park with her eyes of rich sable, reducing the organism to atoms and exploding stardust.

I can stare at myself in the mirror after a kill, watching our eyes marvel at what's left of me. She can see right through me, into my skin, down to the calcium in my bones. My face warps and melts away, mutating into both her and I—me and her.

She is me . . . my world, my one and only.

I love laying here, alone, in my lair. I haven't acclimated yet, but it's growing on me. This apartment was vacant for five years before I arrived. At least that's what the old fuck landlord told me. I can't stop fantasizing about the possibilities. I was fortunate enough to purchase a waterbed with a cheap frame at a used furniture store off Ashbury. It appears waterbeds are finally going out of style.

To hell with the 90s, anyway.

All the girls my age wear baggy jeans and sweatshirts. I like that look, but not around the clock. I find myself missing the 80s. Not my life, but the style and entertainment.

I do have the basics in this one-bedroom hive. I've done a lot in the eight days I've been here. The old rusty fridge to my right works fine and the bathtub water is lava hot. I'd prefer carpet like I had in Kentucky, but this dark hardwood is easier to clean.

Everything looks old, which I'm fond of. The kitchen sink is showing wear, and the cabinets need major work. All I need is the basics, and I've done a good job of accomplishing that.

~~~

It's dark—I'm not sure of the time.

Who cares?

The sole item that remains from the previous tenant is a pink neon sign above my waterbed. Another woman probably lived here before me. The sign reads, 'hello there.' The 't' in 'there' is damaged, somehow. It dangles upside-down, but all the letters still illuminate.

I like the sign and have left it on since being here. I'm staring up at it now. I've moved my writing to the bedroom chamber. All I need is the darkness and my desires. It's not cold tonight, and one of my two little windows is cracked. I don't have a shade or curtain yet.

I'd better change that—for all my *activities.*

The neon buzzes around me. My bed churns like the sea. Only a thin white sheet separates me from the exposed dark. I'm alive and free, but also cursed. My gills grow wet while my fin flips and flops, exposing itself to the open bedroom air.

This Golden State is my arena, my fishbowl of death, my ocean of chaos to do as I please. I must satiate my perversities; isn't that what life is about? Why cheat yourself of your passions, desires, bloodlust and rage?

Who's watching, anyway?

God?

That's a laugh.

If there ever was a God, He gave up long ago.

Can't say I blame Him, or . . . Her.

I can't find a tangible reason why it can't be a Her.

Why do they call it Mother Nature?

If nature is a woman, then *God* is a woman.

I'd rather not go back, but I absolutely must. I can't start in the middle or the end. This is the only way to justify what I've done. Then again . . . how do you condone the art of murder, the abhorrent lust for such a thing?

Allow me to continue. . .

My hand grows tired from all this writing. My mind is warped and overworked. This is the third pencil I've ground down in under a week. I think I'll go to sleep now. I'll escape into my nightmares.

2

'1993'

"Okay, class. Next on the docket is Richard Ramirez."

An uncomfortable Scarlett McNamara sat in the farthest corner seat at UC Berkeley. Her eyes remained bloodshot after a night of solo binge drinking and choppy sleep. It was her final semester of school since being dropped from the FBI's training program in Virginia.

After her last tour in the Gulf, the Marine had come home and gone full speed to land her dream job as a member of the FBI. She thought she could shake off everything that happened over in the enemy deserts of Kuwait, but no such luck. She'd failed the psych evaluation, forcing her to come back to California and continue her studies in hopes of a job in San Francisco.

She'd struggled even more since she'd come home to the Bay Area, bringing dizzying panic attacks and terrorizing dreams with her.

Scarlett realized how shallow she'd been breathing while she gnawed on a pencil eraser. She closed her eyes and took a giant inhale, making certain she wasn't mouth-breathing again. She exhaled through her nose, feeling her slender shoulders relax for the first time all day.

"Miss McNamara?"

The sudden sound startled her, shooting a rush of cortisol throughout her system. Scarlett's hands began to shake, and she prayed that no one else in class could notice. She kept her face forward, instead of gazing out the window at a swaying oak tree in the Bay Area afternoon breeze. "Sir?"

Her professor was a retired fed who had worked twenty years as a criminal profiler. It was the second day of class, with homicide being the last of her criminal justice courses, after gangs and drugs and general psychology. He smirked while the class turned around to look at her. "You don't have to be so formal, Miss McNamara. Mr. Jenkin is sufficient."

With his black business suit and bright green tie, it would be easy for a marine corps sniper to zero him.

I could turn his head to pink mist from a mile off.

She pushed away the intrusive madness of war and dropped the pencil she'd been nibbling to the floor. It bounced with several wooden clinks. She bent down to pick it up while she answered. "Sorry, sir—uh, Mr. Jenkin."

Jenkin folded his hands at his waist, appearing ready to give a lengthy sermon about angels and demons. "That's all right, Marine. Would you like to tell us what you know about Richard Ramirez?"

Scarlett straightened in her seat and reached back to pull at her ponytail, wrenching her black hair as tightly as it could go. "Certainly. Richard Ramirez, aka the Walk-In Killer, the Valley Intruder, or most notably, the Night Stalker. Ramirez terrorized Los Angeles and the Bay Area in the mid-eighties. Serial murderer, sex offender, sadist. An authentic brand of solo spree killer."

Agent Jenkin paced the front of the room. "Good. Why did he kill?"

"There are many hypotheses. Ramirez was tied to Satanism and drug addiction, along with an abusive upbringing. He was known to degrade his victims, with most being selected at random. He used the hot summer months to strike, crawling through open windows and doors. He didn't have a set modus operandi. Ramirez killed with guns, knives, tire irons, strangulation—he used his hands and various ligatures. He even stomped a victim's face to mush with his shoe. Some say he was taught military tactics from an older cousin, which he utilized during his spree."

Jenkin stopped in the center of the room, half of his body disappearing behind his lecture pulpit. "All true, Miss McNamara . . . but *why* did he kill?"

McNamara pulled her shoulders back, working the case over in her head. "He just . . . *did.*"

Jenkin brought a hand up to his smooth face and massaged his ivory cheek before responding. "That's your answer, Miss McNamara?"

"It is, sir."

Jenkin smiled. "It's too bad the Feds passed on you, soldier. You would've made a fine agent."

Scarlett allowed the compliment to wash over her heightened nervous system. "Thank you, Mr. Jenkin."

Jenkin nodded. "Now, class. We're moving on to child killers. Can anyone tell me something useful about the Menendez brothers?"

Scarlett uncrossed her legs, remembering a newspaper clipping that mirrored Jenkin's question, a quick read she'd found several years ago. A teenage girl in Kentucky had killed her police officer father in self-defense. The mother had also been killed, causing doubts about the girl's innocence. The girl was never arrested, and the father's name was dragged through the mud due to a diary of horrors found at their Kentucky ranch.

The Menendez brothers had been accused of murdering their parents with shotguns in their Beverly Hills home.

Scarlett raised her hand, eager to answer her professor's next question.

Instead, he called on another student, forcing her to ruminate about children who murdered their parents.

3

'THE 70S & 80S'

I grew up in Kentucky, a smallish town called Bowling Green. I was an only child and paid the price for that unfortunate fact. My father, Wade, was the local sheriff, the supposed leader of his band of six cop brothers. Mom was a piece of work. For the most part, she just sat there when things got rough.

I can't recall much of the earliest years of my life, except for the smell. The pungent stink of Busch beer and Big Red gum. An occasional whiskey would join the pitiful party, but Daddy *always* reeked of beer and that gum.

An intriguing fact about my father is that he never smiled. I can count on one hand how many times I saw his teeth. He was a miserable sack of stocky nothingness.

I can tell you that she's *always* been with me.

I do remember a bath I was having. I couldn't have been more than five or six. Wade would either finger me or leave me completely alone in the tub. My goddess would speak to me with him in there with me, soothing my lonely abandonment. She'd whisper at how smart she is and how powerful she can be.

He was too dumb to hear *her*.

I'd listen to her soothing voice while my father exposed himself in front of me, surrendering my trust unto *her*.

Tell him to stop.

"Don't touch me, Daddy!"

Wade zipped up and left the bathroom.

I was alone again with *her* and my favorite rubber ducky.

She told me to sink down, immerse my little head of red fire into the popping bubbles. The light was on when I laid back and let the water take me. I was scared at first, but only at first.

She comforted me, told me to stay under and she would help me breathe like a mermaid.

I must've blacked out because the next thing I remember was Wade holding me in his arms. I was sopping wet, and his flannel shirt was drenched. My eyes flickered open and there he was, my grotesque Father of the Year.

I coughed up a lot of water and writhed in his arms. His face was blank, an unfeeling mass of a fleshy void.

Wade said nothing and slapped me across the face.

I ran to my room and slammed the door.

∞

More memories are floating back now. I remember seeing an injured bird outside of the ranch house. Nobody was around as I nearly stepped on it. I bent my eleven-year-old frame down and pushed up my glasses. The blue jay was alive, but its left wing was mangled.

I didn't know what to do. It barely moved; the thing's one good wing occasionally flapped.

Hit it with that stick.

"Why?"

To see what happens.

I looked around, making sure Wade wasn't nearby. The stick was next to the bird on the ground. I picked it up and brought it close to the injured creature. I whacked it, just once. It made a sound, but it was still alive.

I went into the house and took a small steak knife from the kitchen drawer. I went back outside and showed the blue jay what I'd found. Its head darted from side to side, trying to move. I pressed the knife down into the injured wing.

How does that feel?

"Nothing happened. Its wing doesn't work anymore."

Bury it.

"What for?"

Or Wade will find it.

The soil was soft in that area, so I used my little hands to start digging. The sun had just dipped beneath the Kentucky horizon. The air began to chill, kissing my adolescent face.

I buried the bird alive, along with the knife.

And that's that. . .

My teenage years of school were interesting, with the best times consisting of having cheese fries and suicide drink alone in the cafeteria. It was this hodgepodge I used to make, consisting of orange Fanta, grape drink, Sprite, and a dash of Coca-Cola.

It wasn't until I hit a premature puberty when things took their inevitable turn to the dark side.

We had rabbits and dogs on the ranch, even a horse for a short time. I named the horse Roxy.

She was around for what felt like a blink because she got sick one day. I remember fearing her, at first. I was twelve, staring up at a majestic beast with a brindle coat of regal thickness. Roxy glistened in the morning sun and had the wettest nose. Her eyes were jet black, but there was much more to them if you took a moment to look.

There was also a hint of brown in there, a chocolatey richness that humanity didn't deserve. I got to ride her once or twice—with Daddy's supervision, of course.

When Roxy began to take a genuine liking to me, that was when she got sick. Strange thing was she seemed fine up until all-of-a-sudden. Daddy didn't think so. I was thirteen or fourteen by then. Daddy seemed jealous of the horse, like she was stealing his thunder or something.

He shot Roxy with his service revolver right in front of me. He made me watch. I cried in the tall cornfield just outside the ranch house, begging him not to do it.

"Please, Daddy! Please don't do it! We can take her to get a check-up!"

He stood there swaying with one of those stupid beers in one hand and the gun in the other.

I remember Roxy staring down at me while my father grabbed her reins. She looked confused, but I think she figured it out at the very last moment. Daddy laughed while I cried and begged, trying to intervene in my dirty sunflower dress.

The bullet pierced straight through her ethereal skull. Wade was right on top of her, the muzzle of the gun resting on her sturdy head. The sound of the shot made me jump back and wince, causing my ears to ring. Roxy went down in a heap in the wet corn. I collapsed on top of her and listened to her die, along with the last remaining morsels of Kentucky sunlight.

Daddy always wanted me all to himself, to be at his beck and call, to satisfy him in any way he saw fit. I hated him for that, and I always will. He used that badge and gun as the power to manipulate and coerce whoever got in his way. He wasn't even that good of a cop; at least that's what Mom would say.

Speaking of Mom—Mother—Mommy dearest, she never worked or did much of anything. She drank and popped pills like candy, occasionally giving Daddy an uncaring, "Wade, be nice to your little girl." She knew everything that went on and did nothing. She was a despicable mother, and I got her good.

After Roxy, things got worse. Daddy grew angrier as the years wore on. Mom pretty much gave up. I kept to myself at school and had no friends, especially in the boy department. Daddy was feared in the community, and no one dared cross him.

He killed someone on duty when I was nine. He came home that night and laughed about it. He said the lady deserved it because she was abusive to her husband and threatened him with a knife. It wasn't anyone that we knew in town. If I remember correctly, it had been two outsiders passing through that came upon the infamous Sheriff Wade St. James.

The killing happened in a motel on the very outskirts of town. Daddy enjoyed that day so much that he talked about it over and over, especially when he was drunk around the house.

The first time he raped me, I was eleven. I was in my room. It was late. Daddy came in after another fight with Mother. At that age, I needed light in my room to help me sleep. My micro TV was on with no sound. He didn't say a word, just stripped down in the half-dark and got on top of me.

I remember staring at the TV while he moaned, watching the talking black car show with the man and his leather jacket who fought crime.

It hurt the whole time. I was shocked and didn't know what to do, so I just turned off inside. I wanted to tell him to get the fuck off me, but I didn't know how. I was young and afraid.

How could a father do that to his little girl?

4

'1989'

The night it happened was so wild. I still grow orgasmic thinking about it after all these years. There was a tornado warning. I was just shy of my seventeenth birthday. Wade got home drunk—what a surprise—and Mom was stoned in her room.

It's funny calling my own father by his first name, especially in hindsight. I don't mind. It feels better this way.

He was Daddy because I could do nothing about it for so long. I had no choice. You don't get to pick your family. They are pre-conditioned and destined for us from our first cries out of the womb. The trick is knowing if they are worth a damn. If they aren't, scrape 'em off.

I was doing homework when the wind began to whip outside. The corn was getting brutalized as the sky turned a dark gray. The stalks blew with fury, causing some to snap at their roots. The sirens went off as soon as Wade walked through the door. I got up from the table and looked out the living room window.

An enormous supercell was miles out, mere moments from touching down. The clouds were thick and dark, and lightning zigzagged and exploded within them. A blue tint illuminated the very center of the skyward mass. She was an absolute beauty. Such raw power, a force of nature set only to destroy. Whatever got in her way, she obliterated it.

We sat down to dinner right as the twister fizzled out. Mom could barely sit up in her chair, and Wade was just about out of beer. I had this habit of twirling my hair subconsciously. I still do it sometimes. I was twisting it while hardly eating a thing. Wade's chili tasted like ass, but I'd never admit that to his ugly face. It was always "yes sir" and "oh please no, Daddy" up until then.

Wade was going on about some cop business. He noticed I wasn't eating or paying attention. "What did I say, Holly?"

"Oh, um—you caught another bad guy today?"

"Not as bad as that bitch I iced for attacking her husband with a knife. But close enough."

Wade never had any style within his gloating. It was rudimentary babble from a half-wit who thought he was smart. He wasn't much to look at either—barely 5' 7" with a receding hairline. The last day I saw him alive, I was as tall as he was.

Now here I am, scribbling my own justifications and lustful misdeeds with you.

"Awesome, Daddy."

Wade snorted and belched after a giant swig of Busch. He placed the can of poison down, then his hand flung across the table and smacked me square in the face. My glasses went flying and my spoon hit the floor. The metal utensil jingled while my nose was overpowered with what felt like hot lava.

"You weren't listening to me, Holly."

"I'm s-sorry, Daddy. I have a lot of homework, and the tornado was scary."

"You *always* pay attention—or I'll lock you back up in that room of yours."

I looked over at Mom, who sat there like a zombie. She was shoveling food but saying nothing. It was like she wasn't even in there, a shell of a useless thing. My eyes pleaded in her direction for help, but she never, *ever* did.

Mom was jealous because I was having more sex with Wade than she was. She knew exactly what was going on. I would catch them arguing about it.

She was just as much a monster as he was.

When Wade really got going, he'd handcuff me to my bed for days. He'd come in as he pleased and sodomize me, then watch me relieve my bowels and bladder into a bucket. I'd cry and say I'd do anything if he just let me go. There was always a reason why he couldn't.

It almost makes me vomit that I still call him Daddy. I'll stop. Things are getting more intense, anyway. I'm a woman now. A supreme organism who does her best work in the trenches of the dark. My last night in Kentucky changed me for the better. I wasn't broken. I must staple this fact to your little beating hearts and minds. I was never broken by my mother and father. I also don't want your sympathy. That night, I was transformed into a goddess of power and wickedness.

5

The hail began to pelt the ranch house. Another tornado warning snaked its way into the television set. I ran to my room after Wade smacked me, praying he would leave it alone for the night. I lay in bed and stared at the wall, daydreaming for who knew how long, wishing I was somewhere else.

Outside, the rain and the wind gained momentum. The sirens went off again. I rolled over on my left side to stare out the window. The odds of a second twister after one got so close an hour earlier were next to nothing.

Wade burst through the door as lightning lit his average-sized silhouette. My glasses were all bent on my face, and my Mickey Mouse tank top had specks of blood from the dinner table incident.

My breathing sped up when I saw he was still in his uniform.

His badge glistened in the warm light of the table lamp next to the bed. His utility belt and gun were wrapped around him like a bad habit. He'd usually take the equipment off when he got home, but for some reason he hadn't today. He went for the billy club at his right hip.

My heart skipped as thunder rocked the house. I could feel my cheeks growing rosy and hot from the adrenaline rush.

"You owe your daddy an apology, young lady."

I said nothing. I sat up in bed and switched position to get on my knees. My black shorts ran up my legs, offering a kind of power rush in case I needed to move quickly. Something was washing over me, guiding my body. I was being infiltrated from the inside, but there was no perversion about it. I welcomed it, invited it in all the way. It made me choke once or twice, then it was just there with me.

Like a femme fatale prepared for battle.

"Apologize for ruining dinner and the rest of my night, Holly. School or not, I swear I'll chain you to this bed for a week. Answer me, you little bitch!"

I studied him as he raised his club.

I remember the sound of wood clinking metal before the weapon was fully in view. More rain poured, and hail the size of baseballs landed right outside. The sirens continued to blare. I could hear the weather report from the living room TV. Another twister had begun its wrath the next town over.

"Don't you dare touch me with that."

He swung as more thunder coursed through the house. I wanted him to hit me. I took the first blow in the shoulder. I felt so powerful I barely felt it. All I wanted was his gun. I lunged from the bed and crashed into him as he raised the weapon a second time.

Wade may not have been a big man, but boy was he strong. It was like hitting a piece of iron. My bodyweight barely moved him in the doorway. He grabbed me by the throat with his free hand and yanked me away from him.

"I'm gonna bust up that pretty face so all you can do is suck for a month."

Everything slowed. My skin hardened and felt like armor. It was as if I had another whole person inside me, harnessing both of our strength into one fluent unit.

I spit in his face.

Wade didn't like that. He returned the favor, and a huge spraying load of Big Red and whiskey saliva entered my vision. My glasses protected my eyes, but it dripped down my chin and onto my left leg. He pulled me away from himself, allowing a small distance between us.

The club was about to come down again, but I turned my head and bit down on his free hand. Hard.

Wade's clubbing ceased. He shouldered me to the floor and began kicking. Lucky for me, he didn't have his work shoes on. His smelly socks landed a few, but I caught the fourth and pushed. He fell backward with me on top of him. The wood stick scraped the hallway wall, but Wade still had a good grip on it.

We wrestled around for several seconds, but to me everything felt like an eternity. Time slowed to a crawl, trudging forward as if surrounded by quicksand. Daddy was winning, punching me in the head and pulling my hair while he was laid out on his back. Most of his attempts were grazes, but some landed on my nose and forehead. We both lunged for his revolver at the same time. Our hands met at its holster. Mine was underneath his.

I barely beat the bastard to the punch.

I yanked as hard as I could. The holster gave way, releasing the gun into the open. Wade had my hair in one hand and my free hand in his other. All *our* fighting back was an unbelievable rush. I was enraged, loaded with adrenaline, and weak in the knees all at once. My vision was compromised with his dripping spit, but my thoughts were clear. My clit throbbed in the struggle between life and death. My panties became warm and soaked through.

I'd never felt such a thing in all my life.

Maybe Wade thought if he ripped at my hair hard enough, I'd give up his gun.

He was wrong.

I pointed it right at him. The barrel plunged into his right cheek. I went to pull the trigger, but he swatted it at the last second. The gun went off and the bullet landed somewhere in the hallway wall. We separated as I went to shoot again. He kicked me square in the face. My glasses smashed into my eyes. The force threw me onto my back.

The gun went flying.

Wade scrambled up and turned to run down the hallway. For some reason, he stopped and turned to face me as I found the revolver. He charged forward.

I sucked in a deep breath and fired. The bullet blew into his shoulder at close range. The sound of the releasing firearm was deafening inside the tight quarters. I lost my senses while Wade crashed to the floor. His club went flying.

I'll never forget the squeal he made when I shot him.

He rolled back and forth on the floor, his voice high-pitched as he shrieked, "You shot me, you bitch!"

I got to my feet and approached him. My body was in a full shake. I could barely hold the gun on him. I was so excited I almost couldn't stand it. I towered over his writhing meat sleeve and smiled.

"Goodnight, Daddy."

Pow.

I couldn't believe Mother didn't hear the shots. Then again, she was probably loaded on pills or weed. Zombified and incoherent in the master bedroom.

Wade was dead.

A warm corpse, all thanks to *us*.

I stepped over him and dropped the smoking gun to the hardwood floor. Mom wasn't about to get the easy treatment.

Absolutely not.

I picked up the wooden club and headed for the bedroom.

Mom was in bed—like always. Beer bottles littered the floor, and I almost stepped on a syringe a few steps inside. Her frail body rolled over in the bed, the tired springs squeaking under her weight. "What's going on out there, Holly? Where's your father?"

"It's over, Mother. It's *all* over. I feel so good I could scream!"

She barely noticed that I was holding Dad's nightstick. All I could think of next was she had to die. Before I knew what I was doing, I was swinging.

Like father, like daughter.

She didn't scream, plead, or cry. She took all the hits to her head and body. One knocked her out cold, but I kept hitting her until the twitching stopped. She was curled up in the bed, breathing in wheezing gasps. I got on top of her and grabbed her pillow. I looked over at the TV and caught a glimpse of a movie she'd been watching with a silver machine cop that drove around fighting crime in Detroit.

I looked down at Mommy one last time and placed the pillow over her face.

I stopped smothering her when my arms got tired.

6

I started to panic.

The storm wouldn't let up as the hail and thunder grew louder. All three TVs remained on. The one in my room, the living room with its continual weather updates, and the cyborg policeman in my parents' bedroom. The adrenaline rush ceased in several fleeting moments, almost causing me to collapse on top of my mother's broken carcass. My red-orange hair was sopping wet, my face bloodied and mangled. Wade had fractured my elbow, too.

I had to cover it all up, but I couldn't just call Dad's cop friends and claim I killed my parents in self-defense. I needed a real plan. A drastic one. I looked around the house and thought for half an hour. Then I got to work.

I went back over to Wade in the hallway. His eyes were open, and he'd peed himself. I wanted to bash his skull in with his little wood stick. I picked up the revolver and pointed it at myself. I cocked the hammer and did the best I could to aim for the very edge of my side. My shakes were gone when I squeezed the trigger.

The gun crashed to the floor as I fell backward. I had done a good job with the point-blank shot. The .38 special bullet went right through me, hitting nothing of vital importance. It hurt so bad, but she helped mask the agony.

I placed the revolver back in Wade's lifeless hand and limped to the bathroom with his club. I stared at us in the mirror and took off my glasses. I was bleeding pretty good. I could taste the coppery tang. I raised the nightstick and smacked myself in the face two times. I thought about a third, but my pain threshold was wearing thin. I dropped it to the floor and hobbled back to the living room.

My vision started to blur while my limbs grew numb and heavy. I inched to the phone attached to the yellow wall in the kitchen. My pouring blood followed the whole way. My face began to balloon on the right side. I dialed 911 and tried to talk to the operator. I had a flimsy story in my head, but when I started talking my legs gave out and I hit the floor. My eyes fluttered and everything went dark.

7

After what they now call 'The Kentucky Slaughterhouse,' I was assured I was toast. After I came to, our sheriff's department where Daddy worked was aiming to fry me. They never came out and said it, but I could feel it. Wade's friends suspected all kinds of foul play, but my savior was the diary he'd hidden in the floorboards at the ranch.

During the investigation, they searched the place like sloppy vultures, trying to piece together what the fuck happened. I played dumb the whole time, pleading nothing but self-defense. I was guarded and closed-off about most of the endeavor, but I needed all the help I could get.

In his gruesome and vivid telling, he'd bragged about how crooked a cop he was. He went into graphic detail of my abuse and my worthless mother's abuse. He even sketched some of the scenarios he put me through in his little book, like burning me with lit cigarettes. He'd also kept photos of me tied and chained to my bed—the sick little fuck.

After that, Kentucky law didn't go easy on me. I put my best face forward, but the judges and doctors had said there was nothing left for me there. They shipped me away, off to this glorious Golden State, to a place called "The Rock."

The Rock used to be an actual federal prison back in the 50s and 60s, but when three brave convicts escaped, they closed it all down. It's on its own little island, with a lighthouse and lodging for its various employees. They transformed it into a psychiatric facility in the late 1980s, just in time for me to make my way there in '90.

Why can't I write about my imprisonment?

Perhaps it's too difficult to formulate into coherent words.

After all, I'm no writer.

Did it help shape me into the thing in this apartment writing these pages?

Am I seriously asking you, my humble and innocent reader?

Why don't you ask me, darling?

I'm asking myself—right?

What planet am I on?

8

'THE EARLY NINETIES'

I'm tumbling backwards again. I'm no longer in my apartment. My hand moves across the page as the pencil scribbles, but my mind isn't here. It's back inside The Rock.

"Why did they used to call this place 'The Rock,' St. James?"

"Enough talk, Savannah."

"Just asking. Jesus."

Savannah sighed and turned away in her bunk, causing a metallic screech on the gray granite. Afternoon light zinged through the bars and into the cell.

No, wait.

The bars were supposed to be removed after the prison remodel, although that never happened. It was a hospital now. A place for care. Care for the damaged and psychotic. The fellow 'you' and 'me' of marvelous planet Earth.

That's right; I'm looking at *you*.

Nobody's innocent. Not even *you*.

"This is home, Savy."

Savannah flipped back around, and the beaming light offered me a silhouette of her sexy pixie cut. "You call *this* home? I've been here a month, and this place already feels like a prison. I've heard the screams at night. . . and the way that one orderly fuck stares at me."

I stood up and began brushing my hair in the mirror. My natural trestles of red fire were already starting to gray.

Shame.

My reflection looked back at her.

"I've been locked in here for years with no bunk mate. You're lucky I haven't ended you by now."

"Ha-ha, Holly."

I turned back to her wholesome frame on her cot. I flipped my hair and smirked. "Come on, kid. Let's get you some chow."

9

I couldn't seem to keep my head in this place. It was nice to have a roommate besides *her*, but it was all getting to me. I wanted to crack, to satiate on anyone or anything. I couldn't show my cards here or I would be done. I'd never get out.

Why did they play all this Disney trash on the TVs in the mess hall? It was on everywhere, all the time. The sea creature movie with Ariel was stuck on a loop. She was driving me mad. I found myself staring at her, thinking she and I were the same person. She did look a little like me, that little cartoon princess of the sea. I was no princess, but I could pretend.

She was me—I was her.

I was losing my mind.

Did I already mention The Rock was no picnic? It was literally a giant stone cell block planted in the middle of the sea. We were behind bars in solitary for hours at a time. The rules were strict and many of our doctors and orderlies were fucking pricks.

They should have been behind these bars with us. They were no better.

To be honest, healthcare is a psychotic's paradise. Nothing like a playing God complex to the extreme. We were being warehoused. It was disguised from the outside as a psychiatric facility, but I knew better.

It was a void.

A place to reflect on how shitty life could be. There weren't many other teenage killers in that place. Only two or three, including me. There was nothing short of legitimate wackos, freaks, and lunatics.

But you're none of those things.

It was year four in this dungeon. My spirit was fizzling out into nothing. She was the only one keeping me together. My queen on the inside. I'd played it cool the entire time, burying my bloodlust and rage.

I kept to myself and thought about writing, mostly. Sometimes I'd skip meals and just stay in my cell, listening to the sounds of ships go by while I watched day creep to night from my open cell door.

My mind had become more scrambled with the prescribed meds and the mundane routine. I'd lost some weight, but I felt strong. I had a session with Dr. Jamison in an hour.

He was trying to break me.

I'll never let that happen.

He wanted me to admit guilt as to why I was here. We had given him nothing. The little weasel was drawing at straws. He'd never understand that I was more than human. A beast from the face of the deep. If he threatened one of his drastic treatments again, I'd play the indifferent card.

It had worked so far.

10

"St. James. Time for your session."

The orderly was Marv this time. Clay usually dealt with me on Tuesdays. Maybe he was sick or something.

I rose from my bed in my usual orange jumpsuit. I took a quick look in the mirror before stepping out of my cell. My hair was frizzy and my glasses were somehow crooked. I found a black hair tie around my wrist and pulled my mane of red back into a tight pony. I took my glasses off and adjusted them with a little twist and turn.

"Okay. I'm ready."

"Good afternoon, Holly. How are we feeling on this fine day?"

"Peachy, doc. You?"

"Well!"

Always a cringe-worthy introduction with Jamison. I couldn't stand the guy.

Me neither.

He was lucky we weren't out in the world.

I'd chew the fucker up and spit him out in the gutter.

We were in his standard and sterile office that had no style whatsoever. He was behind a desk and I was in an uncomfortable wooden chair in front of him. Jamison's bald head glistened from the cool light above us and his beady little eyes analyzed every move I made.

I pushed my spectacles farther up my long nose and forced a smile. A chameleon's move—joy had left my bones years ago. "What's on the agenda today, Dr. Jamison?"

"Can I be frank with you, Holly?"

I sat up nice and straight. "Mm-hm."

"We've been having our sessions for some time now. Your medications are keeping you stable, and you've been nothing short of exemplary for all these years. However—you're an anomaly to me, Holly."

I crossed my legs and folded my slender hands in my lap. "How's that?"

"Your case is quite strange. I've explained this to you time and again. The facts surrounding your parents' deaths have been worked over and analyzed. Your father was a decorated lawman in your little Kentucky town, although his diary did state that he did horrible things to you and your mother."

I decorated the floor with the bastard's blood, you little fuck.

Jamison went on, joining his plump vanilla hands together and placing them on his desk. The window at his back was screened and barred, but I could faintly see outside of the impenetrable "Rock." Us patients had outside exercise three times a week. It was this concrete yard with high walls and bleachers. You couldn't see anything substantial because the walls were so high, but you could hear the water and waves crashing, or an occasional seabird would join us while we roamed around aimlessly.

Only the women were allowed outside together. The men were separate and had their own time in the yard. I craved to see what was beyond those walls. The view from Jamison's window showed something I'd never seen before. This was a new office. The doc got off on keeping me guessing.

There was a city out there.

It was faint and blocked by iron, but looked so close I could almost touch it.

We must get there.

Some way, somehow. I needed to kill, murder, and maim.

Once you've got the taste, you can't stop.

"Holly?"

"Hmm?"

Jamison tilted his head to the side. He was still in his chair, praying to his desk. "You were daydreaming. Where did you go?"

"Nowhere in particular."

"This is what I'm talking about. I want to go back to the night that ultimately had you sent here to us."

I clenched my fists and craned my head toward the ugly ceiling. "We've been over this hundreds of times, Jamison."

"*Doctor* Jamison." The pint-sized asshole's face was starting to turn red, a tiny cherry tomato that needed a good popping.

I slouched in my wooden seat and opened my legs wide. I had to hike up my baggy jumpsuit to complete the 'fuck you' pose. "Forgive me—Jamison. My story hasn't changed. I acted in self-defense. It was either me or my father that night."

"What about your mother? Who killed her? You've been insistent that your father was responsible. However, the way the crime scene was left, along with the injuries you sustained, it couldn't have been your father. Isn't that right, being that he was already dead? The forensic data has provided multiple reports stating that your father died first. So who killed your mom, Holly?"

"I've already told you—"

"I'll be as forthright as I can with you, Holly. I do believe your father had a mean streak. I can also believe he did some terrible things to you. But I do not believe that he killed your mother. I think *you* did that. I also think you purposefully murdered your father. You could have run from the house after the initial altercation or called the police. I think you liked it, and you staged the whole thing."

My hands were behind my head, grasping at my red ponytail. "You dream all that up on your own, Jamison?"

"*Doctor* Jamison! Half of your mother's face was caved in. Six of her teeth were obliterated with that nightstick!"

I'd never seen old Jamison so on edge.

"You know what I think, Jamison? I think you need some of these candy-coated pieces of psychiatric shit to munch on yourself."

I dug in my pockets and removed a handful of red and blue pills I'd been hoarding instead of taking. I held them out in a fist and opened my hand. They cascaded down, sounding like little marbles hitting the hard floor.

Jamison huffed and clenched his jaw. I could see the strain on the sides of his face.

"What is it, doc? The missus not giving it up after your heroic days at the freak clinic?"

"You need to be taught some manners, St. James. You fail to realize—I'm God around here. I can do whatever I please in the continuation of your care while you're at this facility."

"Going to threaten to shock me, doctor? Throw me in an ice bath again? Like you did to Savannah? Put the lid on and lock me in there for an hour while I scream for help? You gonna change my meds again and again and again until I can't even sit straight to take a piss?"

"This is all part of your care, Holly."

"You can do whatever you want. Everything I've told you is the truth."

"Go back to your room, St. James. Our session is over for today."

Marv opened Jamison's new office door at my back. He escorted me back to my cell.

11

I'd been locked in here for too long now. I was writing all this in my mind until I got out, then I'd transfer it to paper in the present.

If I got out.

My brain wanted to run away on me. This cell was my prison, but also my only escape from the rest of this granite madness. I wanted to crack, but I wouldn't. I had too much work to do on the outside. The added pills and questions were becoming too hard to bear. Jamison was aloof, but he drained me with his stupidity, the pathetic piece of meat.

He thinks he knows.

Maybe he does.

He'll never get the truth.

No matter what.

It was early—couldn't sleep.

Story of my life.

An orderly—well, they were more like guards—came over to my cell. I was sitting up in bed with my back against the wall. My hair was messy and spilled out in front of me, resting in waves on my right breast. I didn't know where Savannah had gone. I put my glasses on and rubbed the sleep from my eyes after he tapped on my cage with his keys. It was too early for a session with Jamison.

I was bound and casually walked to the elevator at the far right of the block. My jumpsuit was getting baggy. I hadn't been eating much in recent weeks. The meds and solitude could do that, even to someone like me. I needed to start taking better care of myself if I was ever to escape.

I thought we were going up, either to the mess hall or another conference room. Instead, the grunt pushed B. Basement. The basement was for the real lunatics at The Rock. If these imbeciles had any sense, we would always be in full solitary confinement. Only my wit and manipulation tactics had kept me in general population.

Something was off.

Jamison was at it again.

A wheelchair greeted me when the elevator door dinged open. Jamison was here, of course. His stupid lab trench fit his blobby little body like a condom. I could tell he'd had the thing tailored by the best in the business to allow the snow-white fabric to gel with such a hideous frame.

I stood tall with my chest pushed out, throwing my shoulders back into perfect posture, and yawned widely. "Good morning, Dr. Jamison."

Jamison smiled smugly. I swear, the guy had the personality of a doormat. "Morning."

"Why the wheelchair? You set on crippling your finest patient?"

"It's quite early, Holly. I thought you could use the added rest for the trip down the hall."

"Aren't you a gentleman."

"Please, have a seat."

"I'll walk. I can use the exercise."

I started toward him, but he moved closer to the seat on wheels, blocking me from exiting the elevator. The lights were dim and cool in the underground chamber, the festering guts of my watery prison. Jamison wasn't having it. His cheeks reddened. "Oh, but I insist."

Two larger orderlies appeared from his left and right. I could smell the dank waft of the one on my left's taxicab air freshener cologne.

Something's wrong. I should change. Change and kill them all. Break their bones and eat their intestines. Feed them their balls while they die choking on them.

Be smart, my queen.

Please let me.

Even if we do win this, there's no way for us to escape.

I stretched and yawned again, moving my hands above my head in the tight space. I moaned a little wave of satisfaction with the obligatory movement. "You're right, Doctor. Think I'll take that ride, after all."

12

I had never been down here before. I was certain this was the first time, but it wouldn't be the last. I was wheeled into a small room with a heavy-looking open door. We all went inside, Jamison leading. The guard who had initially brought me down placed me in the center of the room. It smelled like the ocean. I could almost make out the sound of waves crashing against The Rock formations at my feet.

All the orderlies left. There was no desk or any place to sit. Jamison stood at the other side of the room in the cold morning light. There was a window at his back, higher up from where he stood. It was barred and gated, painted an ugly off-white. For all I knew, we were completely underwater. If a hole was drilled into the wall at his back, or better yet, through his dumpy body and through the foundation, the sea would likely spill in and kill us all.

Except for me.

I didn't care to look around; there was nothing in here to see. It was just another cell, another box of suffocating confinement to stifle my morbid creativity. I wanted to spring for Jamison, but I knew better.

He cleared his throat, a phlegmy sound with a little cough at the end. "Today we will try something new and improved, Holly."

"What are you talking about?"

"You've been a patient with us for several years now."

It feels like we've been here a decade.

My patience was wearing thin.

"Holly?"

"Yes?"

"Where did you go?"

"I'm right here, Jamison."

I thought the narcissist would come unglued when I didn't call him doctor. He smiled instead, a predictable response under the circumstances. He had me right where he wanted me, alone with no one around.

In *his* playground.

The evil warden rearranged his tie before speaking. He rarely wore one. He must've dressed up for this special occasion. "We've hit a wall in your treatment, Holly. Today we will change that."

I flicked my hair of fire out of my face, causing it all to sweep behind my back. "Same old story, eh, Doctor? What are you going to do, bring in a young priest and an old priest?"

"Not exactly. Winston, Elliot!"

The two lurches that helped me down here reappeared. Before I could react, they grabbed my arms. I didn't fight, although my blood boiled infinitely red. I smiled as they stripped me down and strapped me to the wheelchair. It was a good job; these two had clearly done this type of thing before. The one that smelled like a car air freshener was even worse up close. He had hairy knuckles and damp, ice-cold hands.

I couldn't move as the leeches were brought in. It was a woman nurse who carried the slithering mass in a red bucket.

Jamison thought he would win, that I'd fold and tell him everything he wanted to hear. Who and what I *really* was and what I was capable of.

I sat there like a stone. Mr. Air Freshener removed my glasses for the "treatment." My vision turned blurry because I didn't change—didn't unleash *her*. I must never do that in this place. Instead, I stared back at Jamison. He remained a safe distance away, finally choosing to sit on the cold ground with his back against the wall. He looked odd doing such a thing, especially in his business clothes.

He was soaking it all in, but my eyes never left his. The woman who had come in last did the honors, carefully pulling a single creature from the bucket and placing it on my bare skin. She didn't stop, bulking them up in the worst places imaginable. The leeches slithered and sucked, biting my nipples while trying to crawl toward my ass. Some fell to the floor as the more purposeful creatures squished under my armpits. One dangled from my open mouth, struggling to come inside. I ground my teeth and shook my head, causing the slimy mass to fly away and hit the ground.

It didn't hurt.

We don't feel a thing.

He got nothing. He stayed for the full hour and left in a huff. He insisted it was a cleansing exercise, an experimental form of radical treatment to detox and purify a troubled mind.

Once Jamison left, Marv entered with his wavy silver hair shining. He held a long hose, like a fireman's. I thought the color was cream or off-white. He pulled the handle and let me have it. Most of the blood suckers flew off and were washed away, but some remained in my hair and armpits. Marv did his best to remove them all.

After my drenching, he came up to me, dead center in this ungodly torture chamber. I stared up at him, trembling and covered in wounds. My blue eyes pierced through his brown ones, almost causing him to wince.

He pulled my glasses from his lab coat pocket and put them on me. "Jesus Christ, St. James."

He unstrapped me from the chair and hauled me back to my regular cell. I was given a tranquilizer injection from Jamison right as I entered. He had been in there, waiting to stick me. I was still naked, but Marv had tried to cover me with his lab trench. I crawled into bed and slept for forty-eight hours straight.

13

It was deathly quiet. I didn't understand what had happened to Savannah. Nobody spoke to me in there. I was like the black sheep. I finally dozed, listening to the faint sounds of ships at sea around my decaying world. My cell was cold. I thought it was mid-November.

I shuddered and pulled the thin gray cover closer to my chin. I was about to head off to the land of chilling dreams when a flashlight beamed through my barred door. I shrunk away when it landed on my face, blinding me in the otherwise blue-black pitch. Keys jingled as my door creaked open.

"Get up, St. James."

It was Marv. His voice shook in the glacial void of this place.

"Wh-what's the deal, Marv?"

"I'm sorry, Holly, but you're coming with me. Doctor's orders."

"What the hell? You've never done me like this after lights out. Tell me—"

"It's time for your session, Holly. Come with us, now."

Jamison appeared in the doorway. His leprechaun body with a shiny pool ball for a head cut off my conversation with Marv.

I sat up in bed while another large orderly stepped into view. He had a baton in his meat hooks for hands. I shivered as Wade's face and his stale cinnamon breath filled my nostrils and spit at me from his grave. The face of my father washed away and returned to the faceless guard.

"Hold your horses. Just let me get dressed."

"Don't bother!" yelled Jamison. "Gentlemen?"

Marv and his hulking friend converged on me. Marv took my arm as the beast man pulled my hair. They got me to my feet. I wasn't dressed, except for a pair of issued underwear the color of their uniforms.

"Get your fucking hands off me, you bastard fucks!"

I ripped away from Marv and reared back for a swipe at him. My fist struck him right in the face, knocking him backward against my sink. The hulk still had me by the hair. He pulled me close and got me in a bear hug. His body was warm and squishy. I spit in his face after he released my hair.

He stared down at me while I squirmed in his arms. His eyes were stupefied with childish delight.

I was fuming, struggling to get free. I looked over at the doctor as his head caught the moonlight in the icy cellblock.

My attacker reared his large head back and smashed it into mine.

I blacked out in his arms.

14

I woke up in another chair. It felt uncomfortable and wooden, like the one in Jamison's office. The lights were on at full power, causing me to wince and feel the sting in my face. I couldn't move, no matter how hard I tried. I was strapped to an electric chair thing. I'd only heard stories about it while roaming the rec room hallways. A device that had been used to execute prisoners back when The Rock was a different kind of prison.

I was still naked and didn't have my glasses. Goosebumps broke out all over my body. I cranked my head skyward to see what was around me. My hair fire crept behind my ears and head, allowing me to scan the room. Marv was standing right in front of me. The other mountain of a man was gone. I didn't know where Jamison had gone.

Marv came closer, his salt-and-pepper beard settling inches from my face. He sighed before whispering, "Holly . . . I'm sorry. I really am. I don't want to do this, but I'll lose my job if I don't."

"Jamison is a monster. He's going to—"

Jamison appeared like a specter. His white coat and ivory pants, along with his milky skin, fused him into the iridescent oblivion of the small procedure room. "Going to. . .? You were saying, Holly?"

The only part of me I could move was my head. My legs and feet were shackled to this chair of doom. "Shock treatment, Jamison? Is this your last attempt to break me?"

I had to remain calm. I was fucked and I knew it. The only weapon I had left was to give in.

Take it like a woman.

Surrendering can be seen as weakness, but it's not. It's strategy. There was no use fighting yet. I couldn't escape this.

Knowing this inevitability angered *us* to the point of frenzy. I wanted to break free and attack Jamison. Leap on the helpless weasel and tear into his neck like a nubile siren owning her kill. Open him up and watch him die. Bathe in his tears and blood.

Marv left the room after he strapped my head to the chair. I didn't think he could watch. Jamison did the honors of shoving the bit in my mouth so I wouldn't swallow my own tongue. He went to pull the switch, the one that threw its victim into a violent seizure at 40,000 volts, but first gave me a thorough once-over.

He liked looking at my body.

This was his power move, and he was getting off on it.

My chest heaved. My hair was damp with sweat. The anticipation of him pulling the lever was driving *us* insane.

"Are you ready for your salvation, Holly?"

"Die screaming, Jamison."

He looked at my tits and licked his lips.

I smiled back at his rosy, puffy jowls.

He pulled the switch.

15

I endured the same treatment four more times over the course of several months. The shocks were most definitely the worst. I'd been submerged in hot and cold water tubs for hours, even accosted by some orderly prick named Mike.

What a dumb fucking name for a guy.

Mike.

How un-extraordinary.

Anyway. . .

Do you know what it feels like to have electric shock therapy? Your mind gets scrambled into millions of pieces. There's pain—a whole lot more than you can imagine. You can't even hold your piss. It leaks out involuntarily.

Jamison made things worse and worse for me. After each extreme form of his radical "treatments," I was dragged to his office for a chat. The little bastard couldn't believe that my story never changed. My memory had been foggy, and I'd lost a good ten pounds, mostly in my tits and ass. I was fortunate that most of my fat was in those two areas.

Another year sludged by.

It was anticlimactic, although my nemesis had nearly broken me.

If this good-for-nothing fuck Jamison kept going, he would finally get the truth out of me. I hated to admit it, but these were the facts.

You see, being in a place like The Rock was worse than being dead. It was also worse than being alive. It was neither. It was a void, a granite hellscape filled with time and pain. Time could be more awful than pain, sometimes.

I couldn't take much more of this.

16

'1997'

How did I escape?

That prison, that dungeon?

The place where carnal rages and sinister appetites came to die in the coldness of the sea?

Truth is, I had help. The Rock was an invincible opponent. Back before my time, when it was an *actual* prison, three inmates made a break for it one fateful night. They built rafts out of raincoats and used dummy heads to distract the grunts while they dug out of their cells with kitchen spoons to spill themselves out on the roof.

Some say they perished; others aren't so sure.

"The sharks got 'em," they'd say.

Or. . .

"They drowned. Good riddance. That swim is impossible."

Almost impossible.

I'm embarrassed to say I forget the actual night it happened, but I believe it was a weeknight in early July. I was nodding off in my cell;

lights out was hours ago. I was in and out of consciousness, half-there and half-not. The newest pill cocktail from Jamison and the afterburn from all the shock torture were stifling me down to nothing.

I started to flush my pills toward the end so I could stay sharp if the miracle day ever came. I'd envisioned escaping hundreds of times, concocting every scenario an inmate could conjure. Each time, I'd hit the same roadblock.

Getting out of the cell was impossible.

Jamison and the neighboring city had learned their lesson from the old prison days. The cell walls were reinforced iron. Digging or cutting through with kitchen utensils would be an early trip to another form of madness.

～～

I remember coming back from a dream. I thought I'd heard something outside my cell door. I disregarded it and stared at the ceiling, the same dank covering I'd gotten lost in for five agonizing years.

Or was it six, eight, twelve?

Forgive me; my mind is starting to slip.

I sat up in bed. The air in the block was cool, yet stale and damp. It was eerily quiet that night. The barred screen windows out and above my cell bled a rich aqua. The moon was full out there.

I sat on the toilet and twirled my hair. Glanced over at my cell door.

It was *open*. Cracked a bit, as if a moron guard hadn't slammed her all the way shut at lights out.

I rubbed sleep from my eyes, making sure I wasn't seeing things. I looked around and listened, only to be met with silence. The cell next to mine was empty and had been for years. Jamison had done his maniacal deeds with Savannah. I had listened around and heard the rumors. She'd been the only decent person I had, and she was gone.

I crept to the door and placed my hand on it. When it creaked and moved with my weight, adrenaline flooded my body. Who had done this? My initial thoughts went to Marv.

Good old Marv.

He seemed like a decent guy. I knew he didn't like his job or the backdoor doings in this hell. Maybe he felt bad for going along with Jamison's tactics. Either way, this was my way out.

I put on my orange jumpsuit and was about to run right through the god-damned door. Instead, I looked over that cell that had been my cage for all those years. I scanned the vanilla paintings and drawings I'd done. My eyes shifted to all the books I'd read about basic anatomy and human psychology. Then I took a final heaving breath of that wacko prison air and pulled open my cell door.

17

There was nobody around. It must've been two or three in the morning. An orderly came around every hour, so I would need some luck. I could've gone for the stairwell, but I was certain it would be locked. I just stood there, right in the middle of the vacant cell block.

I was fucked.

How was I going to get out of here?

"Psst! St. James! Over here."

I swung my head to the right. The stairwell door was five cells down. I had to squint to see the head popping out from behind the door.

Marv.

His long silver hair covered the exposed half of his face. I ran for him but realized I had no shoes on. I didn't turn around because I couldn't. I refused to go back into that cell.

Marv closed the stairwell door behind us. He grabbed my shoulders with both hands, looking down at me with his eyes of sterling silver. "I'm not one for small talk, St. James. So listen up."

"I'm all ears, Marvin."

"Take my key card. Use these stairs and go up two levels. Once you run out of steps, that door in front of you leads to the roof. It's *always* locked; only us orderlies can access it. Key out with my card, then drop it by the door. I'll need to retrieve it to cover you for as long as I can."

Marv was sweating and wide-eyed. I could hear bars rattling in different cell blocks of The Rock. It was the night shift workers smacking the inmates' bars with their nightsticks.

I used one of those as a weapon, once. Remember? It ended messily for Daddy.

"St. James? Snap out of it!"

Marv still had one hand on my shoulder. I usually loathed being touched, but not this time. "I'm here, Marv."

His striking eyes stared right into me. He was just as tall as me, nearly a six-footer. It was refreshing not having to look down on a man, for once. "Remember, drop the card so I can go up and get it. I'm probably going to get my ass fired for this—or thrown into one of these cells with your friends."

I worked my hands through my hair; I hadn't realized it was damp. "I got it, Marv." I patted his shoulder, like I was one of the guys, then turned away and headed up the first few steps. But I turned back, whipping my hair across my face. "Why are you doing this for me?"

He looked up at me in his white uniform. My orange prison suit and red hair were a stark contrast to him. He winked and said, "I don't know. Maybe I'm crazy."

Aren't we all, Marvin. Aren't we all.

I turned away and began climbing. Marv's final words followed me up the stairs.

"Hope you can swim like a fish, St. James. If not, you're as good as dead."

18

I made it to the roof.

I thought about rummaging around the ground floor first, paying Jamison's office one last visit. It was unlikely he'd be there at this hour, but I could at least piss on his desk.

He can wait.

A guard's tower loomed about a hundred yards to my right. I couldn't tell if it was occupied. A spotlight circled from underneath, turning in a slow three-hundred-sixty-degree motion. I wondered if the guard on watch had a gun or was even a good shot, but I wasn't going to give him the chance.

I soaked in my surroundings for a moment. I'd never seen such a vantage point. All our outside activities at The Rock had been monitored and scrutinized exclusively from the yard, with the sky-high concrete walls of seabird shit where you could only imagine what the ocean looked like.

I was fortunate there was no breeze. The tower with the plausible guard looked more like a lighthouse. The floodlight would work its way around and shine on most everything up there. I remained hidden as best I could. There were fans and concrete protrusions I could hide behind to avoid being seen by the stalking beam.

I shimmied down a long pipe on the very edge of the structure. I was glad I had left my shoes; it was a stealthier approach in my nightly quest. It was a long way down, but the thought of being returned to my cell was more frightening than being shot or falling.

Did I just say I was frightened?

You never have to be when I'm around, angel.

I made the climb down, barely making a sound. The lighthouse nearly got me once or twice. It illuminated a quarter of my body at one point, but it swept past me in seconds. I didn't have time to assess my surroundings until I was off that damn Rock. Once my bare feet settled on a thin sidewalk that surrounded the whole complex, I faced a shallow wall of rocks and a smallish sandy beach.

It was the dead of night, and the air was still. There was no fog, *nothing*.

The moon was directly above where I was heading, out into the watery abyss of the night. The city was out there, too. I'd never seen such a glowing spectacle. From my daunting and doomed distance, skyscrapers rose high into the emptiness. I could see two bridges on separate ends of everything.

A Ghirardelli chocolate factory sign, which bled a bright red, stood out on the shore of the mysterious distant city at my insane distance. I had to squint to make out the richly colored letters. The other bridge glowed like fire, a beauty of a thing that matched my hair. Everything out there seemed so small, too far for me to ever feel or touch.

I stood at the corner of the psychiatric prison, my back to a jagged wall of wet rock. I had nothing except my issued jumpsuit on my back, but I walked to the water's edge and stuck my foot in. It was surprisingly warm, a temperature that welcomed me. The cold never affected me, not really, being that I am as cold-blooded as you'll ever see.

I knew I could make it.

I had so much to do in that mystery city.

So many delights to indulge.

I stripped off my jumpsuit and pulled down my panties. I stood there at the edge of land and sea, on the brink of the stone island that had owned, tortured, and humiliated me for years. Gooseflesh consumed me in the silvery night light as a lone boat sounded its horn in the murky nothing.

As a final *fuck you* to Jamison and his goons, I left my clothes right there to be found. I wanted them to know I'd gotten away. Whether I had help or not, the upcoming swim would be my fight. I didn't turn to face The Rock a final time. I listened and took in a long breath. I felt every ounce of myself, knowing that if I made it to that city of golden lights, it could be mine.

I let the ocean consume me.

19

I was halfway there, a shimmering nude buoy in an ocean of pure glass. The rich moon of white, ever full and hauntingly large, stayed above me. The wind began to stir in intervals but would hiccup to an eerie calm. The endless black water barely moved. My body was weakening, but getting flustered and surrendering to panic isn't in my nature. I turned over on my back several times to rest and stare up at the circular beacon that guided me.

I floated in that position for a long time, allowing the salty abyss to gently instruct my course. Exhaustion doubled, and I'd only made it halfway. I was *never* afraid. I'm not capable of such an emotion, if any at all. I listened to the sea while my ears were underwater. My head dipped all the way under, but I fought back to the surface.

Let me help.

My skin became scaly and rough while my hair fire entangled me in the ocean black. My gorgeous fin began doing most of the work, cutting my lengthy siren frame through the wet glass. A lonely boat horn could be heard in the murk, never showing its face.

I turned back over on my stomach as a blanket of dense fog rolled over me. I did look back then, but only once. The Rock was swallowed whole in the thicket of eerie cloud. The fog seemed to glow, the stunning moon trying to pierce through it with all her splendor. The only thing left to see was that city and her two bright bridges on either side. One made of white, the other an orangish magma.

We're almost there.

20

The dock was so close. I swam and swam, growing more tired by the second, but the wind factor and my goddess were my utmost allies. My transformed skin shimmered in the uncanny moonlight. I glowed the color aqua; my scales and fin owned the watery labyrinth.

The chocolate factory sign was my intended target. I dipped underwater and could breathe. A fish floated by, nearly grazing my bulletproof skin. The moonlight shimmered into the depths, causing my whole body to glow. I sucked in some water, but it didn't hurt me. I felt new life, as if our collective body was designed for the sea. I'd never been in the ocean until then. Kentucky had some lakes and streams while growing up on the ranch, but this was a rebirth.

Did you see that?

In the aquatic murk, a shadow came and went. It looked like a long tentacle slithering toward me. It appeared to glow, reaching for *us*. I blinked, and it was gone. I whipped my head back and forth, but the thing had vanished as quickly as it appeared.

The waves began to rise and chop as I neared the shore. The fog bank at my back begged to follow. It swallowed the glorious circular cookie in the sky, washing away her brilliant yellowish light. A ladder appeared in front of me. I traversed the steps and plopped my feet on the damp dock at the very edge of the twilight city.

Strange. . .

What happened to my tail?

My long legs and slender knees hit the wood instead. My balance was off from the swim, but I'd made it. I'd done the impossible. I'd beaten Jamison and his house of horrors.

The fog thinned and scattered, allowing the huge moon to peek through. My nude frame was ravaged in gooseflesh and smelled of the sea. My arms and legs were heavy and achy. I was one with nature, and she with me. My teeth chattered as I looked around the dark.

Then we moved forward into the unpredictable Golden State.

21

I arrived at a homeless camp. The sun hadn't come up yet. It was holding out just for me. The camp was situated on the first street I entered after walking past the chocolate factory by the sea. Smoke from sewer pipes billowed skyward. Bonfires were choking out, but some still held on in their grungy barrels. Tents lined both sides of the street, with high-rise financial buildings and other skyscrapers taking up the majority of everything.

I'd never seen such things! I'd also never seen so many destitute people roaming around in one large space. The stench hit me first. It was as if all the bad smells in the world had combined into one. My hair was drenched, and I still had no clothes. People shuffled along the street, looking like dark zombies. Occasionally, one of them would hoot or scream at the top of their lungs, thrusting their heads skyward to go berserk.

One guy almost bumped into me right in the middle of the street. I had no shame and was right out in the open, with no fucks to give. His complexion was black as midnight, and he donned a salt-and-pepper beard. All he wore was a Ninja Turtles T-shirt that was several sizes too small, even for his average frame.

Looks like a kid's shirt.

He wore it like a crop top. The turtle on the front was the red one from the cartoons. The one who carries those two lame stabbing weapons and is always angry, like he's constantly on his period or something. The weirdest thing about him was he had no pants on, unabashedly naked besides the shirt.

The fog followed me inland, a fitting display to match who had landed on these sorry fuckers' doorstep. I was happy to find another person in their birthday suit. He mumbled something and twirled around in the street. His penis flopped around, slapping his thighs. He almost bumped into me.

"I need to get those space toys, space toys—space toys. Whoop!" he said on garbled repeat.

And I thought *I* was insane. . .

I found an unoccupied tent and hurried inside. Nobody noticed me. It was as if the wastes of oxygen were all in their own worlds of madness, lost in translation inside their own mutated flesh prisons.

Then again—aren't we all like that? One bad day from transforming into something like me.

Okay.

I know what you're thinking. You're thinking you could never be like that. You could never be that sorry fuck drinking his own piss and eating out of a dumpster in a back alley.

Well, I've got news for *you*.

We're *all* capable of madness. It's in every one of us. Sometimes, all it takes is one diseased thought to manifest a whole army of mental decay, one horrific experience to open the floodgates to inevitable doom.

I found a pair of baggy sweatpants and a men's navy blue polo shirt. I put them on and, feeling somewhat complete, I wrapped a large blanket around me and left for the heart of the city. We were hungry and tired. I needed to act fast.

22

There wasn't anything around except houses for a while. I walked along like a wrapped-up specter, alone in the night with my new bum clothes. The blanket smelled like piss and shit, but a lady must improvise when things get thick.

Desperation was sinking in.

The last thing I wanted was to be forced to sleep on the street, but block after block, I saw nothing but homes. The houses were bizarre. I was used to spread out ranches and farmland. This was the total opposite. They were scrunched up in a line against each other, all looking the same. The only real difference between them was their pastel color schemes, a half-hearted attempt to stand out on the heavily inclined streets tilting upward into the night.

The fog scattered, peppering itself about as it tried to follow me. Several streetlights were positioned on either side, casting a hazy, warm light. A single porch bulb was on, but most of the stacked abodes were dark. I didn't know what time it was, but soon the sun would begin to bully its way to the surface.

I was on the verge of giving in and sleeping on the sidewalk until an alleyway jumped out on my left. I'd been walking to a crawl when it appeared. About halfway in, a small neon sign read, 'J&J's Liquor and Spirits.' Underneath that in smaller letters was, 'Open 24 Hours.'

～∽～

"Scram! I don't have time for *your* kind in here."

His voice sounded like honeysuckle. Even while bitter and angry, it bled friendly tones.

I had the blanket pulled over my head like a hood. I removed it and stared into him with my hair fire and bright blue eyes. "Forgive me, sir. I was admiring your sign from outside."

My appearance seemed to do nothing for him. I tried to change my voice and kill off anything that sounded like Kentucky. I adopted what I thought California sounded like on the fly. I think he knew I was a foreigner.

"Admire it from outside."

There was nobody behind the counter, as if I were talking to a ghost. I considered grabbing some candy bars and fleeing, but he appeared from the floor area behind the register. He must've seen me through the glass and thought I was one of the diseased psychos from outside.

Well—aren't you?

His name was Stretch. He was average in the looks department, acting out his whole life in the Golden State. He should've been bald, but he held onto the side sections of his light brown hair for dear life. He had the patches situated in a comb-over like a modern-day Pablo Picasso. He even donned a shirt like the famous Spanish artist, a white and black thing of striped hideousness. He came off looking like an old spicy convict in front of all his shiny bottles of booze.

"I don't think you understand, sir. My name's Ariel. I'm in search of employment."

Stretch seemed surprised. I told him I had moved here from Canada and had fallen on hard times, been sleeping on the streets for weeks. Plus, I think I reminded him of his daughter that had moved away to school.

In addition to the job, he also had a small room attached to his business. He lived upstairs, and he gave me the downstairs unit. He fed me a steaming bowl of macaroni and cheese and showed me to my quarters.

There was nothing to the job, really. Stretch had just lost his wife and was the only one running everything. He didn't want to have to close the liquor store for hours a day because he needed the income. He was wearing himself out trying to man the store around the clock.

That's where I came in. Stretch worked the days while I took the nights. He taught me intricate things about liquor and specialty beer and gave me lots of pointers on the inner workings of the Golden State. I even helped with inventory, counting bottles and making orders.

I only stayed a few months.

We had other plans.

23

"Ahh!"

Scarlett McNamara thrashed in her bed, but she quickly came to terms with her recurring fit. She was damp through and through, her raven hair sticking to her bedroom pillow. She blinked her brown eyes and sat up, covering her face with her hands.

"Another nightmare?"

She was startled by her lover's voice, but she'd never show it. She removed her hands from her face, choosing to stare into her vanity's shadowed silhouette straight across the room as her girlfriend switched on the nightstand light. "I'm . . . fine."

Her other half came over and rested her head on her slender shoulder. "Same one?"

Scarlett sighed, an effort that could be heard clear across the room. "Same one. Never changes."

Her lover kissed her on the shoulder, as gentle as a feather grazing a baby's cheek. "Lie back now, soldier. I've got you."

Scarlett looked over at her. They'd only been dating for six months. She wasn't the type to fall so hard for someone. She was consumed by work and her own demons, but she was in fact falling in love. Elsa had been a comforting force that she'd never had or known before. Scarlett pulled some of her locks out of her own face and brushed through Elsa's short auburn hair with the same hand.

They kissed and were about to make love, but another interruption greeted the grizzled McNamara. She turned over and reached for her cell, almost knocking her badge off her other nightstand.

"McNamara."

The other voice cleared his throat. It was the freshman Ramirez. "Apologies for calling so late, Sergeant."

She gripped her forehead around her eyes with her thumb and middle finger, pressing her eyes closed tight. "Spill it, rookie."

"It's Captain Mitchell, Sarge."

"What about him?"

The rookie removed more phlegm from his voice box. "Mild heart attack. He's fine but needs a lot of rest. He's requesting that you take lead on homicide."

She swallowed and turned back over to face her companion, removing the phone from her ear. They kissed long and hard, knowing precisely what was going to happen next.

She put the phone back to her ear, keeping eye contact with her darling Elsa. "I'm on my way."

24

I'm forced to do this because I have no choice. Besides, it'll be fun.

I've taken a long walk toward the ferry building. The skies are gray, and the city has a chill to her that can cut through lead. I've passed by joggers and tourists, all laughing and enjoying their measly little worlds. I haven't eaten a thing all day.

You must remain sharp.

I've tried to hide my appearance, covering my mane of fire with a black baseball hat and dark sunglasses. I tied my hair up and scrunched the hat down to eye level. I lifted the items from a homeless encampment on a street I can't remember.

I'm across the way from the ferry dock entrance, overlooking the ocean that leads straight to The Rock. It's the first time I've been on this side of the city since my escape. It's strange looking out at the floating asylum from the other side. It doesn't possess its gory intimidation from this cool distance.

There are people peppered all over, so I don't have to be too careful. Some seabirds fly around, jetting out toward the prison disguised as a psychiatric facility.

I tried looking in the phone book for *our* friend's exact address; however, his last name is common enough to show more than a dozen entries. After all these years, I don't even know his first name. I do remember how he'd gloat about being helicoptered in on Wednesdays. I tore out the section in the yellow pages, providing me the various addresses.

Today is Thursday, I think.

The bright silver of muted skies lessens by the minute, ready to give way to the cover of another chilly night. A ferry approaches the dock as the choppy waters slosh at its undertow, causing the boat to bob up and down in the vastness of the sea.

He's on this one.

"How do you know?"

Just wait.

I remain across the street and duck behind a bush. I remove my sunglasses and squint to see the passengers as they get off the boat. I start to perspire; I don't want to miss my chance. I think everyone has gotten off and I begin to grow angry. I'm about to abandon my post when a straggler comes into view, holding a black briefcase.

See? There he is.

I hold my position, trying not to explode with excitement. I study every nuance of his walk, his portly body lumbering across the street away from me. It takes restraint not to chase him down and maul him right there in the middle of a busy intersection. He disappears toward a sprawling parking lot a few hundred feet from where I stand.

Move.

I hurry to catch up, careful not to draw any unwanted attention. I put my sunglasses back on and peek around the corner, watching him get into a convertible red Corvette. The engine purrs as I watch him go, rumbling up a hilly street with no name as the remaining daylight goes with him. I watch as his headlights disappear, leaving me crawling with heightened senses.

"See you tomorrow, Dr. Jamison."

25

I hope he likes what I've prepared.

It looks so good.

All I had to do was visit a couple locations late last night until I saw his red Corvette in a driveway at the far edge of the city.

His house is like a castle. It's the only one around for a quarter mile. You have to come up a long, twisty driveway to reach the *actual* driveway.

From the outside, the house is loaded with sprawling windows. Some curtains are pulled, concealing large sections of the overall interior. The paint job lacks style, though. It's a boring medium tan color. Fitting that the wealthiest seem to have the most abhorrent taste in just about everything.

I didn't do much scouting or lurking around last night, but I covered the basics. The sun has just gone down, throwing the warmth of the candlelit kitchen into a symphony of sunset purples and flickering oranges. I made sure to close most of the curtains from inside the house.

You forgot the thyme.

"Let me stir it first!"

I've already spiced the pot with oregano, onion powder, garlic, and chili pepper for an added kick. Oh, and some black pepper. I found the candles in the living room, tucked inside a cabinet next to a white grand piano.

He's almost home.

I can feel it.

Is this what playing house feels like?

The door unlocks while I'm still in the kitchen. Keys jingle at my back in the shallow distance, along with a heavy sigh from a pint-sized blob of a man. I remain fixated on the dinner, making sure not to burn anything. I've borrowed some clothes from the nearest bathroom, diligent to hide my hair in a white shower cap.

Footsteps approach, and the smell of cheap shaving lotion somehow overpowers my makeshift cuisine.

"Blanche, why are you cooking in your bathrobe?"

I continue to stir.

"What'll it be for tonight? Pasta?"

I say nothing as he moves closer, almost touching me. I'm hunched forward to settle into character.

"Blanche?"

He grazes my shoulder, the sweat from his clammy hands oozing into me. A surge of power pulses through me, as if it had laid dormant for a thousand years.

Now.

"I'm trying to make dinner!"

Jamison leaps backward, nearly sprawling to the floor. I turn around with a smile full of teeth, like some cryptic wooden mummy in a bathrobe and shower cap. He doesn't seem to process what's happening. He looks at me, then at the boiling pot, and finally down at the floor by my feet.

"Blanche!" he hollers.

His sudden fear courses through me like a crashing wave of ecstatic delight. My eyes roll back as I allow it to wash over me. I remove the cap and whip around with my fire mane.

Blanche's severed head is in the pot, ready to be served medium rare. The rest of her partially nude body lays at my feet, a contorted mess of gore. I surprised her while she tended the garden out front.

The hedge trimmer she'd been using was used on her.

Jamison mumbles something, but finally finds his words. "Oh, dear God! It can't be . . . *you!*"

I peel the robe off, stepping out in my black leather pants and oxblood red shirt. "Nice to see you again, too, *Jamison.*"

He starts to cough, grabbing at his belly with his right hand. "Holly, what have you done?"

I throw my hands in the air and do a little twirl, settling back to face my arch nemesis. "You don't like your dinner? I worked very hard on it."

He turns to run but stands no chance.

I grip his chubby neck. I aim down because he's a full head shorter than me. He chokes and gasps as I pull him in. My eyes go black while a red haze washes over my superior vision.

I lift him from the floor.

Wait . . . I think *she's* doing it.

Jamison's tongue pops out while he fights for air. My hand sinks deeper until I feel his fluttering pulse in my palm. He's inches from my face as I watch his eyes bulge from his skull, ultimately understanding *everything.*

He sees me.

He sees me.

"Well done, doc!"

My grip is so tight my wrist starts to go numb. Before he goes un-conscious, he reaches up and grabs at my forearm. It's a feeble attempt, and we shake it off. I loosen my hand as he reaches his other one up and tries to claw at my face. I catch it with my free hand, then swallow his index finger with my palm and *twist*. The bone snaps like a wishbone. Jamison cries out in agony. I still have him by the throat, so the variation in sounds is quite funny to me.

It's as if a dying pig is squealing and wheezing at the same time.

I think he tries to speak, but I can't care less. We rally our strength as I squeeze even harder, shaking the little prick until he goes limp. I drop him to the floor and twist my head up toward the ceiling. I'm left panting with indescribable energy, as if fireworks of every color are exploding inside me.

I check Jamison's pulse to make sure he's still breathing. His work necktie made it up toward his throat when I dropped him. I move the blue and yellow piece of neck cloth away from his face, watching his flushed cheeks inflate, then deflate.

"Rest now, Sleeping Beauty. Our session has just begun."

26

"Honey?"

I've moved things to the bedroom. You'd be surprised how heavy dead weight can be to carry from one room to the next. The sleeping chamber is on the first floor. I wasn't about to lug Jamison all the way up the stairs. The room has a classical darkness to it, with walls painted dark gray and a king size bed constructed of thick and heavy wood. It's spacious and elegant, especially for a weasel like Jamison.

"*Honey*, wake up!"

Jamison's eyes flutter open. I slugged him in the nose before I carried him in and onto the bed. Both fresh and dried blood have collected on his mouth and chin.

"Ahhh!"

I don't care that he screams; no one can hear us, anyway.

He tries to move but cannot. "Blanche? My God—*Blanche*!"

I stand over him while he's tied up and on his back. I hold the severed head of his wife in front of my face, imitating her as he returns to consciousness. The seasoning I used in the kitchen smells delightful. Her blondish hair has melted off in patches from the boiling, but chunks of hanging dampness remain. The hag's skin feels like jelly in my hands, red and puffy. Her mouth is agape with one eye open. The other eye may have fallen out in the pot on the stove, causing one side of her face to droop and sag.

I back away from Jamison and allow him to throw his fit. He shrieks and wriggles, finally realizing I've tied him by hand and foot to his own bed. He appears like an upside-down version of da Vinci's *Vitruvian Man*, but much uglier. His head lays nicely at the very foot of the bed. He's forced to crane his head up and scrunch his forehead to look back at me. I got lucky that the gaudy bed frame has four large posts in each corner. I've secured him real nice with sections of thick rope from his garage.

I pull the boiled head of his wife away from mine, exposing my face of death. My teeth have narrowed and sharpened, seething for something decadent. I change my voice again to mirror the wife, but it comes out deeper and more alien.

"Your wife is pretty, Jamison. Well . . . she *was*."

He says nothing, instead choosing to snivel and try to move.

I turn the sopping head over in my hands and grin. "Kiss me, Blanche."

I lift her to my face and kiss her, pushing my tongue down her throat. I feel around for what's left of her tongue and take a bite, sawing my new teeth into it. I yank her away and throw the skull to the floor. It rolls along the carpet and smacks into the wall by a TV stand, making a final squish as my Blanche surprise comes to rest.

I look down on Jamison while I chew. I swallow most of her tongue and spit the rest onto the floor between us.

He is so shocked he doesn't scream. I study him on the bed, proud of how I've positioned everything.

He's going nowhere.

Jamison shakes his head, as if struggling to wake from a nightmare. He finally speaks with some degree of mortified lucidity. "I was right! You're . . . *you're. . .*"

His voice trails off, so I walk over and retrieve my regular glasses from the nearby cabinet. I almost forgot where I left them.

I step over the Blanche head, choosing not to pulverize it under my shoe. His eyes follow me until I return to my position at the foot of the bed. I cross my arms and smile, pushing my glasses to the bridge of my nose. It tickles, and I shake my head to smother an unexpected sneeze.

"Yes, Jamison? You were saying?"

He thrashes and cries for help.

I laugh. "If you scream again, I'll staple your mouth shut. Understand?"

Jamison freezes, realizing his defeat. "How, Holly? How did you escape the facility?"

"*Magic!*"

"You're pure *evil*, St. James. I know that now."

She demands that I silence him, squash his tomato head to pieces. I battle with *her* and stand my ground. I crack my neck and sigh, causing a flood of pins and needles to creep up through my left temple. "Takes one to know one, eh, doctor?"

Jamison snorts and gags on his own blood. "Ow. You broke my nose, you bitch."

I place my hand on my hip. I've always thought my ass looks great when I do this. "Your nose is the least of your problems."

Jamison returns to his bewilderment, and his milky face turns beet red. "How, Holly? Who helped you?"

"You're no longer eligible to ask questions, *doc*. Your privileges have been revoked."

He huffs like a bull. I can practically see the steam pluming from his ears. "When I get out of here--"

"Hold that thought!"

I turn around and skip away from the bedroom.

⌁

I return to Jamison with a chair from the living room. There were two of them next to a minibar in the corner near the piano. It's backless with a soft leather cushion of steel gray. The legs are a brand of dark wood. I push it up to the foot of the bed, making sure my measurements still add up. Jamison's head has a little room to move, so I grab him by the hair and rest his skull on the chair.

Perfect!

His eyes are tightly closed, causing his sweaty body to shudder whenever I get close. I stripped him to his underwear before securing him to the bed.

I go to leave the room again but instead gloat about my handiwork thus far. "There's one useful thing Wade taught me, doctor. How to tie a good knot."

The color drains from his face. "You mean your father? The one you killed?"

"Sure, if that's what you wanna call him."

"Holly, please untie me. I'm your doctor. Why are you doing this to me?"

Shut him up!

"Stop asking me questions. It's *my* turn to ask *you* something."

Jamison tries to move but gives in and goes limp. The bed makes a gentle squeak with his pathetic effort.

I move to the side of the bed, allowing him to stare up at me. "Savannah, doctor. What happened to her?"

Sweat beads on his forehead. His white briefs soak through, showing off his baby dick. "*Who?*"

"Don't fuck with me, Jamison. My cellmate at The Rock."

Jamison's nose begins to bleed again. He turns his head to the side and lets it run down his face and onto the chair cushion. "She was released, Holly."

Liar.

"You're lying. I wouldn't recommend doing that again."

I'm getting bored, so I take my shirt off in front of him. I'm not wearing a bra, so he's already noticed how hard my nipples have become. I slither down toward his face, bending and contorting my slender frame. "Remember the good old days, doc? The leeches and the torture?"

He looks me over, licking his lips like he did back at The Rock. "I *remember.*"

"Good. Now tell me what you did with Savannah. Or . . ." I pull a giant butcher knife from my back pocket—another handy gadget from Jamison's kitchen.

"She died in treatment! It was a tragic accident."

I wave the blade in front of his face, causing its sharpness to catch reflections in the warm bedroom light. Crickets are chirping outside during the beginning stages of dusk. "A half-truth. I'll let it slide."

I lean closer and bring the tip of the knife down toward his eyes, mere centimeters from piercing through. Jamison slams them shut, forcing wrinkles to break out across his pale forehead.

"Now here's what I think, *doctor*. Savannah's purpose was to spy on me. When she came back with nothing useful against me, you killed her. Tell me I'm wrong."

I hold the knife steady, ready to plunge it into his right eye socket. I can't help but notice a whole galaxy living inside his icy eyes of dread.

"You're not wrong, Holly."

He shrinks away when I snap back up, straightening my posture away from him. "*See*, I knew it!"

Jamison opens then closes his outstretched right hand before responding. "Yes, but . . . what do you care?"

I don't.

"Come again?"

"I said, Holly . . . what do *you* care? Savannah means nothing to someone like you."

I switch hands with the kitchen knife, gripping it with my left. I slap it down against the palm of my free hand, the sound like a dude smacking a girl's ass while fucking her from behind. I blink several times before answering. "That hurts my feelings."

Jamison smirks. He looks like a hairless opossum that's just been surprised in a smelly dumpster when shining a flashlight upon it. "You have those, Holly? *Feelings*?"

"Touché, Jamison."

His body relaxes in the restraints as if he believes he's winning. His breathing slows, and the redness starts to fade from his skin.

"You know, doc, you should thank your wife for giving me those gardening shears. Woah, are they *sharp*! It only took two big cuts to remove her head. I also can't believe how talented a pianist she is. I had her serenade me with a song before I chopped off her hands."

His body sags, sinking into the mattress. "You're a monster, St. James."

I'm on him so quick I nearly faint.

She's pulling me now.

I/*she* grips the knife and rests the point just below his left nipple. *She* begins carving into him—nothing lethal, merely surface cuts.

"No, *ahh!*"

She stops and moves around the bed, pulling a pair of dress socks from a nearby dresser. Blood leaks down Jamison's chest while he shrieks like a stuffed pig. *She* jams the sock ball into his mouth, stifling the piercing noise.

"Shut your fucking mouth! You're making me lose my concentration!"

She's in total control. I allow it, melting into *her* otherworldly strength. I'm still here but in intervals, as if a flashlight is running out of batteries in a dark cave. Tears stream down Jamison's face while the cuts continue, carving *her* symbol into his chest. He bleeds more than *she* wants, forcing *her* to drop the knife and lick his stomach, slurping up the sweet hot red.

"You know, Jamison, you truly taste like shit."

Jamison starts to pass out, but we don't let him. I remove the sock and smack him across the face.

"Stay awake, you little fuck!"

I leave the room and return carrying the microwave.

He's still bleeding, but nothing fatal.

I cradle the clunky food warmer in both arms. "You know what I like most about your kitchen, Jamison? Your microwave is portable."

I'd already planned on needing an extension cord, so I found an orange one in his garage. I set the device on the bar chair at the foot of the bed to stick Jamison's head inside. I had previously smashed out the rectangular window in front, making sure I didn't have to open the door to stick his slimy head in.

I return to my position on the side of the bed, watching him writhe and moan. His head fits securely enough inside the microwave; the only movement he can muster is a few inches side to side. His head whacks the sides of the oven, attempting to free himself from the inconceivable.

"Holly! Please!" His pleas are muffled from inside the radiation box.

"Are you ready to be reborn, Dr. Jamison?"

"*Holly!*"

I climb on top of him, thinking my added weight will help hold him down. I switch on the microwave and bounce on him as it hums to life. Jamison hollers for God to save him, but he's pleading to nobody but me.

I am God.

His body quakes beneath me. I watch as his face gets puffy and melts away, the shrieks turning more feminine with each passing second. The bed shifts a little but holds up fine. I remain on him with my hands folded and pushed up into my chin. I flick my nipples and rub my breasts while Jamison's whole head catches fire inside the microwave, causing the hissing sound of radiation waves to sputter.

Once he's dead and I cum, I roll off him and get to my feet. I'm dizzy with delight, finally able to scratch an itch that has tormented me for countless years.

Reality sets in while I stand there, watching the mutilated psychiatrist and his exploded head in a box. The microwave dings and stops, then starts smoking. The smell of overcooked meat fills my nose.

"Do we burn the house down?"

No.

"What, then?"

Just leave. It'll give you more time.

"Okay."

I clean up the scene and grab my things. Before I leave the house for good, I head back to the bedroom and stand in the doorway. My bodyweight gives into the foundation, allowing me to rest for the first time in hours.

"I told you you'd die screaming, *Jamison*."

27

"You wanted to see me, Captain?"

"Come in, Mac. Close the door behind you."

Captain Mitchell's desk was twice the size of hers. His was also on the top floor of the precinct, with a stunning view of the city. Mitchell was behind his desk, sipping morning coffee from his United States Marines mug.

McNamara stood before him the way a soldier would before saluting her superior.

"Have a seat, Mac. I hate looking up at people."

She sat and rubbed her nose, catching a whiff of her sweet chewing tobacco on her hand. "How's the ticker, boss?"

Mitchell leaned back in his chair, setting the coffee down first. "Hell, I thought this job would kill me ten years ago. But here I remain."

"Amen to that, sir."

Mitchell looked over at a picture of his wife and kids on his workstation of black marble. "I don't know, Mac. Shit's getting thick out there. I almost want to call it a career and take the family back home to Nigeria. I've gotten to a point where I think I've done enough. My sister always asks when I'm coming home for good."

McNamara peered over at the family photo. "I wouldn't blame you, sir. I can handle it."

Mitchell perked up, causing his leather chair to squeak. "That's why I called you in. You holding up okay? I understand you were thrust into lead sergeant because of all my health shit."

McNamara had been feeling the burn, but soldiers never quit. "I'm all over it, sir, but I do have a question."

Mitchell rummaged through his desk drawer and pulled out a pack of Newport cigarettes. He lit one with a white lighter that rested beside his computer. "One more cancer stick won't kill me, will it?"

McNamara licked her lips as she watched him suck, then release a billow of smoky nicotine.

"Want one? Just don't tell the wife," Mitchell said.

"No thank you." McNamara shifted her weight sideways. "I used to smoke the shit out of those things after the Gulf."

"Now you've got that pipe hanging out of your mouth all the time. It does suit you; I'll give you that."

McNamara looked down before grinning in response. "As I was saying, sir. Some of the guys have been chatting about a murder up in the hills. A shrink and his wife. Apparently, he worked out at The Rock."

Mitchell took another puff, clearly savoring the powerful menthol stick. "You know we can't touch that case, Mac. For starters, it's not our jurisdiction. It's on the border, making it Sausalito's problem. Second, we don't deal with any personnel out there on The Rock. The feds are taking care of it. Federal institution, FBI's problem."

McNamara placed her hand in her pantsuit pocket, trying to locate her Savinelli. Her heart skipped a beat when she realized she'd left it back on her desk. "I understand, sir. Do you think that case has anything to do with the shitshow we've been having in the city?"

"Unlikely, but who the fuck knows. Everything is classified out there. It always has been."

"Right. Anything else, Cap?"

Mitchell put out his Newport in a clear ashtray next to his keyboard. McNamara wanted to rush over and snatch it, to get one last puff before it died. "Just making sure you've got your shit together, Sergeant. Your plate is full; I hope you've got an appetite. Be smart and stick to what we're in charge of."

McNamara found relief in knowing that another unsolved case was being dealt with elsewhere.

"Hungry as ever, Captain."

28

"I'll give you a chance."

"A chance at what, Ariel?"

A fitting alias.

I catch Stretch sitting by the fire, a glass of bourbon in his hand. His robe of red velvet moves with the flickering flames. The smell of burning cedar and pine enter my nose.

"A chance to live."

He takes a sip of the whiskey before answering. I stand in the doorway, blocking his escape. "What are you talking about? Are you drunk again?"

Maybe *he* is too drunk to notice my body has changed. I'm taller and my skin is rough. My voice is deeper, an intense rasp.

"I'm leaving, Stretch. I'm giving you a chance to stop me from *killing* you."

He uncrosses his legs and turns toward me in the upstairs doorway, pulling his attention away from the fireplace. "Where are your clothes?"

My eyes go black while my nipples harden. I salivate at the thought of violence. "You know too much about me. I can't risk leaving you alive."

He sees me now. The *real* me.

Stretch's eyes grow wide as he stands. "I've been nothing but good to you. I took you in when you had nothing."

I just smirk, a hollow contortion of blank wickedness. "Pick up the knife, Stretch."

A sharp letter opener is on his desk. It's close enough for him to reach over and grab.

Stretch does as he is told. "Please, Ariel. Don't do this. I don't want to hurt you."

"Stop calling me that!" I charge him head-on, allowing him to ready his blade. He almost fumbles it but recovers and raises it above his head. He comes down for a strike as I catch his hand at the wrist, stopping the motion dead.

I look through him and laugh, owning him with my eyes of sparkling sable. I wrench his wrist with my hand, causing it to snap as the knife falls to the floor.

"Ahh!"

I shoulder him to the rug. His robe flies open, revealing a hairy chest with a Yosemite Sam tattoo by his heart.

I find the knife and slither on top of him. He tries to grip his shattered wrist, but that's the least of his problems. I raise the blade high with both hands, and Stretch shields his face with his arms.

As if that will save him.

I plunge the knife into his chest. He heaves and gags, choking up blood. I pull it out and stab some more, flinging blood everywhere. His gurgled screams become muffled with the amount of fluid that fills his mouth. Each new strike covers me further in his hot death.

My mind enters a strange autopilot after his spraying crimson touches my lips. When I come back to the room, Stretch is there under me, dead and mutilated.

I don't know how many times I stabbed him.

87.

His eyes are wide open and so is his mouth. His tongue is out, frozen in an eternity of dread.

"Stop looking at me," I snarl. I pull the blade from his stomach and sink it into his left eye. It looks fun sticking from his head like this. I look around for another knife but get frustrated that I can't find one. I notice a fork on a small table. A half-eaten meal with vegetables rests on a small dinner plate.

I bring it over and hover it near his face. With a forceful thrust, the fork pierces through, eliciting a sickening crunch as it embeds into his skull.

He's perfect now.

Festering fantasies must be quenched.

I cover my tracks with Stretch, cleaning the scene and burning his body. It is a sloppy attempt, but I'm certain it is enough. I simply drag him toward the fireplace and watch him go up. The wood smell mixed with melting hair and human skin invigorates my basic senses. I rob him and finally have enough dough to scratch things together on my own.

Yep, I hit the lotto landing on Stretch's doorstep that first night. It's as though destined by the powers that be, an allowance to inflict as much torment as I can upon this city.

After all, Stretch was a somber and lonely man.

The perfect target.

29

'1998'

I need another a job. Stretch's gig was fun while it lasted, but I can't stay idle. The thought of making my own way is exciting. I'm beginning to feel a sort of freedom I've never had before.

The possibilities are endless.

I don't know exactly where to start. I have no newspaper in my new apartment. No pager or fancy cell phone. I'd have to be a high roller to own a cell phone. I've seen a few people in the Financial District roaming around with them. They'll saunter down the street in their suits and pretty dress-up clothes, talking business or nothing at all.

Seems weird to me.

What's next?

A cell phone that can give me directions or tell me the weather? Or one I can order lunch on without talking to an actual person?

Preposterous.

My wardrobe hasn't been established yet. The apartment remains barren. I pull out the fanciest jeans I can find and a collared shirt that isn't too wrinkled. It's a men's dress shirt that I stole from a consignment store while working over at Stretch's. I've always been drawn to men's clothing.

I stare at myself in the mirror before I leave. These jeans are a little baggy, but the shirt fits nicely. I roll up the sleeves to complete the look.

There you go.

I really must dye my hair. My mane of orange fire draws too much attention.

It'll have to wait.

What about breakfast?

"Who needs it?"

I'm out the door and into the city. It's almost noon as the sun blinds me. The light breeze feels wonderful on my long arms and face.

You forgot to brush your hair.

"Oh well."

This city is so damn big. Cars are everywhere, and people move along like over-caffeinated zombies. One random street can be spotless and inviting, with lush homes stacked neatly next to each other. No litter or garbage anywhere. Then you can cross over to the next strip of asphalt and be consumed by the decaying transient community. That's how unpredictable the Golden State can be. Maybe that's why I like it one second, then suddenly crave to slaughter the lambs that cross me while they suck in their dead air.

Dead air.

We are *all* dead air.

30

After days of searching, I land at a place called "The Blue Lagoon." I am somewhat put together today. I have to get my shit together and make this happen. The late-morning air in my City of Gold offers wafts of Belgian waffles and eggs Benedicts with bacon and hollandaise sauce from a place next door called "Doug's." Gourmet coffees of custom pedigrees fill the autumn air.

Sunlight bleeds halfway down the other towering buildings on the street, giving everything around a Jekyll and Hyde appearance. My gray slacks and white button-down feel good with the occasional breeze, causing me to take in healthy breaths of fresh breakfast air. My hair is pulled up in a high ponytail. My hands feel a bit damp as I push them through to slick down some flyaways.

The sign above the door isn't elaborate, but altogether classy. "The Blue Lagoon" is written one word above the other, all in thick cursive writing. The bulbs are blue, which means it bleeds the same color when the city gets dark. There is a large anchor behind the letters, appearing as a steel gray through-and-through. The circumference of the bar is dressed in a thick white brick that really stands out. It's the only structure of its kind on the whole block.

I remove my wayfarers and step inside.

31

I've never seen such a fancy watering hole. Back in Kentucky, all us locals had was Woody's. I was nowhere near old enough to drink, but Wade would take me in from time to time while he got sauced with his cop pals. I could always tell he was trying to flaunt me around, his own darling daughter, to show off his dominance over me. He'd make me bring beers back to the table and remove the empties when the boys were dry.

Woody's place was merely a smallish red barn that had been converted into a bar. There was a long police light above the simple sign, which was a clever design idea from the proprietor. It was always on, beaming white, blue, and red all the way into the witching hours.

When you walked in, the bar top was right on top of you. Woody was always the only guy back there, built to last in a cowboy hat and black shirt. Some days, he would have a piece of straw sticking out of his mouth. He'd hold and chew it while serving Wade and his goons. He was always nice to me, and I think he knew something was amiss with Daddy. But hell, I'm far worse than that reckless fuck ever was.

We're superior, angel.

Thank you, love.

Wait—where was I?

Oh yes, back to The Blue Lagoon. The double doors to enter are made of solid steel and quite heavy. Two circular windows are the only way to see inside from up close. There are no big windows to look through from the street, only a sea of white brick. The handles are long and smooth and have an industrial feel to them.

Once I step inside, I feel the *rush*. It is visually stunning to look at, as if every corner and enclave was meticulously decorated with intense forethought. It's almost noon. The joint is empty. There's a uniformed lighting system, a swirling of blue and green throughout the place. To my immediate left is a large fishing boat wheel. It's glued to the floor and held up by a piece of iron. Fishermen's nets line the walls, along with other aquatic paraphernalia, like starfish and huge plaster shark displays.

There's nothing cheesy-looking about it. The high tables are made of thick dark wood and fancy marble slabs. A candle display with a quaint holder sits in the center of each drink table.

The best part is the bar.

It's hard for me to describe, but I'll try.

It's a sprawling clear countertop with every spirit you can think of. I've been around long enough to know my booze and take note that the many beer taps have stylish and uncommon selections.

Nothing worse than having piss water served in every keg.

I notice an Alaskan red ale and a few dark stout options on draught.

Anyway—there's a fish tank above the bar!

Like, this giant tank that stretches as long as the whole counter. It looks like an aquatic paradise, filled with salt water and real, actual fish. It's unbelievable! I stand there staring, not realizing I'm being watched.

"Help you?"

I think he said it one more time. I look to my right and settle my eyes on him. He looks to be the only person in the place. He smiles while he polishes a beer stein with a clean rag.

"I'm interested in the bar back job. I saw your flyer on a telephone pole a few blocks up."

He's middle-aged and harmless. His accent is intense, hailing somewhere from the Middle East. "Two of our bar backs just quit. Both back to school."

I sort of look through him before responding. "Yeah, well—school's for suckers."

He keeps grinning. "What is your name?"

"I'm. . ."

Don't use your real name.

"Ivory. Ivory Blake."

"Obi. I own 'dis place."

Before I can respond, the front door swings open. A bartender type comes barreling in. She's young, like me, but with bright blonde hair. I have a way better body and exude more confidence. I can tell she has no idea who she is inside.

The new person yells at us, "Obi—I better not get a bunch of shit tips again tonight after getting in your glorious tank."

"But Delilah, you look so good doing your act. You are a natural! And 'da drinks fly off 'da shelf when you are in 'dere!"

Say something.

"Forgive me, but what are you two talking about?"

"And who might *you* be?" the bitch Delilah snaps back, shifting her large backpack to her other shoulder.

"Do not mind her. Delilah has been wit' me for a while."

Delilah can't help herself. "It's a mermaid tank, rookie."

"It's Ivory, *De-li-lah*."

Obi laughs and winks at me.

"Awesome, *Ivy*. Kind of sounds like a stripper name."

She can't even say your fake name right.

She'd be fun to slit ear to ear.

Delilah breaks the three-way silence.

Don't you mean four-way?

"I costume up as a mermaid and flop around Obi's tank during prime time. It drives the drunk-y boys batty."

We'll do fine here.

Obi hires me on the spot.

I start tomorrow night.

32

Took the day off from the bar. Not sick; just can't concentrate on work. This is the first day in three weeks that I've called out. Find myself wandering around this city. The sky is gray today and the fog consumes the streets. If you stare straight up to take in the huge high-rise buildings, they almost get lost in the murky mist. Even now, this place remains foreign to me.

There's a little coffee shop on the corner of Van Ness and Gibraltar that I've been frequenting. I take the cup of Sumatra with a splash of cream to go. It is six-thirty in the morning and the weekday rush hasn't gotten underway. There are still some honking cars and cabs, along with screaming kids with backpacks trying to chase down an early school bus. The noise always adds more fuel to the city fire of decay.

I need some solace in this madness.

I walk several blocks. The fog is there, a brooding presence keeping everything blanketed in damp gray. It's windy and cold, a recurring theme in my new hometown. I haven't read much these days, but I remember what Mark Twain once wrote about this place. Something like the coldest winter day he'd ever spent was a summer day in this Golden State. I don't mind the cold; it keeps me sharp. I'm dressed in tight black with the only real color coming from my dyed merlot hair.

I want out from the cars and the people, so I walk several more blocks. I hang a left on Hyde and go toward the water. The creeping clouds are getting thicker toward the sea, almost forming a wall trying to cut me off. I want to disintegrate into the mist, to transform into what I *truly* am.

Several more streets from the gray-washed coastline, I stop at a magnificent cathedral. The doors are shut and padlocked from the outside.

Looks like God doesn't work at all hours. . .

I don't know if I even believe in such a thing.

Why would a god create *me*?

I can't tell if the gothic-looking structure was designed for the Catholics, Protestants, Presbyterians, or Jews. I'm ignorant to the idiosyncrasies of organized religion.

My coffee has turned cold, so I look for a garbage can next to the holy house entrance. I find one off to the side near the few steps leading up to the gigantic double-doors. As I throw the half-full cup away, my heart skips a thudding beat.

It is merely a notice; you *must* remember that I am emotionless.

The cup remains in my hand while I claw into it before finally giving it to the can. It doesn't make sense what I am looking at, but then again, does anything in life make sense?

She is homeless, heavy-set and pants-less. Well—she has pants, but they are down to her chubby ankles. She cranes her head up and gawks into my soulless entity.

"Why are you shitting in front of a church, lady?"

The thing cackles and squats lower, her ass almost to the floor.

"Hello? What's your deal?"

She won't stop staring at my superiority, but she is wholly ignorant to my dominant presence.

"What I do is *my* business, you stuck-up bitch."

I notice her two front teeth are missing while I watch her squeeze out her feces. I try to feel something for such a person, but nothing comes. To feel for someone so—despicable?

But wait—I know what *you're* thinking. . .

'You ain't no saint either, St. James.'

You're not wrong, being that you've probably written me off pages ago.

I consider walking away, just turning around and getting lost. But as I look down on her, kind of getting trapped in my thoughts, I smell her.

The filth.

I finally turn to walk away, but something hits me in the side of the face.

"How do I taste, miss priss? Ha *ha-ha*!"

The cunt rears back to throw another mud biscuit at me, but this time I dodge it. I haven't thought about killing anyone today, but I am fucking livid. I didn't bring my purse, but I have the ice pick.

If you work at a bar, never leave home without one.

The pick sticks out from my right jeans pocket. It remains hidden with my long shirt, but it occasionally pokes me while I walk.

It feels good.

I slither toward the bitch while she pulls up her messy britches. She chuckles as I move in. My weapon is already in my hand, gripped tightly behind my back. I kneel gracefully while she fumbles with herself, like a snake wrapping itself around its next meal.

The waste of oxygen doesn't even see me coming.

I take a long, smooth breath and speak on the exhale. "That wasn't very nice."

Before she realizes I am still around, the ice pick is in her neck. The piggie gurgles and chokes, falling back onto her own soiled ass. I rise to my feet and watch it all unfold. She gasps as her dirty beanie falls off, revealing patchy hair and an olive complexion within her grime.

I think she tries to speak, but I am transfixed on her actions. It's better than sex watching a wretch pull an ice pick from her neck as her gore spills and splashes. It jets in streams, her body squirming and seizing like a glorious display of satisfying death. She claws at the small patch of grass where she lays, ripping up handfuls of wet earth.

She looks to the gray void above us and chokes one final time as steamy piss pools under her. I touch my face, not realizing I was smirking the whole way. I smear some of her stink onto my hand, but it doesn't take away from my incredible high. I crouch down after she stops kicking and pick up my weapon.

I don't run.

I walk away like nothing happened.

Nobody saw.

I got away with another one.

We're invincible.

33

Time has slipped away once again.

I may have slaughtered another homeless wretch.

I'm wandering the streets. What a surprise.

It's almost night; not too late. The sprawling mall across the street is just closing. The sun hasn't fully gone down. The clouds are scattered formations all around the upper ethos. They move quickly in this Golden State, like thoughts whizzing by. The sky tonight has all kinds of colors—aquamarine, sherbet, and a kissable shade of reddish purple. It's a beautiful evening and I've never felt better.

The wind strikes through me while I stand on the sidewalk with a Woolworth's store at my back. There's a 'Closing Forever' sign on the door that says everything must go. People rush by me, barely noticing even themselves. I've dyed my hair again, this time a raven black. My natural waves of fire are transforming to gray at warp speed. I stole a generic brand of color from a small drugstore a few blocks from my apartment. The old guy in there is as good as blind. The cool thing is there's a hint of a deep red within the black. It's subtle and can only be noticed in a certain light.

Why can't I remember what I've done or where I've been?

I didn't work today; I know that for a fact.

I look down at myself, studying my body as a random pedestrian grazes my shoulder in passing. A trolley hitches along, bursting with tourists. The usual wooden shell of the city's riding system glows a rich hue to match the lovely sunset sky.

Let's see.

I'm not covered in blood.

Check.

There are no corpses around.

Check.

It's fine. Everything's *fine*. . .

I'm starving. I probably did unleash my wrath on someone, and that's why I'm exploding with incredible feeling. I look across the street and see a restaurant called Tad's Steakhouse. The sign looks like a Vegas casino. I've never been to Vegas, but I've seen enough of it on TV back on the ranch in Kentucky. The letters light up green and black and are surrounded by huge oval bulbs that give off a bright yellowish light.

I follow my curiosity.

I'm dressed casually in black yoga pants and a *Pantera* sweatshirt. What kind of mermaid dresses in all black?

I do, motherfuckers!

I'm outside, staring at the menu. It offers a substantial selection, with burgers and fancier steaks. They even have an expansive coffee bar. The door beside me opens and a worker steps out. He invites me in. I don't mind the approach, so I oblige.

I sit by myself and scan the joint. This place is strange, but in a good way. It has a unique style to it. I settle in at a two-seater table next to the bar. I look to my right and study its arsenal of spirits. They have some juggernauts back there, such as absinthe and chartreuse. No one's tending the bar and no patrons are around.

Way over in front of me is the kitchen. It's an open arena and I can see what the chefs are up to. Smoke rises, and a flame bursts up from one of the stoves. The air smells of dead cows and coffee.

It's empty inside. Only two other tables are occupied, on the other side of the restaurant. Some generic family with a baby sits at one table, and the other seats a group of three, two girls and one guy.

I kind of want to go over and kill them all.

I sit some more and stare off into nothing. I don't know why a waiter hasn't come over, but then I realize I have to order at the counter. It's in front of me and off to the right, between the dining area and the kitchen. I sigh and rise more slowly than expected.

Must have gotten into something good out there. . .

I'm at the counter, looking over the menu once more. I order a dish that's a hamburger patty, cooked medium and smothered with mushrooms, onions, and gravy, served with mashed potatoes and two massive pieces of garlic bread. To go with it, I order a classic cappuccino.

It's nice having my own money. Sure, I still steal when I get the chance, but my bar has provided a freedom and independence I've never had.

I do have a lot of extra cash on me, though.

Maybe some of my jumbled thoughts are returning.

Did I get in a car with someone?

Fuck, I'm hungry.

A Vietnamese lady finally comes over with the food and coffee. I'm pleasantly surprised by the whole presentation. The cappuccino steams in a fancy white saucer and a leaf design is carved into the foam on top. I've always wondered how they do that.

The hamburger steak is a perfect medium. Each cut I make forces the blood to ooze from the slab. I slice a section, then soak the meat thoroughly in the gravy and excess blood. The dinner is divine. I enjoy it as if it were my last meal.

I'm dozing off while sitting. I'm halfway through with my bloody burger and find myself just staring down at it. The front door of the restaurant opens and in comes three cops. Two are in full uniform, hats and all, while the other is her own thing. The uniforms are both male and the lady is dressed in black—just like me.

She's even tall, with a similar frame and stature. Her hair is jet black, and I can tell it's her natural color. She looks to be in her late thirties, maybe early forties. Her hair isn't as long as mine, but close. The monkey-suited dullards appear dumpy, with their overstuffed police belts weighing down their saggy attire. They have some serious wooden clubs on their hips, even more imposing than the one Daddy used to carry.

Both dudes look like they're one donut away from a heart attack, while the business-looking lady is neat and put together. She towers over her companions while they follow her to a booth next to the front window.

The one sure way I know she's a lawman is from her firearm. The fellas have plastic-parted weapons attached to them, ones that probably carry a dozen rounds. Hers is strapped to her shoulder, attached by a thick dark brown leather material. I see it underneath her jacket as she sits down. The gun she carries appears to be a revolver, a *big* one, even bigger than Daddy's.

I'm not staring and making it obvious. They don't notice me. I'm on the other side of the restaurant, anyway.

The men are boisterous when they order, but the raven woman with her hand cannon orders stoically, gesturing at the little Vietnamese waitress.

I wonder if they're on to us.

I continue eating, enjoying this unexpected rush. The loud idiots order some macchiatos while she gets a large black coffee. While they wait, she digs into her blazer and pulls something from a hidden pocket. It's a tobacco pipe, a slick one that matches the color of her leather holster.

While her friends talk about this or that, I study her from my distance. As I chew, she manifests a tin of tobacco along with a shiny tamping tool. She has a book of matches, no lighter or modern technology to disgrace her methodology. She packs her pipe at the table, lost in her own little world. I can't help but admire how different she seems. She lights up with no hesitation, right there in Tad's Steakhouse.

The waitress hurries over with two plates. It looks like just coffee and tobacco for the woman. I thought the waitress would say something about her smoking, but instead she runs off and fetches an ashtray.

Time slows to a crawl as I watch her.

She's strangely captivating. I wonder what brand of tobacco she smokes.

"What are they talking about?" I ask aloud.

Keep your voice down!

I wince and cover my mouth with my hand.

"Just tell me."

The ugly one is talking about the uptick in crime around the city. The slender woman has interjected, mentioning a recent cold case . . . charred remains in a fireplace above a liquor store.

Stretch.

She's looking at you. . .

I bite into a buttery piece of garlic bread and avert my gaze. I remain with my food for several seconds but have to peek back over. She's not looking at me. She's scanning the restaurant while her smoke rings billow as the sun disappears outside.

I finish before them and get up to leave. I'm not intent on sneaking by or anything like that. I'm playing it cool. Her phone rings just as I leave and enter back into my dark city playground.

"McNamara." She signals to her two morons by snapping her fingers at them. "Another body—in the Tenderloin. Let's move."

That one was probably me.

Pleasure, Officer *McNamara*.

Until we meet again.

34

In the weeks that follow, work goes well. My appetites for flesh and bone remains constant and intense, but somewhat bearable. Being a bar back in a place like The Blue Lagoon has its perks. I do a little bit of everything, from pouring beers to cleaning up after drunken shitheads.

I stay many nights to help clean up, whether it be arranging chairs or washing dishes. I even get to feed the fish in the tank. Obi is cool and never asks too many personal questions. He pays in cash, everything neat and under the table. He doesn't have to, but I'm glad it was offered.

I watch Delilah doing her little performances. Patrons line up around the block on her nights in the tank. We also have a guy named Tomas that performs on the slower nights. His boyfriend doesn't like his act much, but it helps pay for the watches and jewelry that Tomas buys him. Tomas is all right and plays the merman thing well, if I say so myself. He has longish brown hair and is a little chunky, but he takes his performances very seriously.

I feel bad for him when Delilah produces an army of men and women to come in and see her.

You don't feel anything.

Tomas couldn't fill the room if he tried, although he swims much better than Delilah. That's why Obi has him perform on Monday and Tuesday nights. Delilah has the prime-time slot on Fridays and Saturdays. Nobody is in the tank the rest of the week. Obi can't afford any more help.

35

Not sure of the day. Is it tomorrow or the day after? I can't believe I let this happen. I let my guard down and I paid. All I know is I'm sore all over and I can't remember . . . much of anything. There are glimpses of consciousness, like a dream that is patchy and vague. As if a flashlight were running out of batteries, and no matter how hard I whack it with my hand, it won't cooperate.

I feel it, too.

I tried to fight.

I know you did.

Someone had the upper hand. I'll try to unscramble the night. I think it was last night. I'm going back to sleep.

36

I was on my usual bar back duties. I was feeling good, too. My body count was rising, and the blood never stopped flowing. I'd built a bank roll to treat myself to this or that. It was Delilah's night to swim in the tank, but she got sick last minute. She wasn't the type to miss work, even if she was barfing her lungs out. At least that was what Obi had said when I arrived.

Other than that, the night was ordinary. I wore a gold necklace I'd pulled off some random fuck that I'd ripped to shreds the previous night. I had left him behind some donut shop uptown. It was hidden under my shirt with a splash of blood still on it. The symbol was an upside-down triangle that I had to have. Each time I touched it, my legs turned weak with delight.

It was a younger crowd, and it had just gotten dark in the city. The lights inside were dim, except for the dozens of blue bulbs Obi had placed everywhere. The cool aqua straddled the ceiling and all over everything. The brick walls were overshadowed with thick fishing nets, of course.

That's what I love most about my bar.

It looks like a giant boat inside, like we're all rocking in the sea.

Inside *my* dominion.

〜✄〜

With Delilah out of the picture, there was nobody to perform. Bar backs weren't allowed to swim—bartenders *only*. I was helping Maverick pour a red ale for some jocks as the line began to swell around the bar top. We call him Maverick because he always wears aviator sunglasses indoors and is obsessed with that one flying movie with the short actor who runs a lot.

The chilled liquid turned thick and chunky, as if the tap were bleeding out, and my mind fell away to my latest kill. I could recount every detail, each feeling so vividly.

Someone tapped my shoulder. It was Obi.

I hate being snuck up on.

It was loud, so he had to lean into me. He smelled like his famous homemade chicken tikka masala. He brings it in occasionally for all of us to try. It's good.

"What do you say you be 'da mermaid tonight, Ivy?"

Funny how they call you Ivy now.

I kept pouring, but I was getting excited. "Get real, Obi. We're swamped and I'm not an *official* bartender."

He didn't respond, so I turned around. He pointed at my beer. "You are doing great as my newest bartender, Ivy."

I winked and touched his shoulder. You know, just applying my psychopathic charm. "I'd be honored to be gawked at by all this sauced-up fresh meat."

He leaned away and stiffened, really looking into my shark eyes. "It's a performance. Consider yourself an artist. A showgirl!"

I placed my full beer of blood back on the drip tray and crossed my arms. "A showgirl?"

He raised his hands in defense. "I was going to say a showman, but I do not want to offend you."

I grabbed my ponytail with both hands and pulled it apart, tightening it hard at the back of my glorious skull. "Relax, Obi. I'm all over it. I don't have an outfit, though. I know Delilah's stuff is tailored, and she carries it around like she's a real mermaid."

I'm so good at throwing people off my scent.

I'm the real mermaid, Obi.

I passed the blood beer to Maverick.

"There are a bunch of clothes in 'da closet by 'da break room. All 'da way in back by 'da empty kegs."

"You got it, boss."

He reached into his back pocket and handed me a key. I smiled and disappeared to the back of my bar.

37

Alice in Chains whirred from the speakers. I closed the break room door as the lead singer's raspy, yet beautiful tones mixed with the jumbled outbursts from tipsy patrons. It took me a second to find the light, since I'd never been back there before.

It was a small room with a little desk and computer. Obi disappears to crunch his weekly numbers there when he wants some quiet. The costumes were scattered on the other side of the room. It wasn't really a room, more so a large closet. It was rectangular and just wide enough not to become claustrophobic.

I hitched my glasses up on my nose and squatted down like a catcher requesting the hard stuff at the bottom of the ninth. There were a few Halloween-looking things, wigs and cheap glittery materials. Most everything looked like something you'd see in one of those horrid Disney cartoon movies that I was forced to watch as daily entertainment back on The Rock.

I'm not wearing this shit. . .

"I'm not wearing this shit."

I was forced to echo my better self, my . . . *righteous* self.

There was a single locker with no lock on it to the right of the mermaid clothes pile. I opened it and found folders of papers and other insignificance. A small mirror was on the inside of the metal door. I leaned in and stared at myself.

My eyes had turned black, as dark and rich as the midnight waters on a moonless night. They practically matched my newly dyed hair of the same color.

"Hello, gorgeous."

I smiled and saw my new teeth, sharp razors that were jagged and closer together than the *other* me. My skin darkened and I felt the scales come forward, pushing through and hardening to match the hell that is my playground.

It's showtime.

38

I climbed the ladder at the rear of the tank and dunked in headfirst before I transformed all the way. No one saw me make my way over. My tailfin began flapping, a slow-motion seduction of grace and power. I morphed into my surroundings, not paying any attention to the crowded room below me.

The water was salty, and my sea-nymph gills used it to breathe. Some fish swam by, then scattered. A big one with multicolored stripes got brave and almost touched my shoulder of scaly armor.

I had left my glasses next to my clothes in the back. I could see so well in the water that it almost alarmed me, a red hue of clarity mixed perfectly with my black eyes of nothingness. Everything was perfect when I became the *real* me. I flipped around to face the crowd as I got more comfortable. I swam around several times, never needing to go up for air while loosening my long and muscular frame.

It was as if the entire bar had stopped moving.

They looked hypnotized, like they were soaking me in. I could still hear the music playing through the glass, some other rock song crooning about how blue a woman's eyes can be when she says she loves her man. Even Obi and Maverick were left staring. They all looked at each other and began smiling and pointing.

I'd never seen Delilah get *this* kind of treatment.

The bar was packed with fresh meat. I swam for as long as I desired, making eye contact with the insignificant humans below me. The bar was right below me and the entirety of the rectangular tank was clear, so I could see from inside how much booze was flying off the shelves.

I wanted them all to cower, to be petrified by my superiority. I stared at some women and several men, offering the best show I possibly could. It didn't feel cheap, at least not to me. It felt real and authentic. I had stripped away a façade of myself, an outer shell that was also real but hollow and a lie. The real me was right *there*, swimming and frolicking above the inferior masses.

Why weren't they afraid?

I wanted to taste their fear, their horror and disgust.

We'll show 'em, angel. We'll show 'em.

39

I got out after Maverick reached up and tapped on the glass. He was pouring another beer while shaking his head. He looked almost embarrassed, rosy in the cheeks and everything. When I hit the last step before the ground, Obi was standing behind me with a big towel. His brown arms were outstretched, practically erasing his body but leaving his silly head.

I looked down at my fin, but it was gone. It vanished as soon as I got out of the water.

Obi stepped forward and wrapped the towel around me. "Now 'dat is the most daring show I've ever seen!"

I wasn't expecting to change back so suddenly. I didn't like the feeling; it nauseated and weakened me. My confidence was erased, back to being simply Ivory Blake, or Holly St. James—or whatever the fuck my *real* name is.

Obi kept talking. "I knew 'der was something about you, Ivy. I 'tink you made me ten 'tousand dollars tonight!"

Why wasn't he trembling?

I was, instead—and it sickened me.

"I don't feel well, boss. I need a minute."

Before he could respond, I disappeared back to the empty break room.

I wrung out my hair and removed the towel. It was just the other me, naked and second best. My clothes were in a pile next to the open locker. I didn't remember taking them off, but I felt so strange right then. I righted myself and made sure my siren was locked away. I needed her to comfort me, to tell me everything would be okay.

Why is she doing this to me?

My shift wasn't over for another two hours. When I returned behind the bar, I was greeted with claps and whistled cheers. Maverick was pouring another red ale. When he saw me, he stopped mid-pour and came over.

"You've got brass balls, Ivory Blake."

I squeezed more water from my hair and pulled it up in a twisted ponytail.

At least someone has a little respect.

"What are you talking about?"

His cheeks were still flushed while his eyes fluttered around my whole body. "No, nothing. I just can't believe you got up in there in your birthday suit. You swim like a fish, girl."

"I'm *not* a girl."

"Huh?"

I looked at him, his eyes meeting mine at the same height of just under six feet. The music continued to blare on all sides. "I said I need a drink!"

Fuck yeah. . .

40

I only had two beers. Everyone wanted to buy me one after my swim. I told one after the other to piss off. The boys, especially. They couldn't help themselves. I could sense their beady little eyes scanning me the rest of my shift. The bar was rocking, an energy that could only be felt. I'd never seen so many people in there.

Things died down around two. I hadn't had a drink in hours. Obi was in the back office, and Maverick had already gone. I left and almost ran into the doorman.

"Hell of a show tonight, Miss Mermaid."

I scratched my head until it hurt. "Thanks, Ralph."

He was standing by a small overhang next to the bar, smoking a Dunhill. Ralph is wider than he is tall, but he's all muscle. I'm guessing those biceps are all for show. "Call you a cab?"

Isn't he a sweetheart? Perhaps I'll eat it one day after I carve it from his chiseled chest.

"I'll walk."

41

I'd only gotten a block when the car rolled up. The first thing I noticed was the tinted windows. It looked like some flavor of BMW, a nice German piece of shit. He thought he was being sly, cruising alongside me like a little midnight stalker. I pretended not to see him as thunder boomed through the night. The clouds opened and rain cascaded down with a fury.

I was almost at Ferguson Street when I stopped walking. I turned toward the street as the car braked to a squeaking halt. The streets were surprisingly mild at that dead-of-night hour. His car was jet black. The water-speckled paint lit up yellow then red to match the streetlight on my left.

I didn't wait for him. I walked over and tapped on the window. It rolled down halfway. I backed away so I could stare while standing nice and tall. "Can I help you, stud?"

I couldn't see much of him. The sheets of rain were doing a fine job at shielding everything.

"Oh, please don't be scared. I'm sorry I'm following you. You must think I'm a sicko."

I'll show you a sicko. . .

His voice sounded like he'd swallowed a flute. He switched on the light above his head. The phantom silhouette went from dark to visible in an instant. He was decent looking, that clean-cut average appearance. He looked maybe half Asian and the rest some flavor of white. "I'm Mick."

The deluge intensified as the 800 bus screamed by at warp speed. It cut through puddles like they weren't even there, making whooshing sounds and sending water flying all over the black street.

"What can I do for you, Mick?"

He looked away before turning off his engine and switching on his hazard lights. "I saw your show."

He looked embarrassed, timid, and sheepish all rolled into one.

Just what I'm looking for.

"You want an autograph?"

Then I recognized him. He had been standing in the middle of the bar when I first got in the tank. He couldn't stop staring. That was the only reason I'd noticed him. He had looked to be alone throughout the night, but there was no way for me to tell with certainty.

Mick didn't smile or laugh at my snarky question. He put both of his tiny hands on the steering wheel and stared ahead while he spoke, looking as though he were talking to himself while driving nowhere. "I thought I'd fix you a drink back at my place. I saw you walking in all this rain. Just wanted to get to know such a bold woman."

He was so unassuming it was confusing—even to *me.*

I already wasn't feeling my best with everything that had happened during my shift, so I guess I was looking for a glimmer of a good time. I was only two beers deep, and it was pushing three in the morning. I stared down at him in his warm car, flooded with all kinds of yummy scenarios I could act out back at his place.

"Come on," he urged. "You're getting soaked."

I got in and we sped off.

42

We got to Mick's loft shortly after three. We didn't talk much on the drive over. My mind was somersaulting inside itself. We parked in a big garage next to the high-rise apartment building. His place was on the nice side of town, the Russian District. I was at least fifteen blocks from home.

Mick switched off the Nirvana song and got out. The rain had stopped, sputtering to silence in the early morning city. He said he had a roommate but wasn't sure if she was around. He was vague and dodgy, almost calculated with his words and actions.

We took the elevator almost to the top, somewhere in the high thirties. When the door opened, we were already in his apartment. It opened to a vast space of modern warmth. I wasn't quite dry yet. My hair remained damp and my thin leather jacket was still heavy and water-logged. He took my coat and disappeared into another room.

There were candles everywhere. The big main room was lit by firelight, with the only window being a semi-large one straight ahead leading to a small balcony. I didn't care where he went, being that he was five-foot-six on a good day.

I felt comfortable, probably the most comfortable I'd felt all night. I took to the window and looked out. There were no curtains or drapes, only the glass offering a breathtaking view. Kentucky has her way with captivating an audience, with her rolling hills and scattered ranch houses, but this was something different.

I could see the whole city, my entire playground. I smiled to myself while beads of fresh rainwater inched down my face. Both bridges were out there on opposite sides. The one shone a bright white and the other was dipped in fire. Huge boats and transport vessels were scattered about at sea. I was above it all, looking down on all the carnage I'd inflicted thus far.

I wrung out some water in my freshly colored raven hair and pulled out my ponytail. I let my hair drop down past my shoulders and mid-back. It felt cool with the natural warmth of the edgy loft. I turned my head to the left, losing myself in the vastness of the view. The Golden State almost seemed still, with scattered clouds and a crescent moon oozing down, giving everything some drama.

I could even make out, *way* out there, The Rock.

It looked so far away, but never far enough. I cast my hateful soul toward that little speck, that horrid prison where I sat captive for years, and couldn't help but smile. I'd beaten it, that unfeeling purgatory.

I'd beaten Jamison, too.

I took a huge breath and scanned the panoramic scene, finally exhaling for what felt like eternity.

Some music kicked on behind me. I think it came from an old vinyl player. I could hear the faint scratch of the needle before everything hit my ears. I swayed at the window with my better self—just for a moment. I wanted to unleash her and go crazy, but this was a peace I hadn't felt my entire life.

"You like the view?"

I turned around and saw her.

The roommate.

"It's breathtaking."

43

She called herself Snow—just Snow.

"Please, have a seat."

I followed her to the sprawling couch in the center of the room. All the candles were white, resting and glowing like little mysteries of light. Some dripped down tables that were scattered around, the hot wax drooling toward the floor. The candles were scented; the room smelled of cinnamon and vanilla. I took another huge breath in before joining her on the ivory couch.

She had a gothic look, but it wasn't trashy. Her hair was white, fitting her unique name. She wore all black with no letters or insignia. I admired her skirt and her fishnet stockings. She was slender, even more so than me. She looked feminine and wholesome. I struggled not to stare in the dimly lit pitch.

"So . . . how did my *glorious* brother coerce you into coming back here with him?"

She crossed her legs and turned toward me, reaching over for a glass of red wine. The caged liquid looked dark and thick, like the finest blood from a fresh kill.

I faced forward, not showing my desire, and reached a hand up to my hair. It had dried nicely in such a short time. I created another ponytail and grabbed it with both hands, giving it a satisfying yank at the end. "It wasn't much coercion. I got off work and was walking home. Your guy was creeping alongside me. Guess I just gave in."

"Sounds about right."

I kind of like this one.

"I *so* wasn't creeping."

He appeared from the side someplace with a joint hanging from his mouth.

"Oh really, Mick?"

I couldn't help but join the petty small talk. "Yeah, *really,* Mick?"

Snow looked my way and smiled, a toothy presentation that was hauntingly beautiful. Her facial features were striking and original, a distinctness that radiated like a gravitational pull. Her lips were full to match such a large smile and her face was long and godly. She was maintained from head to foot. Her eyes looked black in the candlelight—not as black as *mine* can get, but close.

Mick stood before us with his dirty blonde hair and white T-shirt. He'd changed out of jeans and into a pair of pajama pants. They were all black with white skeletons all over, with crossbones and everything.

Real cute, Mick.

"Two against one, eh? Looks like I'm screwed." He sunk his average-looking ass into a recliner chair next to the couch, then immediately clambered back to his feet. "Wait—where the *hell* are my manners? You need a drink."

He was looking at me. I didn't have time to answer.

"I'll get her a drink, brother. I need a refill, anyway."

"It's your world, sis. We're all just living in it." He turned my way and rolled his eyes.

THE MERMAID KILLER - JOSEPH MIGUEL   149

Snow looked down at me and placed her right hand on her hip. Two gemstone rings on her fingers sparkled in the coziness. "Wine, darling? This red I'm drinking is divine."

I trusted her—I really wanted to.

As for him, I didn't trust him as far as I could throw him.

But her. . .

"Sure, thank you."

She returned quickly, holding two full glasses. She handed me one and snuggled up next to me. My hand grazed her leg, shooting an intensity into me that I was nowhere near used to unless I was killing.

Mick broke me loose from her long legs of smooth vanilla. "A toast—to Ivy the mermaid and her wild antics at The Blue Lagoon!"

44

Dozens of candles continued their burn in the fancy loft, providing the only light that neared picture-perfect. Things seemed so surreal, cuddled next to Snow with her dumpy brother over there stealing our oxygen.

It was all small talk before she said, "You have such gorgeous black hair, Ivy. Do you dye it?"

"I have once or twice."

It was unsettling answering such a personal question, like I was giving something away. I should have lied and said it was my real color. She leaned closer, and her white mane grazed my shoulder. Her breath smelled of cherries and dark chocolate mixed with lip gloss that smelled of rich honey. "I can almost see some fire red in there."

"Yeah, uh, I dyed it red but didn't like it." I leaned forward and grabbed my full wine glass. The first sip went down with a tingle in my gums. The thick elixir had just the right amount of sweetness and intensity.

"Would you mind if I try ASMR on you?"

I settled back and turned toward her, getting even more comfortable. "ASM—what?"

Snow giggled, but not to insult me. It was genuine and forthright. After a large swig of wine, she explained, "Autonomous Sensory Meridian Response. It's a sort-of new phenomenon that very few know about. It's a tingling sensation that usually begins on the scalp and moves down the back of the neck and spine. It's supposedly a little different for everyone—I think."

"Sounds . . . advanced."

Mick exhaled a large plume of weed smoke with a little cough. "Sounds lame, more like it."

"Bite me, Mick."

I grinned and looked at her, enjoying her comeback against her brother.

Snow left for a moment, and Mick looked to be plotting something. I was too tired to care. She came back with a few tools. "Here, let me show you."

She had me sit up straight on the couch. I faced away from her and out toward the sweeping window. The skies remained dark while the city slumbered. Sheets of sideways rain whacked the glass every so often.

She began by running her fingers through my hair. I had some tangles from the work night and the rain, but she gently worked through them. She used her hands like a brush, gliding them through small sections of my hair. Then she gathered all of it up and moved it over my right shoulder, resting it in front of my breast.

My neck was exposed, along with my arms in my tight work shirt. She glided her fingers along my nape, drawing swirls with her smooth tips. My eyes were open, but they soon closed against my will. My breathing slowed and my mind relaxed. Her hands were made of gold. The softer she touched me, the more intensely I felt. She brushed out my hair with a wide-toothed comb, a rare wooden one that she tapped on before using it on me.

The tapping made me break out in tingles all over. She ran the brush through my scalp all the way down my back, releasing any knots I had. The wooden brush made it sound like ocean waves next to my ears as she used it, always taking her time, never trying to rush or hurt me.

Snow occasionally brought her other hand up and ran it through my hair, or she'd caress my neck and shoulders like I was something delicate and prized. My body exploded with sensations. I was experiencing tingles all over, like a pleasurable hypnotic trance that heightened all my senses.

Snow put down the wood brush and picked up a black comb. She ran her fingernails across it while it made a noise like a zipper being slowly pulled up and down. She whispered in my ear that on one side of the comb were standard bristles, thin and tightly together. On the other side was what she called the 'rat tail' side of the comb.

I think she called it a 'rat tail' comb.

She brushed me with the bristled side, all over my head and exposed skin. Then she turned the comb over and began drawing on me with the pointy side. She picked up my hair with her free hand and ran the tail up the baby hairs on my neck, causing me to moan and break out in thick gooseflesh.

I no longer knew where I was.

My dark half didn't care. She craved more of Snow, just as I did.

Snow drew random squiggly lines on my back through my shirt, scraping her way to random sections of fleshy bliss. She ran her tools over my exposed bra straps. Then she reached over and grabbed them, adjusting them back to the heart of my shoulders when they slipped down a bit.

She finished by parting my hair in a zigzag pattern right down the middle of my skull, using the pointed side to snake down my part. She braided my hair and secured it with a white bow at the end, then quickly took it out and released it all.

It was pure heaven.

I was in and out for most of it.

Imagine having a faulty flashlight in a pitch-black attic. You can see a little in an immediate direction if the light shines bright, but when it sputters and leaves you, it all goes dark. You whack the bastard thing as much as you can in the darkness, trying to ignite the beam, but it's wildly inconsistent.

You're blind, really.

You don't know what's happening.

It kind of feels like that.

I had more wine with Snow and Mick after he came back with another cigarette. I had two puffs of it and that was it. The long night began to shift into dawn, turning the dark skies into a lighter purple. I remember my limbs going completely dead on the couch, slumping on Snow's lap while she slept soundly.

She must've woken up because I could hear them talking while Mick carried me to the bedroom.

"Mick, what the fuck? What did you do to her?"

"Stay out of this, sis. She's obviously wasted. She probably had too much of your stupid wine."

"Bullshit!"

"Okay, okay! Maybe it was the weed. It's some powerful stuff."

I couldn't speak or move. I was being carried away into his own little hell. I could still hear Snow.

"Mick, goddammit! What did you slip her?"

Yeah, Mick. You little bastard.

"Relax. It's a concoction I dreamed up at work. She's perfectly fine, sis. I'll take good care of her. Just be a good girl and go off to bed."

He laughed—or coughed—after he nearly dropped me to the floor. "Man, this lengthy vixen is heavier than I thought. It's like there's two of her in there."

There are two of us in here, you filthy fuck. I'll g-et y—. . .

She was fading from me, my anchor, my supreme being. She'd been drugged too. This wasn't just a mind thing. Jamison had tried every piece of psych candy he had to break me. None of it had worked. This stuff was different. It was affecting our nervous system and our muscles.

I was scared, but *she* wasn't.

I think Snow tried to intervene and grab me from him. I heard the smack, then my eyes went dark again as Snow cried out.

"This is the last time, Mick! I don't want any part of your creepy bullshit. You're lucky you're my brother."

That was the last we heard from Snow.

We were his.

45

He tossed me on the bed like a piece of meat.

By then, everything was in and out—in and out.

I think he was surprised that I had slivers of consciousness left at that point. I could tell by his eyes when I opened mine and looked at him while he fucked my lifeless body.

He could barely stay hard the whole time. I think he would have preferred me dead. The room was modern and spacious, the bed large with all black sheets. A deep red accent wall was at the head of it, brooding down on his helpless victims and their average assailant.

I opened my eyes again with him on top of me. He was wearing some type of mask. It looked like a goat with horns, a shaggy white animal thrusting into me. I wanted her to wake up and help, to unleash her incredible wrath on such a petty piece of nothing.

She could not. She was fast asleep.

I tried to move, but it was no use. He choked me out at the end of his play time. The last thing I remembered was thinking I was going to kill him.

46

I woke up near a bus stop by Coit Tower. The wooden seat was damp from the previous night's rain. The sun had just broken free out in the distance, blasting through the scattered morning cloud formations. I looked down at a large puddle at my feet, fancying itself a shimmering mirror of pooled rainwater.

I looked like hammered shit.

I scanned my body and went through my pants pockets. I was fully clothed and had all my belongings. I hadn't been robbed, at least not for cash.

It had been much worse than that.

I got to my feet and looked around the cold city. I needed sleep and painful solitude.

I walked home.

47

"Scarlett?"

She gently opened her eyes, as if coming back from a spell. She was laid out on her back, staring straight up into a sky of eerie blankness. No clouds were visible, the sun nonexistent. The atmosphere was a blanket of hazy green, the color of radioactive ooze. She lifted her head, realizing she was at the beach.

It was quiet, except for the crashing waves.

No seabirds squawking—nothing.

It all looked so familiar, but . . . *not*.

It almost resembled the same beach she had taken Elsa to on their second date.

She stretched her whole body, contorting it while lifting her arms above her head with delight. She must have been laying there asleep for some time. Her belly and the front of her legs were beginning to burn. She sat up, cradling her knees with her arms.

The sand was gloss black against her skin. She took a breath, but there was no air. The sable sand shimmered like scorched glass. There were small stones peppered around, as slick and shiny as exploding dark crystals. She looked around. She was alone.

"Scarlett!?"

She wiped the sleep from her eyes, realizing her movements were all in slow motion, and peered out toward the ocean. A blurry figure caught her eye, floating out in the greenish abyss. The waves crashed with fury close to her bare feet.

"Help! Scarlett!"

Scarlett called out toward her drowning Elsa, but her voice box wouldn't cooperate. She scrambled to her feet and dove in, allowing the watery wrath to take her. She tried again to call out to Elsa, but she had become mute.

Elsa thrashed and bobbed in the blue-green swell, pulverized with each crashing wave.

Scarlett swam and swam.

She came up for air to check her position, but just as she thought she'd made progress, Elsa was pulled further away. She took a huge breath and went under, punching through the water like a madwoman.

She came up again and almost had her.

Before she could corral Elsa, a pair of gangly tentacles erupted from the water behind them. They were thick and black, with large glowing pustules of a sickening neon pink.

They both screamed, but only Elsa made any sound.

The tentacles crashed down on Elsa's shoulders, dragging her down into the slime-colored nothing.

Scarlett thought to flee, but she buried her fear and took another wheezing breath, diving after Elsa. She whipped her head all around the depths, but there was nothing but murky black.

No Elsa.

Scarlett couldn't hold her breath any longer and started back up toward the surface. Before she reached the light, something grabbed her by the ankle. She shrieked, an underwater muffle of piercing dread.

It pulled her down, down, down.

All the way down.

⌒⌒⌒

Scarlett's eyes shot open.

She choked and gagged, gasping for air.

It took a moment, but reality flooded home.

Another nightmare.

Scarlett turned from her back to her side in the pitch black of her bedroom. Elsa was next to her, sleeping and at peace. She studied her for several seconds while her eyes adjusted to the dark, listening to her girlfriend's gentle breaths.

Scarlett felt wet, as if she'd recently been underwater. She could still taste the synthetic salt of her night terror. She pulled back the sheet and realized she was drenched in sweat. Careful not to wake Elsa, she slid out of bed.

Scarlett shivered in her underwear all the way to the bathroom down the hall. She turned on the shower and cranked the knob as hot as it would go, then flicked on the light and stared at herself in the mirror by the tub.

Her captain was expecting her for a meeting in three hours. The department had become restless with the sudden insurgence of violent crime. Now that she was lead Sergeant of Homicide, all fingers were pointed at her.

Scarlett studied herself in the mirror, raising a slender hand to her face to wipe away a tendril of damp dark chocolate. She never thought of herself as pretty, although she undoubtedly was.

Marines turned detectives didn't have such luxuries.

She looked herself right in the eyes, gelling with their grizzled animation. "Get a grip, McNamara."

She smiled a little; her grit had come back to her. Her teeth chattered as the mirror fogged over with steam, and she peeled off her drenched panties before stepping into the hot water. She leaned on the tile closest to the shower head, allowing the water to cascade down her long body.

Tilting her soaked head to the floor, she became hypnotized as the fright washed down the drain in swirling circles.

48

I didn't work for several days after the rape. Obi understood. I said I had the flu. I bathed several times a day, never quite getting the stench of Mick off me. I didn't eat much, but I did try some blood. I gathered it in an empty coffee cup from a hooker uptown that I stumbled onto near Land's End.

The night is quiet in my lair. All the lights are off except for the pink neon above my bed. It now reads, 'hell here' in cute cursive. The 'o' and 't' have burned out completely. I'm drawing a bath in my large tub. The steam rises to the ceiling as I strip down and get in. I light some tea lights and place them around haphazardly. I boosted a box of black ones that smell like licorice from a little place in Chinatown.

The door is open while the pink crawls in after me. The colors form a symphony of orange and pink meshing together in the dark bathroom. I draw a lengthy breath, stemming from deep within my diaphragm. The small window above the tub is cracked, now frosted over from the hypnotic heat. I dip my head under the steamy water, drowning out the occasional screaming bum or police siren screeching in the adjacent street.

These days, whenever I hear a siren, I think they've found me.

I wonder if the authorities are growing a brain.

The woman cop seems purposeful.

She won't win.

I come up for air after what feels like an eternity. No matter; I can breathe for hours under there. I stare at a candle on the very edge of the tub, barely clinging to life. I watch it with my legs bent, my glistening knees breaking free from the inviting deluge. I'm hypnotized while the tea light flickers out, dancing smoke skyward in a lasting effort to maintain life.

I have one wine glass in my whole apartment. I fill it with the life source of the street walker I recently conquered. I've been saving her for several days in my fridge. I drape one of my legs over the rim of the tub before taking a sip.

She goes down with a choke. I can feel her trapped inside me, kicking and screaming, a lasting bond where I have complete control. I put my finger in the glass and stir her around, then bring it back up to my lips and suck her down clean.

Not too much. You must savor.

From the still steaming water between my legs, bubbles form and the water churns. She rises right there in front of me, a towering goddess that nearly touches the ceiling. Water overflows from the tub, hitting the floor and wiping out several light sources. Her blue-black skin is scaly, and her head is shorn, a hulking form of superior grace. Her fin is visible in short sequences, her splashes emptying the tub even more.

"You're *so* beautiful."

She settles down into me, infusing us until the candles go out and the blood is no more.

49

I venture to an area of the city that's wholly unfamiliar. I don't know what happened, but I wind up on Broadway. It's like a dead zone in time, maybe a blackout that teleported me here. An unexplained phenomenon to continue its torture upon me.

It's dark and wet. Maybe I went for a walk because I couldn't sleep. The buffet of prescription pills I took for years at the "hospital" are no longer a part of my daily diet. I did give in to some street drugs, pills, and weed. I tried cocaine for the first time last week. A faceless guy offered it to me at a bar, and I snorted it from his sweaty hand.

I didn't kill him, if that's what you're thinking.

All the white powder did was make me more restless.

Broadway doesn't seem to sleep. Strip clubs and bars line up like candy to junkies and perverts. Block after block of buzzing neon and hustlers at entrances of their meat markets entice the scumbags to come in for some action.

I'm a substantial distance from home. At least ten blocks. My legs are tired; I must've walked a long way. I have nothing on me except a little cash and my charming personality. I look and feel like a drowned rat out here in the rain for so long, but I'm still sexy and saucy as hell.

I can make anything work.

I can deceive anyone.

I think about turning back for home when I pass a skin joint called The Garden of Eden. Umbrellas and other soaked pedestrians sift through the mirrored streets of wet glass. Taxis and cars move up and down, honking at each other even in the dead of night.

The Garden of Eden's sign catches my attention even before the jackal at the front door starts in. The illumination is a large box above the establishment, with a huge thorny rose surrounded by a bed of glowing apples. The name of the club is immersed in the brightest red, glistening with eerie enticement.

"Step right up, step right up! The hottest dames in the city are right inside. No cover charge after midnight."

I want to avoid the creep, but I can't help but notice his outfit. He's dressed in a red velvet tuxedo with a single rose sticking out of his jacket pocket. His shoes are bright green while a black top hat sits lopsided on his head. He's all belly and I literally dwarf him in height. He may be a midget—you know, a little guy. I don't know the proper terminology, but maybe he's half-midget? His legs are extra short, but the rest of his body offers better proportions.

But that gut . . . Jesus Christ.

At this point, I'm drenched from the rain. I stop in front of him. "No cover, eh, shorty?"

He cranes his rosy little tomato head upward to meet my water-speckled glasses. His voice has a weird squeak to it. He looks middle-aged but sounds like a prepubescent boy. "Absolutely correct, pretty lady. My, are you tall!"

I sniff without looking down. "My, are you short, *shorty*."

He bellows a laugh and almost loses his hat. Then he whips out the rose from his little breast pocket and holds it out. "Heck, I like you, kiddo! If you're thirsty, tell sweet cheeks at the bar that Malcolm says the first one's on me."

I'm shivering from the cold and have no jacket. I scan myself with uncertainty and see all I have on is a skimpy T-shirt and extra tight jeans. "Appreciate that, Malcolm. You can keep your flower for your next victim."

I remove my glasses and wink at him, then disappear inside.

50

It's another realm in such a dark world of sleaze. The music pulses through my ears while I walk a short hallway. Framed pictures line the black walls on both sides. They're all various strippers posing for cheap photographers. Some are partially nude, others all the way.

There's one at the end of the hallway, right before the room opens into a tight box of glowing red. It's of a girl on her knees in a hotel room. The picture is monochrome and dramatic. She's wearing lacy lingerie with her hands behind her head, grabbing at her long locks of wavy dark hair. There's a fierceness in her eyes, like she's in control. She owns the picture, frozen in time, standing apart from any others on the sable wall space.

Once the room opens, the smell of tobacco and heavy cigarette smoke hits me in the face. The atmosphere has a haze about it, with puffs and ringlets of vapors filling the air. It's very dark, with rich red lights buzzing from the ceiling. They are positioned every foot or so, hanging by a rod with a single bulb. They blanket the scene in crimson drama.

Small tables loaded with fat and ugly men are in front of me. American beer cans and dry martini glasses glisten in all the red. On the dozen drink tables are lit candles to help with the ambiance. They flicker and dance, offering their own show that nobody else seems to notice.

Some women are seated here and there, but the men rule the territory. It's warm and stuffy in the main showroom as my hair begins to dry and frizz. The stage is off to the left, a vacant arena with a deep green curtain of ornate velvet. It's drawn down to the floor with no woman of the evening in sight. I look for a place to sit down and settle my eyes on the bar. It's on the other side of the tight square room. Surprisingly, no patrons occupy this stretch of space.

I go over and am greeted by a woman in a men's business suit. She wears the hell out of it, looking simply gorgeous. My glasses remain littered with raindrops and have fogged up, so I take them off. "I love your tie. You look stunning."

She straightens the striped dangler around her neck and offers a smile. "Thanks, darlin'. Looks like the rain is ugly out there."

I shrug and wring out my hair.

"What'll it be?"

I scan the smallish bar. It offers a few beers on tap, but gross IPAs and Lite garbage was the theme. "Buffalo Trace on the rocks. Oh, and Malcolm said to tell you the first one's on him."

The slender brunette in her fitted suit looks me over, then turns toward the whiskey at her back. "I bet he did. Whiskey girl, huh? My kind of gal."

She hands me the healthiest drink I've ever seen and pours herself a shot. Then she turns back to me and smiles. "To our health!"

We clink and I leave her, taking a seat in the very front of the vacant stage. I'm prepared to let the night slip away.

51

A silence sweeps over the red garden until the music begins to play. I take a long sip of whiskey as the speakers bump and vibrate. There's whistling and hollering from some of the prick men behind me and around in the darkness, but it remains respectful for such a place. The smoky little world trembles and comes alive with the catchy tune.

I'm halfway through my drink when the curtain begins rustling. The club isn't too packed, but it feels comfortable. The velvet rises and a girl stands there. She wears clear high heels and sports a white fur overcoat.

She's more of a dirty blonde, her hair not too long or short. It's her statement piece, a risky effort that she pulls off somehow. It's parted down the side of her head and longer in the front. The sides are also short, almost shaved. She's extremely young but doesn't look nervous.

The song lyrics melt into my soul, if I have such a thing.

The singer wails on about ladies coming and sugar baby butterflies.

Without warning, the dancer flings off her coat. She's not coy at all, wearing absolutely nothing underneath. She goes straight for the shiny pole feet from where I'm sitting. We lock eyes, and I look away. The lyrics sync with her body while she takes several twirls in front of her shadowy onlookers.

After her performance I get another drink. Other sex workers in bikinis and tassels prance around taking drink orders, but I go to the bar if I need anything. I can't recall how long I've been here, but it's been at least several hours.

I'm bushed and don't even care what time it is. If I had to guess, it's somewhere between two and four in the morning. As time flies and the night churns, the crowd thins out. I'm getting restless and want to go home.

I crave something else.

"What?"

You know.

Another chance to show a weaker organism what I'm capable of. . .

I scan the darkness and realize I'm the only woman left in the crowd besides the bartender and performers. I'm paranoid and leave. The midget doorman isn't there and that makes me happy. The side alleyway beckons to me, and I sense something beneficial might come of it.

I'm so hungry I can almost taste it.

The rain has let up, but I can tell it wants to come roaring back. The night sky is consumed with clouds, the street and sidewalks are full of puddles and slick dampness.

I do admit I'm a little tipsy.

It feels good, a type of relaxed reckless abandonment. Although the outside air is moist, there is no wind. This helps keep me warm despite my thin T-shirt. Another song kicks on inside while I press my back up against the outside brick. A large dumpster is beside me while graffiti lines the side of the strip joint. It is just scribbled babble, nothing artistic or stylish.

I'm on the verge of abandoning my position when the door to my left swings open. It's one of the back doors to the Garden of Eden. Out comes a guy a hair shorter than me. He's stocky and sports that T-shirt and jeans look. His hair is short and average like any other guy. A good old-fashioned slice of mediocrity.

It's been a full minute and he hasn't seen me. He figures it out after he pulls another drag of his Marlboro Red. "Jesus! You scared the crap outta me."

My back remains pressed against the cold wall. I turn my head to stare silently at him.

"What the hell are you doing back here?"

I make him sweat a little before giving in. "You almost dropped your cigarette."

He goes straight to the tough guy approach. Nauseating. "Bullshit. I was trying to make you feel more comfortable for sneaking up on me."

I don't move or acknowledge his words. "Some show in there, huh?"

He shuffles his feet and crosses his arms, fighting the cold death of my presence.

"Why do you men go to places like this?"

He's drunk. He takes a swaying step backward and rests his back against my wall. "Why are *you* in a place like *this*?"

Cute, asshole.

"Hunting."

"Huh?"

"Oh, nothing."

He looks around and finds some courage, taking several staggering steps toward me. "Say, you're *way* prettier than any of those sluts in there. I noticed you inside. You don't work here, do you?"

"Aren't you clever. Do you work here?"

He leans in, far too close for comfort. His breath reeks of stale booze and white trash cigarettes. "You kidding? I wouldn't be caught dead in here, but a guy has needs."

"A woman does, too."

He lunges in for a kiss, but I step away from him. He's clumsy and stupid, not knowing what the fuck he's stepped into.

Me, on the other hand—I'm sharp and alert.

There's nothing more dangerous than a relaxed and focused killer.

"Easy there, pal. You should probably buy me dinner first."

"I've got some dinner for you."

He pulls the knife rather impressively from his back pocket. It's a shiny butterfly type thing. With a flick of his wrist, the blade is out and ready for me. He's so close that I let him grab my hair with his free hand. It takes incredible discipline to allow him that at such an intimate range, but I'm still in complete control.

"You're going to suck me dry—or I'll cut your fucking throat." His eyes are glazed, but he knows what he's doing. His seeing windows are pretty, a deep ocean blue. It goes to show that not everything is as it seems.

I'm full proof of that.

He unzips his pants, then presses the blade to my cheek. It's cold and sharp as the rain begins again. He pushes my head down while I squat and take him into my mouth. The fuck can't even get hard. I can't see where he has the knife, but it doesn't bother me. The uncertainty fuels the excitement.

When I sense his body relax, I bite down. I start with a gentle nibble, then lock my jaw and chomp. Blood pools into my mouth. He shrieks. There's a strange delay in it, like he never in a million years would suspect a woman do such a thing with a knife dangling over her head.

I hear the weapon hit the cement as he cries out again. He tries to pull away, but I don't let him. Blood drips down my face and pours to the ground. I straighten in time for him to hit me. We fall together to the alleyway of soggy newspaper litter. It's dark back here, the only illumination coming from a warm light a hundred feet further down.

All he cares about is his mangled dick.

All *I* care about is the knife that he's dropped.

I find it first as he wraps his soggy hands around my throat. I'm on my back and he's all the way on top of me. He's moaning and crying, sounding like a real piece of shit. There's no way he knows I've found his blade.

I blindly stab him somewhere in the back.

He doesn't like that—not one bit.

He lets go of my throat. I think he wants to flee, to run away from me. He stiffens to stand. We trade glances for just a moment, his heightened surprise and terror causing me to giggle and go crazy inside.

Before I can get up, I flash the knife in front of his face. He follows it on instinct, just long enough to allow me to sink the dagger directly into his right eye of blue. It enters his skull with surprising ease, like it was always destined to wind up there.

He takes a heaving breath as I let go of the knife, causing it to stick straight out of his stupid head. He fumbles to remove it with a bloody hand while I laugh up at him. He kind of gags and whimpers, then shoots blood on my face and collapses on top of me. I wriggle out from underneath him and get to my feet. The rain starts pouring in buckets, washing away my crime scene of vital evidence.

The shitbag is on his face, the soggy garbage and a green dumpster becoming his final resting place. I want to take something of his, a keepsake to remind me what I've done.

There's no time.

This wasn't a calculated act.

His lukewarm blood is still in my mouth, along with the foul taste of his cheesy dick. I rip open his shirt at the neck, exposing a hairless surface, and stick my left index finger in my mouth to draw out some red ink. I scribble my signature on the dead waste of space, in his own blood and gore, authenticating my beautiful masterpiece.

I tilt my head up to the gray black world and swallow the rest of him down. I savor every drop while my black eyes roll back into my mermaid skull. I gather what I can and turn toward Broadway, disappearing back into the remaining night of the gritty Golden State.

52

Feel awful today.

Can't even bring myself to look in the mirror.

My mind is mush, a jumbled psychosis of pain and wicked angst. My apartment is filthy, and the rain hasn't let up in the few following days since my strip club conquest. I never thought I'd rely on such things as psychiatric drugs, but without them I fall to madness.

I remain functional when I need to be, but mundane tasks seem difficult. Showering is a chore and eating "normal" food just as bad. I sit here alone and write, feeling not the slightest bit human.

The walls in my lair seem to move in the twilight hours, rocking back and forth as if I'm at sea. I peel myself from the waterbed and lie on the floor, naked and exposed, desperate to cease the swimming feeling in my head. My eyes won't close. I just stare up at the ceiling, rehashing my icky conquests. My scaly skin feels rough and exotic to my own wicked touch. My fin twitches and sways, slapping the hardwood in my state of comatose.

What am I?

Am I human?

What has been done to me?

Sometimes she won't answer.

The world doesn't seem real—but instead a stage. Some cheap show where I can still act out and reign supreme.

I can't tell you how many I've killed—and I don't care.

It's not enough.

It'll *never* be enough.

I have to try—die trying, if need be—to shave the bloated masses of inferiority.

When did I become this siren, this menace stalking these streets of fake gold?

It's strange knowing I'm not the result of *anything*.

It's just me. It's always been *me*.

It's morning and I'm still on the floor. I've hardly moved a muscle, but that's all right. I have more work to do. There's much more blood to spill.

53

The truth is, I'll always be a Kentucky girl. I've tried to beat it out of me, but the warring inside is futile. Bowling Green is a micro town where everybody knows everyone. Milk and sugar are exchanged with neighbors and all that crap. Most families would never think of locking their doors at night, especially with Daddy on active civil duty. He was king of Kentucky Podunk until *we* ended his reign of terror.

It's all different here. This city is a wacky funhouse, a roaring playground with people all over and cars at every intersection. You can be anyone and do anything—at least that's how I see it. That's probably why I've been so successful with my work thus far.

My mistake with Mick was letting my guard down, just for a moment. You can't do that if you're someone like me. Trouble always finds us.

It's not a victim mentality; it's simply stating truth.

Evil attracts evil. Diseased souls attract the same brand of filth.

I'm in no way dumbing myself down, because as you know by now, I'm something much more complex. But even I can slip up. Even *she* can make a mistake.

I must continue to evolve.

54

Hailed a cab after work. It's late and this rain is a menace. I would've walked, but I'm feeling frisky. I made sure to hike a few blocks away from The Blue Lagoon before flagging one down. I'm drenched as one finally stops for me on Pine Street.

I hop in the back and tell him to go to some bogus area of the city. It's desolate and close to the majestic bridge of fire. The dummy can't understand why I want to go out that way so late. I say I'm meeting a friend to sightsee the view, then they are going to drive me all the way up to Oregon to see my folks.

It's amazing what people will believe if you have a pretty face and a quick wit.

We drive block after block and reach the city's edge. He tries making conversation and says his name is Paul. He's wearing one of those painter hats and has a belly the size of a beachball. He's wearing big square glasses that practically swallow up his round little face. The car smells of hot dogs and damp body odor.

I want to roll down a window, but the rain keeps coming. The traffic was light on the way over while I sat in the back seat to scheme. The wipers of his yellow cab are hypnotic, entrancing me along with the pitter-patter of the powerful deluge.

We've reached Fort Point. The fort is no longer used, of course. It's more of a tourist attraction in this grandiose year of nineteen-ninety something-or-other. No cars are in sight, not a soul to be found. The ocean is right next to the car and the bridge gleams directly above.

She's so close it feels magical.

Although the sky pours down like silk, thinner clouds are scattered in some sections. A green light illuminates the inside of the taxi as the vehicle comes to a full stop. On the way, Paul blabbed on about his kids and his wife, saying he has driven a cab for years and loves getting people where they need to go.

I don't understand why humans reveal so much about themselves to absolute strangers.

Especially ones like *me*.

$\sim\!\!\propto\!\!\sim$

I grow deathly quiet.

I'm still in his backseat, right behind him.

The wipers swing their dance and Paul coughs, a phlegmy kind of gross. He turns around and asks what sort of game I'm playing, attempting to exude his masculine confidence over what he presumes is a weird little girl.

He goes to get out of the cab as I stick the knife to his throat. It's a large one I'm lucky to have found in my closet at home. The previous tenant must've left it on accident or didn't care for it any longer.

Or. . .

They were hoping someone, or *something*, like me would find it and put it to good use.

The dagger is light and unique. The blade is razor sharp and de-lightfully long. It curves and breaks off into two sections, like a slit in the overall design. You can wrap your hand all the way into the custom handle. The outside of it is surrounded by sharp metal spikes. It's been in my purse for most of my hunting thus far.

I haven't pierced Paul's skin, but I've really scared him. He closes the door and begins shaking. I make him take off his belt while he snivels like a little fruitcake. He begs me to let him walk away and keeps saying his wife will be worried and his kids will miss him.

Yada yada. . .

"Please, lady. *Please*. I don't know what this is about, but you can have anything you w-want. H-here, take my wallet."

He tries to lean away from the knife as I reach my other hand over and rip off his hat. I grab his thin bed of receding hairline. "Don't you move, now."

He has this accent, like maybe Boston or New York. I've never been to either place, so who fucking cares.

"Give me your belt, Pauly."

He maneuvers a bit and gets it off. I grab it from his right hand.

"Put your arms behind the seat."

"W-what?"

"NOW."

He complies while the cab engine idles in the midnight hour.

I tie him up good with the leather strap. His hands are sweaty, so I knot the belt several times. I remove the knife and sit back in my seat, giving Pauly some breathing room.

"Don't kill me, lady. What did I do?"

I remove my glasses and put them in my purse.

He tries again, practically sobbing. "W-what's the matter with you? Jesus!"

I look down. His little hands are trying to move in the restraints behind his seat. He's not going anywhere. I slither forward as my brown leather pants gel together. My feet become one long stem. I can see my fin and can feel my skin becoming reptilian. My eyes roll over in my skull from blue to black. I can still see, but better. It's as if I have a film over my eyes, enhancing everything.

It's always like this when I transform.

My voice deepens, but I'm still female, sultry, and dominant. "What day is it, Pauly?"

He's lost in translation.

"What?"

"I said . . . what—day—is—it, Pauly?"

"Monday?"

"I just don't like Mondays."

There's a plastic bag in the passenger seat. I reach around and grab it. It has some food and crap in there. The good news is its double bagged.

How fun!

I dump the shit out and bag the fucker's head from behind. He doesn't know what's happening, I can tell you that. The windshield wipers are the only other sound during the struggle. They wash the rain away every few seconds with a gentle squeak.

Pauly is rather strong, a deceiving little specimen. He writhes and squirms something fierce. I don't want to pull with all my might in fear I'll break the bags and allow him to breathe, so I ease up when I need to. It's a clever game of knowing when to apply force and when to release some slack.

The shithead's legs are flailing, his hands going crazy. I'm giggling and laughing while his head thrashes and his tongue and teeth try to bite through.

Pauly does *not* want to die.

He's holding on for dear life. I'm so fucking wet between my legs I can't think. I sense the useless life of this loser warring with me. The engine revs in park while his shoes nick the pedals. The windows fog with my heavy breathing and his gasping and heaving.

His last words are whimpers.

～⌒～

I want to stay in the car with him, to cuddle with my fresh kill. Stay the night and enjoy my conquest. Instead, I find his wedding band on his chubby finger. It's right here, all tied up with his own belt. I can't get it off, no matter how hard I try.

I look in the rearview mirror while the rain never stops. Everything is quiet, except for the outside world. The taxi stops shaking and the laughing and dying cease. I smile at myself with my huge black eyes and my jagged set of toothy grinders. My usual human teeth have given way to my authentic mouth bones.

I bend down and bite hard, grinding into his flesh and bone. His finger remains, but I got the stupid ring. Maybe I'll keep it under my pillow and kiss it every night before I go to sleep.

I spit out the piece of finger I mutilated. It tastes like hot fear and death.

I untie him and remove the bags from his head. I really don't care how I leave the inside of the car. I just want my prize and my own things. I get out and put the cab in neutral and press his lifeless foot down all the way. I lean in over him and give him a little kiss on the forehead. His tongue is out, and his eyes are bugged from his skull. His mouth is halfway open with drool coming out.

"So long, Pauly."

I slam her in drive and get the heck out of there. The yellow cab careens off the narrow path nearest the bridge of fire. It catches air and ends up in the black ocean. I drop to my knees and finger myself twice while I watch the cabbie sink into the murk.

My siren self leaves quickly. It's just plain-old Holly out in her midnight madness.

I walk several miles back to a more populated area of my Golden State, then take the bus home.

55

By the time McNamara arrived on the scene, it was light out. The sun peeked over the Sausalito mountains, causing shimmering water to pinball off the relaxed ocean. Seagulls could be heard and occasionally seen, with the fort holding up the Golden Gate from one side. A sheet of mist blanketed the water bank nearest the sunken cab, but the sunlight was quick to burn it away.

She pulled right up to the action. Divers were standing by along with the heavy equipment that had pulled the car from its forced resting place. She slammed the door of her black Firebird just in time to take one last sip of coffee from her Styrofoam cup. She aimed and chucked it in a defaced garbage can with a giant seagull perched on the rim. The bird didn't flinch.

As she walked on scene, the rookie was standing next to Fleming. Fleming was her long-standing partner if she needed help. Since the promotion, she usually worked alone.

"What do we got?"

The rookie itched to go first. He started but stopped when McNamara pulled down her dark aviators and scowled at him.

Fleming looked at the rookie, then to his partner, then back to the rookie.

McNamara looked at Fleming, eyeballing him with a smooth annoyance. "Come on, Fleming. Just the meat and potatoes."

"That hot rod seems to get louder by the day, Mac. What are you feeding that thing? Rocket fuel?"

McNamara turned around to face her custom car. The seagull from the can had made its way to the center of her hood. The sergeant cringed at the sight, then turned back to face her crime scene.

The rookie was staring at Fleming with a look that read something like 'what the hell is *her* problem?'

"I'm always like this before breakfast. At ease, rookie. You can burn through lead with that stare. If you want to make yourself useful, walk over and remove that rat with wings from my car."

He took a few steps on command but stopped when Fleming grabbed his shoulder.

"It's a joke, Ramirez. She's fucking with you."

"Am I?"

The two smiled at each other.

"*Okay*, Fleming. Let's have it."

"The deceased is Paul Gimanelli. Local cabbie, forty-seven. Has a wife, two kids, pays his taxes on time. Just your typical guy out trying to make a living."

McNamara walked over to the driver's side of the freshly fished-out tomb. Paul was situated in his seat, slumped over with sludge and algae draped over him. A small fish lay dead on the passenger side floor.

Fleming kept talking. "I only had the chance to look for a second because we just fished him out."

McNamara crouched low like a baseball catcher, craning her head and two gloved hands into the car. "He was murdered."

"How can you tell? You just got here. He doesn't have any wounds that I can see. For all we know, his heart gave out and he zigged instead of zagged."

"What was he doing way out here?"

Fleming ran his hands through his flat top of gray and pulled his notepad from his back pocket. "His wife reported him missing seventy-two hours ago. According to her, he never failed to come home. Didn't have many friends. Was a family man until the end."

"I believe it. His ring finger is missing. Almost looks as though it's been sawed or chewed off."

Fleming wasn't good with the whole blood-and-guts part of the job. He winced and rubbed his forehead. "Good catch, Sarge."

"It's right there in front of me. Not all of us are blind, partner."

Fleming took no offense. "You said *chewed* off? What kind of psycho would chew off a guy's ring finger?"

McNamara disregarded the question and leaned farther in. A leather briefcase was on the floor next to the dead fish. She rose, knees popping, and went around to open the passenger door. She grabbed the case and pulled it from the cab.

The sun had risen fully, gracing the Golden State with another unpredictable day. The case was standard, a classic piece that any older businessman would carry. The inscription next to the number lock read 'PG.'

McNamara tried to open it, but it was locked. She reached into her pocket and pulled out the switchblade she always carried.

Fleming walked over. "Jesus, Mac. You still got that thing?"

"I won't tell if you don't."

She drove the sharp dagger into the crease, popping the assembly open with remarkable ease. The briefcase was waterlogged on the outside but dry as a bone on the interior. Inside were random documents and miscellaneous notes of Paul's, loose receipts and writings while he waited out the long nights for a fresh fare.

McNamara leafed through and found a page in the stack. It was scrawled in blood, the bizarre fish fin symbol coming into view right in front of them.

"Almost looks like . . . a mermaid."

The rookie had snuck up on them, offering his two cents. The gory drawing was an abstraction that could have meant anything, but the rookie may have been on to something.

McNamara had never dealt with anything like this. Not in the Golden State she'd sworn to protect. They walked away while Paul was pulled from his car and carefully prepped for transport and an official cause of death.

She was almost back to her car as Fleming called out, "Mac?"

"That's right, boys." McNamara opened her car door and turned back to them. "We've got ourselves a fucking serial killer."

56

Inside every television set is some kind of horrific news. I'm thankful I can't afford one at my apartment. Even if I could, I wouldn't. Those stupid tubes rot your brain. Whenever I'm in a bar or passing by a restaurant window or moseying around town looking for my next bit of fun, it's the same regurgitated programming.

Humans *love* bad news.

They pretend they don't, but they can't get enough. Murder, rape, suicide, war, explosions, some guy in a suit fucked that guy in a suit.

I'm no different.

The glaring difference between me and the majority is I act on my nature.

It's strange how humans violate each other willingly, with some form of reason. Look at a lion or tiger in the wild. They hunt and kill because it's in their nature, not because they enjoy it. They murder to survive; it's all instinct.

I guess I'm kind of like that.

An instinctual hunter, always on the prowl. I possess a human brain, but I run on something more basic. My brain hardly gets in the way of my primal needs. Being human makes it that much more fun. I can ruminate over what I've done, study it and play it in my head repeatedly.

It's the best of both worlds.

There's another thing—the high road that humans take.

They shudder at a gangbanger frying his baby in a microwave, but they'll watch and engage in the story endlessly. It's hypocritical. At least I own who and what I am, with no guilt or remorse.

I wish I could discuss my true self with another. Could that ever be possible? Could someone understand what I am? Comprehend my cravings and accept my justifications? Doubtful, but none of that is relevant. I've got me, and I'm all that matters.

I'm all you need, angel.

"I know."

I've pondered what this world could look like in thirty years. What will 2010 have to offer? 2030?

If the only choices left are fear and anger, I choose *anger*.

The world tries so hard to dominate with fear, punching everything and everyone down to literal nothingness. As of now, the distracting rage is Pogs and whiny boy bands. Computers are taking off and technology appears to be the major advancement for the human collective. I shudder to think what the future holds.

57

Didn't go in to work. Wasn't in the mood for all that pretending. My appetites have been insatiable and overpowering, draining me to my core. I was supposed to start at five but went out around noon to cruise my playground. I may have to invest in a typewriter or something. My left hand grows tired with all this scribbling. I've even switched to my right when the left goes numb.

You never know how talented you are until you give it a go.

I didn't eat breakfast. Don't have anything in my rotting fridge, except the heart and spleen. They're wrapped in newspaper next to a bottle of Tito's.

Those are for later. . .

Yummy.

I went to a fast-food restaurant. Had a little cheeseburger with ketchup only. Found myself wandering again. The day is so bright and the traffic is running smoothly. I pass by bums and businessmen, hotel staff and uniformed bellhops.

That's the thing with such a city. One street can be littered with schizophrenics and psychos, while the next boasts million-dollar homes stacked almost on top of each other. There's always China and Japan-town, too, with their interesting smells and cheap shops.

Everything seems to breathe out here.

Not the people. Not these . . . cattle.

My cattle.

The city itself, I mean. It has a hundred heartbeats, with each night and intersection being different and unique. I will never grow bored of such a place.

The quick burger has given me some fuel and the cola's caffeine has kicked in. I slither through the Financial District and wind up near a hospital. It's on the other side of the street, some fancy-looking thing named after an emerging tech giant. The hospital is his real name, apparently.

Talk about being an arrogant little fuck.

Who am I to talk?

I shouldn't judge so harshly.

The air is warm, and I'm again covered in black, a baggy sweatshirt and some tight jean shorts. They're ripped in some areas and are really comfy. I have my hood on, with my dark messy hair spilling out into my face.

I miss your natural red.

It's a frantic scene in front of the hospital. There's a traffic jam with cars honking and pissed-off people. I'm a safe distance away, across the street leaning on a streetlamp by the corner. It looks like a mini riot, with hospital employees in scrub suits and red shirts marching back and forth, holding little blow horns with their plastic badges gleaming in the sun.

A breeze comes through, kissing my face while a large pickup truck comes into view. All the boisterous employees stand chanting about diseased hospital politics and unfair wages. They're really getting turned on when they read what the guy has on his truck. He's hand-painted all kinds of phrases on the truck, telling how horrible this hospital is with how they treat staff and patients.

On the truck bed door, he's even written names of doctors who are not performing at their full potential. They all look like lunatics. The city's "finest" have stormed in to break it apart. Ordinary citizens are getting involved, whether they're randomly passing through or coming in and out of the hospital.

The chants grow incessant from the hungry horde. I cross my legs and increase my lean at my post, folding my arms across themselves.

"WHAT DO WE WANT!?"

"FAIR WAGES FOR OUR MENTAL HEALTH PROFESSIONALS!!!"

"WHEN DO WE WANT IT!?"

"NOW!!!"

On and on.

The cops have finally dragged the guy from his truck. He was trying to mount the curb and almost took out a fire hydrant in the process. He's been laying on his horn the whole time, screaming bloody murder.

Two women cops drag him out with guns drawn. One's lost her hat, and her blonde hair spills down her back. The trucker is big, with a huge beard and long hair. They have him in cuffs as he hits the floor. As they pull him to his feet, he's spitting and cussing, going ballistic.

"THERE IS NO HEALTH WITHOUT *MENTAL* HEALTH!"

I admire this type of rage in people.

I love it.

It's getting more insane out here—and *we're* helping to make it worse.

I'm doing everything in my power to crumble the human collective, to bring these pitiful peasants to their knees.

In the end, they stand no chance.

58

"You coming to bed?"

No response.

"Scarlett?"

The off-duty sergeant remained at her kitchen table. The latest autopsy report had just come back on the sunken cabbie by the bridge. A small army of empty beer bottles were scattered among the paperwork.

"*Scarlett*!?"

She replied without turning away from her work. "Hmm?"

Elsa stood in the entryway, hugged tightly by a silk nightgown. Her hair was wet, and her lotion smelled of fresh strawberry candy. "How many of those beers do you plan on drinking tonight?"

McNamara leafed through some things, settling on a photo of the cabbie's face and mutilated hand. She spoke, but to herself. "He was dead before he hit the water."

"Are you listening to me, Scar?" Elsa crossed her arms. "We can't keep doing this."

McNamara picked up the closest beer bottle, realizing it was bone dry. "Fuck. We're out."

"Out of what?"

"Beer."

Elsa scoffed and ran a hand through her recently conditioned hair. "That's what you care about? You're sinking again, Scar."

McNamara still had her work clothes on. Her white dress shirt was unbuttoned, showing off a black bra. She'd rolled both sleeves up to her elbows. She stopped her obsession and got up from her seat. "I'm fine, honey. I need to study this case. It's ugly."

Elsa stayed in the kitchen entryway, using the wall to hold up her slanted posture. "You've been home for hours and have barely said a thing to me. You're still wearing your gun, for God's sake."

McNamara needed more booze. The handful of beers she'd swallowed wasn't cutting it. "I can't do this right now, Elsa. I need to concentrate."

"Concentrate on *what*? That dead guy's picture on the table?" Elsa took a step forward. Her eyes began to well up with fresh sadness salt. "I know your job can be difficult, but you're spiraling. All you do now is smoke that pipe and drink."

McNamara took a long breath and bit her lip. She placed both hands in her slacks pockets. For the first time all day, she felt her revolver's bulk under her armpit. "Elsa, you don't understand."

"You're right, I don't! I do hair for a living. I don't deal with death and dying all day."

McNamara leaned her head toward the floor. Her ponytail slipped over her shoulder and touched her firearm. "Consider yourself lucky."

"I don't *feel* very lucky, Scarlett!"

With the nightmares, long hours, and excessive alcohol consumption, her ability to have a rational conversation with a loved one simply was not there. "We need more beer."

Elsa stepped into her path. "That's your answer!?"

McNamara looked into her eyes. The tears rolled down Elsa's face, and her cheeks were beautiful and rosy. She reached out and touched her lover's delicate face, wiping away a stream of gushing sadness.

"I'm sorry, angel . . . but I *need* to keep working. Go on off to bed. I'll be in as soon as I can." McNamara leaned in and kissed her on the cheek, taking in her freshly showered aroma. "You smell amazing, Elsa."

"And you smell like booze and pipe smoke, Scarlett."

Elsa stalked toward the bedroom. She turned around as McNamara gathered her keys to hit the nearest liquor store. Before the front door closed, Elsa yelled, "Have it your way, Sergeant!"

59

The whole world feels distant, not real or concrete. If I try to reach out and grab it, it slips through my fingers. I move about, day or night, inside a bubble of my own morbid decay. I'm forever hungry, but I do not crave human delights. It's as if this city I've inherited by the sake of my need to be free has become another form of prison.

I should've stayed in the ocean, just sank to the bottom.

My home is there.

It simply must be.

It calls to me, now more than ever.

Have I done enough damage here?

60

"Hello."

"Hello yourself."

I'm staring at nothing, distant and lost. I'm in a bar uptown to which I've already forgotten the name. It's not a sleaze joint. It has a punk rock vibe, with stickers covering the bar and whiny bands bleeding through the juke.

I haven't killed in over two weeks. I don't know, maybe I'm trying to stop.

Who are you kidding?

"Who am I kidding. . ."

"Sorry?"

I shift on my stool, watching myself morph from the usual me to the ghastly me. She's laughing through the mirror, reminding me she's the itch I can never fully scratch. The ocean devil on my shoulder, the one who says take the candy bar instead of paying for it.

I'm not expecting her to be interesting. I'm not looking for anything tonight. I'm mostly just trying to get out of my apartment for a bit. The smell is getting troublesome, even for my exotic tastes.

You'd better work on that.

"How can I help you tonight?"

She places her purse on the vacant stool next to mine, a subtly bold move. "You look familiar. Don't you work at that mermaid bar?"

"Anything's possible."

Careful.

We talk over the punk rock. The lone bartender is a real prima donna. His hair is red like mine used to be. It's longer and nicer than mine ever was. He has a full beard to match with some nice muscles. He's wearing a tight tank top to try and get better tips. He looks all right, but I can tell he thinks he's the best thing in the room. I have some Jack with a few ice cubes in front of me.

At least he hasn't screwed that up.

<hr>

She says her name is Elsa. I'm surprised how forthright she is. She's given away so much of herself while I've reciprocated nothing. I think that's what's attracting her to me.

We play pool and she buys me another Jack. The punk switches to metal, these intense squeals and screams with angry lyrics and insane riffs. I can tell Elsa likes girls, but she doesn't fit in this equation. She almost dresses and talks like a cop, or she's trying to disguise that she is one. I'm not sure if that makes sense, but I'm going off my instincts.

I'm liquored up good and so is she. When the pool game goes stale, we switch to pinball in the corner. I want to play the Ghostbusters machine, but Elsa demands Dirty Harry.

I let her have it . . . for now.

Things change when the football game ends on the television above the bar. I think it was the Raiders and Chiefs who were playing. The Raiders were up big, but they blew a huge lead at the end.

I barely paid attention.

Elsa's demeanor changes as the lead lady cop enters the little TV frame. There she is, speaking at her police podium with cameras flashing all around. It's another 'Special News Bulletin' about the killings in her precious city. I got lucky and saw her once at Tad's Steakhouse, but at this point I've begun to enjoy listening to her and her team fumble around trying to catch me.

You better say something to this cunt.

"You seem rather enthralled with the TV. Am I boring you?"

We're standing at the bar top. The TV is right in front of us, with me facing Elsa. She's turned toward me, but her head is twisted toward the tube. Nobody can make out what the cop is blathering about. I think the set is on mute.

Even *I* don't care.

She knows nothing of what she's dealing with.

Elsa has responded, but not to me. "Hey, Mike. Can you turn that up, please?"

The long-haired ginger obliges; however, the heavy metal remains dominant throughout the speakeasy. She speaks after sipping a beer that I have just paid for. Her cheeks are rosy, and her eyes house a guilty pleasure within them, like she's being naughty and knows it.

"Can you believe all these random killings?"

I almost grin while slinging another sip of Jack. "I don't watch TV. Rots your brain, ya know?"

She's not listening.

I slither closer to her in the late-night vibe. She's a lightweight, I can tell. She's trying to keep up with me, but she's losing the battle. Rain pours from the window leading outside. Red neon from the bar's sign makes it look like it's raining blood.

I caress her face and turn it toward me. I lean in and kiss her. She offers me her tongue, and I suck her cold wetness. It tastes of malty beer. I bite down just a little, causing her to moan and sink into me. We separate as she opens her eyes at the very last moment.

I think she savored every moment.

"How about one more drink, then we share a cab?"

She still has half a beer left. "I can barely finish this!"

"Those are the rules. For your last drink, you must have what I'm having."

Her eyes grow bright, and she perks up. "What on earth even is that?"

"Have a smell."

I bring the whiskey glass to her nose, and she gags. "What is that? Motor oil?"

"The best money can buy."

I wait until she drinks her whiskey, then I ask where she lives. The neighborhood is thirteen blocks from where we are. She says her place is off limits. I offer to take her home with me. My lair isn't far. We fool around on the short ride back.

61

"Why were you so fascinated with that cop on TV?"

I hand her a beer laced with something to put her out for good. I have a couple red label Budweisers in my fridge, right next to a severed hand. She doesn't look around or comment on the smell.

I should clarify that I am extra careful about leaving rotting flesh inside the apartment for too long. I cook what I need, refrigerate the rest, and dispose of it when the maggots arrive. I've been scrunching a heavy towel in the crease underneath my front door. That prevents most of the aroma from leaking out into the hallway.

Elsa's laid out on a recliner I just got. I found it in an alley nearby and lugged the thing all the way back here. I bring in my special chair from the kitchen and sit in front of her before removing my sweatshirt. My halter top and black skirt are still a bit damp from the outside elements. I cross my legs and watch her take a sip of the Bud.

"What kind of a chair is that?" she asks.

"Sorry?"

"Your chair has a bone for a leg."

"I made it."

For the first time, she looks uneasy. She's unbelievably drunk, but such a strange sight is fueling her with survival clarity.

Say something.

"Relax. I work at the college, and I'm surrounded by fake skeletons in the biology department. The leg snapped off this chair, so a girl *must* improvise."

She's just staring.

"I didn't steal it. We were throwing one away, so I put old bony to good use. How's your beer?"

"Strong." Elsa giggles and takes another sip, but her demeanor switches and the air in the room becomes serious. "The cop on TV is my girlfriend."

I uncross my legs and open them as wide as they go. I lean forward and study every nuance of her. I can smell the lingering remnants of her leave-in conditioner. "Bullshit."

"No, it's true. We live together." She puts the beer on the floor and places her head in her hands. "My God. I can't believe I'm telling you this."

My feelings here are bordering indescribable. I'm being suffocated by an avalanche of fear, lust, rage, vengeance, and wrath—all at once.

Elsa looks up and sees my suggestive posture. She leans her head back and stares straight up my skirt.

"Go on. . ."

"It's this horrible case she's working on. It's been hard on her. She and I have never been more distant. She works all the time. It's like she's taking each murder personally."

She has no idea it's us.

I rise and inch toward her. I tower over her where she sits, as if I've grown a foot in the last half-minute.

"What's with all these papers strewn around? Are you writing a novel?"

"More like a manifesto."

I slither down and kiss her. My eyes roll over as red fills my vision on all sides. I tell her to strip right here in the living room. She chugs most of my drink and does what she's told. Her frumpy clothes drop to my dirty hardwood, revealing a miraculous woman.

Her stark white bra and matching underwear hug her natural beauty in an enamoring way. She swings her body from side to side, allowing the alcohol to guide her sultry movements. She wipes a flood of tears from her face as she looks up at me. Her perfume is sweet, and she has a dainty tattoo on her left side.

It almost looks like a mermaid.

"You're mine now."

62

"We've been at this for three hours, Sarge. My eyes are starting to cross."

"Try some of this." McNamara pushed the wine bottle at the corner of the table toward him.

"Works like a charm."

They were huddled on her couch at her apartment, case files and photos strewn all over. Raindrops pelted the living room window to their left. Headlights from passing cars down in the street occasionally crept up the walls where they sat in the warm half-dark.

"You know I gave that shit up, Mac. By the looks of it, you should too."

Fleming's water glass was empty. McNamara grabbed her own glass and put back a huge swig of pinot noir. "Christ, Flem-wad. You sound like my mother."

Fleming turned toward her, his white and blue Hawaiian shirt opened at the top of his chest, exposing some white chest hair. "I'm serious, Sarge. How much of this are you slinging every night? Where's Elsa?"

McNamara sat back on the couch. She brought her hands to her face, rubbing out the drunken sorrow. "Don't want to talk about it."

"About Elsa, or about *you?*"

"What do you want me to say, Fleming? Just be a sport and tell me what you see in these files."

They both leaned forward, sifting through the dozens of crime scene photos. McNamara got up, then came back with a full glass of wine and another case folder. She filled her partner's water glass.

"It's hard to tell if all these are related, Sarge. There's no consistent MO. But you already know that."

McNamara took two gulps of her new glass before responding. "It may appear that way, but I don't think so. Sometimes organs are removed, eyes are taken. The blood signature isn't there at all the crimes. Sometimes yes, sometimes no. There is one minor consistency, though."

"Which is?"

She turned toward him, bringing her left leg up and over her right. Her baggy gray sweatpants allowed the sudden movement. "On the surface, most of the murders look clumsy and brutish. But there's something more to them, like an art. As if she's painting a picture, not caring about staying in the lines or if things go as planned. There's a strong femininity inside the hate, a wild unpredictability. But they are *all* related."

Fleming sighed. "It's the wine talking, Sarge. You and your 'woman killer' theory. I'm not seeing it."

"Of course you're not."

Fleming looked around the apartment. "Seriously, where's your girlfriend?"

McNamara grabbed her pipe that was next to the wine glass. A book of matches sat beside it. She plucked one and fired it up with one hand, like a vintage cowboy would do in a spaghetti western movie. "Think she took off on me again. She didn't come home last night. I guess I don't blame her."

"I'm sorry, Scarlett."

"She's probably back in Oregon with her mom. She did that to me once when we first started dating. Elsa's extremely non-confrontational. I feel like such a bitch."

"You're doing your best, Boss."

She turned toward him with tears in her eyes. "Am I? We're losing out there, Robert."

Fleming turned away and folded his hands together in his lap. "We're not at war anymore, Marine."

McNamara stiffened. "Yeah? Tell that to my nightmares. I'm back in that hell every fucking night."

Fleming's leg started to twitch, but he turned his head to face his superior. "I know you got into some shit over there, Scarlett. When I was in Afghanistan with the Rangers, we didn't see anything. We saw bloody aftermath, but never active combat. I know how that stuff can mess with your head."

A huge billow of pipe smoke plumed between them. McNamara put down the Savinelli and went after the wine again. "Well, know this, Robert. There is something else . . . the real reason I had to come back home. Only my shrink knows."

"You can tell me, Marine."

⋯⟨⟩⋯

The wine had settled in, freeing the closed-off officer to talk. She turned away from him and faced the dark television screen. Then she confided everything to her own defeated reflection.

"It was me and Spencer, alone on this mud hut roof. This was after the *other* incident. We were up there relaying intel to our squad down below. After the first shot rang out, I didn't know what happened. I fell to the floor and checked myself, wondering where I'd been hit. I turned to Spence. He was down. The bullet was clean, right through his shoulder. He made this sound when he got hit, this agonizing surprise that I can still hear. I wanted to stay down with him and cower, just give up, but I didn't."

The tears ran like a faucet down her slender face. She took a heavy breath.

"When I got back to my feet, I heard another shot. I didn't cower that time. I hugged a wall and poked my head out. The third shot blew my helmet off my head. It rolled away from me, and I could see that a bullet had gone straight through. Blood leaked down my face and I thought that was it . . . that I was done. The round missed my skull, but my helmet had cut me when it flew off. I got low and poked my head out again. I thought for sure it would have been a man, but it wasn't. It was a girl, a teenager dressed in full military gear. Her face was covered, but I knew. The rifle looked ancient, like she couldn't have been shooting such a thing at us."

Fleming listened, allowing his sergeant her time.

"She fired again as I ducked back behind the wall. After that, I just threw myself out into the open . . . to face her. My legs were quaking, and I could barely hold my fucking weapon straight. I got off a burst of fire, then she disappeared behind a roof wall where she'd been hiding."

Scarlett wiped her face with both hands, then continued.

"I wasn't sure if I'd hit her, but then she popped out from the lower portion of one of the buildings below. She was limping and she'd abandoned her rifle. I took aim while she crossed a dusty stretch of roadway. I was this close to unloading on her—*this close*—when a truck carrying vegetables entered my view. She stopped in the road and looked up at me, right through me, just as the truck mowed her down. It didn't even brake, just kept going. I can't get her out of my head, Robert. Her eyes haunt me."

Fleming moved toward her, allowing her to collapse in his lap. "At ease, Sergeant. Your job is finished. It's time to sleep, now. Just sleep."

The two colleagues fell asleep on her couch of black leather.

63

I want to get out of the city. I'm still working as much as I can, struggling to remain an inconspicuous monster. I've been afraid because many of my kills have been out of thrill, with no elaborate planning or forethought. Fear is an emotion that has never truly consumed me until now. I doubt mine is authentic human fear, but instead a skewed perception due to my *unique* views on life.

I think it's more the captivity part, always wondering if I'll be caught, knowing that I'd be forced to stop my work. They *all* think a man is the one capable of such senseless destruction in their little funhouse of a city.

I should write the police a letter. I'll enjoy every nuance of creating one to send, a toy to fluster the ignorant men and women working tirelessly to solve my impulsive puzzle.

I'll show them.

I'll show them *all*.

I'll never be caught.

We'll never be caught. . .

64

I'm taking the DART train to get out for a while. An essential to this Golden State is the fact you can move around easily without a car. I've never had one—haven't even been behind the wheel of a car.

Pauly the cabbie's sunken tomb doesn't count. I merely helped it along into the ocean.

What a fun night!

It's dark as I get on the train. The underground stops whizz by in a blur while the train makes an intense whine and lurches on the tracks below. Several lights are going out inside. They flicker in dizzying fashion.

I'm not dressed up or anything. Ripped jeans and a fitted hoodie will suffice. These Chuck Taylors I lifted off a joint on Market Street fit like a glove. My hood is pulled up over my hair. A large section of hair spills through, swallowing up half my face.

A vagrant is close by. She sits two rows up in the handicap aisle. The seats face sideways in that section. She's wearing a clean Santa hat and is decorated in all sorts of grunge. Her shopping cart is next to her. One hand drapes over her life's savings while the rest of her slouches and snores in her seat.

She looks so pathetic, dead asleep and vulnerable, almost begging to be sacrificed. I study her sloppiness for several stops, watching as her head moves from side to side, up then down. Her diseased tongue occasionally shoots out between huffs of broken sleep breath. I'm salivating up until she begins pissing her baggy gray sweatpants. It pools in her lap and runs down her right leg, jetting and dripping into a steamy yellow puddle.

And these people call *me* sick.

The highlight of the ride is when jolly old Saint Nick comes aboard. The pisser has gotten off as he gets on. I tried to like Christmas in Kentucky, minus living with Wade and my deadbeat mother. The beatings always intensified that time of year, as Wade revved up the drinking.

It's me and him.

I'm not staring, but he comes right up to me.

"Fancy a candy cane?"

He's a skinny version of Santa, but his suit flatters him. He's tall like me, maybe a six-footer. I can't see his whole face with his huge fake beard pulled up to his nose. His eyes pierce blue, like two glassy snow globes.

I look up at him without answering.

His body sways as the train takes off again, almost losing his footing in his clunky black boots. "How about a drink, then?"

He reaches inside his pockets and pulls a thick candy cane from his left and a silver flask from his right. The flask sparkles in the dying train light. His swaying gets more prominent as he speaks again. "Come on, kid. I won't bite."

"Aren't you worried that *I* will?"

There's a long pause, then he looks skyward and bellows a jolly laugh even I can't help but smile at. "Ooh, you're no candy cane gal. You're a straight gin sort of lady, aren't you?"

"Whiskey. I like my booze like I like my men."

"And how's *that*?"

"Bitter and murky."

"Ha! . . . HO-HO-HO!" The lean Santa pockets the sugar stick, then twists the flask open with two white-gloved hands. He takes a big swig and chokes it down. "This here is the *finest* gin from the North Pole. The secret ingredient is a splash of good old-fashioned OJ. Vitamin C is key for jolly old Santa Claus!"

He holds it out and I take it. I have a whiff before throwing some back.

"To you, young lady. Santa hopes you get *all* that you want this year."

The train clunks to a stop at Main Street in a town called Pleasanton, or Pleasantville. I give Santa a wink before stepping off into this new uncharted territory.

"Merry Christmas, miss!"

"*Santa. . .*"

I'm gone.

65

It's pushing midnight. There's a dampness in the air, but no rain. The DART stop I got off on is near a residential area. Nothing fancy, just normal houses lined up like cattle for my slaughter. I'm wandering, smelling real wood fireplaces and tree sap from large swaying oaks in housing fronts. The streets are dark, except for the occasional streetlamp, all warm colored at this hour. The moon is ever full, providing most of the light on a mundane street of average America.

Many of the inside lights are off, with their perfect little families bedding down for a holiday night. I'm hungry, almost nauseatingly. This stretch of Earth is an untapped resource, and I can taste the opportunity.

If a car rolls by, which hasn't been often, I duck behind a bush or tree.

It's too easy.

There's nobody walking around, which makes moving block to block easy at such an hour. My appetite increases with the pale moonlight crunching down on me. My insides grumble, demanding satisfaction.

I'm thinking of heading back toward the DART train, but I've come upon a house at the end of a random street. There's no real significance to it. It looks like all the others, but this one still has their Christmas lights on.

How festive.

The lights inside are off, but the Santa and reindeer are alive and glowing on the front lawn. There are multicolored lights lining the gutters, tight and in a neat row displaying large classical bulbs.

Go say hello.

I'm around back where there's a small door that goes down a few steps. It's not locked and opens right up. I peer in the blackness like a still menace and allow my eyes to adjust. They roll over red and now I see as clear as daylight.

We're together--as *one*. The way it should *always* be.

We puff several billows of chilled night air before entering our newest playground.

It's incredible how humans are so trusting of each other. How can they leave their doors and windows open at night? Even in Bowling Green, we *never* did that. Wade made sure to keep his prison tightly secured.

Would we have entered this house if the door was locked?

Found another way in?

I'll allow my reader to assume.

I'm in a wine cellar. It smells old, and I run into cobwebs on my left. The room is small but has an extensive collection of vintage bottles. There's a rustling off in a corner by another door leading deeper into the house. It's a two-step approach that probably enters the kitchen. The foreign sound does nothing but heighten my senses.

All I'm thinking is I feel bad for what's over there.

I approach with boldness that a normal person does not possess. There's no artificial light, only my bulging blacks and the richness of their vermilion saturations.

It's only a black cat.

The furry thing makes a jingle of its collar and pops out from nothing. She caresses my pantleg with her body, snaking around it with her back arched high. She purrs with animalistic delight.

I reach down. My hand has grown twice its size, with sable nails long and sharp like knives.

The cat peers up in wonder, our eyes meeting with my hand around her neck. I gently remove her collar, giving the gorgeous feline a pet behind the ears.

"Good girl. That's a good girl."

I bring the collar to my face. There's no name—only a bell attached like a simple necklace. I pocket it and open the new door in front of me.

66

The kitchen is micro. The overall size of the house is no more than a thousand square feet. The stove is an old gas thing. The cabinets are uninspiring and everything is drably decorated. A window with sunflower half-curtains welcomes in the moonlight. A set of knives catches my attention underneath the window. They're next to a single serve coffee maker with a grinder attachment. The whole beans in the clear casing are down halfway. I open the lid and bend down, smelling hazelnut and pumpkin spice.

The knife set isn't in a block, but instead lined on a slab. It's an expensive Japanese set, magnetically standing upright next to each other from largest to smallest. I grab the biggest one, its wooden handle comfortable and powerful in my grip.

A thought strikes me before I creep further.

Get another weapon.

I tiptoe back into the cellar, taking my time, and find a hammer on the water heater. It's resting halfway on there, as if someone forgot about it after completing a job.

Knife in my left, hammer in my right.

You get one . . . *I get one.*

I creep deeper into the house. A fire breathes its last breaths in the living room. The Christmas tree is flocked and decorated with shiny garland and ornaments. The tree's lights are on, and a Santa statue rests by the fireplace. It's either electric or battery operated. The head and right arm sway in a circular motion. This one wears glasses, unlike the booze hound I conversed with on the train. The little mirrors shimmer with the rainbow tree lights.

I stand in the center of the room with my head cocked to the side, listening for any sound or signal, like some raving menace.

Nothing.

I take my own glasses off and pocket them, being that *she's* now running the show.

There's nothing complex or miraculous about this house. I think that's what drew me to it from the start. Fewer surprises to deal with. The single hallway is nonexistent, just a thin walkway with a bathroom on the right, a larger bedroom adjacent, and one other room in the middle.

My two guides are the Christmas tree lights and *her*. . . my queen.

We enter the larger room on the left because the door is ajar. A bed is right in front of me, and I can see two people sleeping in it. A simple window in the back of the room spills more outside light on the scene.

My breathing intensifies and my muscles tighten.

They're mine.

All mine.

I approach the figure closest to me. Light-colored hair spills over the dark pillow. I'm lucky that she's laid out straight on her back. I lean in, bringing the knife to her throat.

I make a long, quick slit as if I'm fileting a fish. I think she realizes what's happening because she makes a sound. I put the hammer in my back pocket and use my free hand to cup her mouth. She squirms and dies too fast for my liking. Her wound gushes like I've spilled an entire bottle of wine down her. It jets and flows to my delight.

Check the other side of the bed.

I've done a wonderful job at making little to no noise thus far.

He rustles and stirs, but I'm on him before he can get his bearings. I plunge the knife outward in the darkness, finding a home near the center of his chest cavity. He gasps and sits straight up in the bed, as if waking suddenly from a nightmare. I *need* him to see me, so I run over and turn on the light. He's trying to talk or say something, but I don't care to listen.

He springs from the bed and faces me. He's young and handsome, mid-thirties or so. He has a nice body and great abs. His white boxer shorts have reindeer on them. The smell of fresh blood floods my nostrils. My hands are doused in his lady friend's gore. He glares into me with the knife plunged deep in his chest. His eyes are wide, practically bugged from his face. I lick my scaly hands clean right in front of him, giggling the whole time.

I think the fright of it all is killing him—the actual sight of *me*.

He manages to pull the knife from his sternum with a scream, but he hits the ground shortly after. He writhes and moans, a despicable motion picture of pathetic humanity. I pull the hammer from my back pocket and stand over him. He reaches for the knife next to him, but it's no use. I bring the hammer down on his face, using the small circular side to start, then finishing with the jagged side.

The bedroom light blazes in the little house of death. *We* stand panting together, grinning from ear to ear.

The black cat makes her way into the bedroom. I didn't hear her come in. She struts to her owner on the floor in front of me. She meows and smells him, then comes to me for a sultry purr on my leg. She moves like a dancer doing a twirl, showing off.

I turn to leave when I hear crying from the other room. I leave the cat with my corpses to go investigate. A wooden crib is in the center of the room, with cliché blue wallpaper and shit. I inch over and hover over the tiny human. I thought he'd scream, but he does not. He studies my face in such a serious way, like he's taking notes for later in life.

I have the knife again because the hammer is stuck inside the guy's head in the other room. It won't budge. I raise the blade and lean into the crib, swallowing the baby's world. I place the bloody instrument on the farthest side of the crib, in the very corner of the Ninja Turtles blanket he was wrapped up in.

"Here you go. A gift."

I need a chair for the final piece to my on-the-fly artwork. I find one in the kitchen and bring it all the way back. I rally some more blood from the woman still in her bed. Brain and skull from the guy have flown to the white walls. My strength is unmatched while performing my art.

These two are gushers!

I get my hands nice and saturated, then go back to the little guy's room. This time he's up in his crib, holding on to the ledge of his prison. His eyes are bright and alive while they follow me around. The cat is also here as I get up on the chair. All I hear is purring, and the kid stares up at me in silence with bright, stupefied eyes. I leave my mark, my signature on the ceiling above the baby's crib. An average-sized woman would not have been able to reach the ceiling on such a chair, but it's no problem for me with a little stretch.

I sign my abstract masterpiece while my young friend watches. I start to get restless, knowing I need to get the hell out of here. It feels darker than when I first arrived. The moon's movement signals me.

I don't care about cleaning up. I thought about setting fire to the house, but that would stir too much attention. I've relied on stealth, and it's worked. I do my best with fingerprints and don't leave anything of mine behind.

Even if the pigs get a print, it won't be mine.

It'll be *hers*.

Good luck with that.

I carefully wash my face in the small bathroom, making sure my clothes aren't covered in death. There are a couple specks, but the darkness masks the carnage.

I catch the last DART train back to my Golden State.

67

'1999'

I t's been raining more and more. A philosopher or writer guy once wrote that the wettest day he spent was a day in my Golden State. I read a book of his at The Rock. Or maybe he'd said the coldest day he'd ever spent was a summer one in San Francisco.

Didn't I already tell you that?

My brain is scattered with meds some days and nothing on others. Running on whiskey and blood is an altogether different high. For years, I was on whatever Jamison saw fit. Stopping cold turkey hasn't been easy, but I'm starting to notice a change.

I feel fractured, more so than ever.

My queen feels it, too. She's so powerful, yet her laser focus of keeping us safe and organized tends to slip.

Is it just me that's slipping, tumbling down the rabbit hole to hell incarnate?

It's the little things, like what days I'm supposed to work or remembering to pay the rent on time before the landlord starts snooping around.

My apartment is my studio, with each new pound of flesh becoming part of my canvas.

Outside of work and my nightly bloodlust, I've mostly been here. The heat is on out there. The cops and my cattle they call "innocents" are growing restless. They demand to know who's doing this devilish work.

There is no Devil or God.

They are both human beings.

The only true *god* is my queen, my beloved siren of land and sea.

68

"Thought you wouldn't show."

"At ease, Jody. I've missed two sessions in four years."

Scarlett McNamara had thought about going for three, but she needed some clarity. She was reeling, with Elsa still missing and the rest of her death plate becoming too much to digest.

Jody didn't respond, but she did perk up in her chair to study her.

Crime was winning, and not just petty thefts and purse snatchings.

It was serial murder, defilement, and scribbling bizarre calling cards in victim's blood at every scene.

The sergeant chose the chair, which she never did. She always went for the couch. Rain pelted the large window in the high-rise precinct on the top floor. Sarge thought the shrinks belonged in the basement, not the cushiest views of the city.

McNamara was in street clothes, having been awarded one day off in the last three weeks. She felt defeated as she stared at the steaming cup of coffee on the glass table between her and Jody.

Jody was an intrigue, even to Mac. They considered each other as friends, although they never formally hung out or got together outside of the shrink room.

Going for drinks with your work psychiatrist was never a good idea.

McNamara shifted her tired browns left to face the sprawling window. Sheets of rain were pelting the glass, like the water came down sideways. It was gray out there in the city at noon, with wind gusts rallying to almost twenty miles per hour. She could see her whole city from her seat, the one she'd sworn to protect.

"What's going on out there, Jody?"

"What exactly do you mean, Sergeant?"

McNamara removed her casual sport jacket and leaned over to rest it on the nearby couch's thick velvet arm. "Christ, Jody. Cut the formalities."

She went back to her coat and pulled out the Savinelli. The matches and the Captain Black tobacco were in the same pocket. She'd been puffing on it like mad since the killings first hit the papers.

Jody was unflinching, her petite frame and doe eyes in complete restraint. "I'm sorry, Scarlett. But we do have *two* firsts from you this afternoon."

McNamara postured up with her supplies and began digging in the tobacco pouch. "You know I smoke, doc. I've just never smoked in *here*. Do you mind, just this *once*?"

Jody brushed through her shoulder length curls of blonde with her hand, accidentally nicking her pearl necklace in the process. It was a therapeutic sound of nails tapping jewelry. "I don't mind if you smoke, Scarlett. However, that's not the most glaring of our two firsts."

Scarlett had packed, tamped, and lit her pipe cooler than a sea captain spiraling on a death course with the horrific Moby Dick. Plumes of sweet raisin-scented tobacco joined the two cups of fresh coffee between them. The gelling of the smells was intoxicating.

"What the hell are you talking about?"

Jody crossed her legs before responding. "Your gun?"

McNamara dangled the pipe from her lip freehand, then looked down and crossed her arms over herself before leaning back in her chair, a feeble attempt to shield her leather shoulder strap. "Fuck. I'm sorry, doc. I'll take it off—I completely forgot. My mind's been so fried since the beginning of this godforsaken case."

"No, no. It's fine. You can leave it on."

"You sure? It can disappear in two seconds."

"I insist. I suppose there's a first for me this afternoon, as well."

69

They talked, with McNamara doing most of the work.

Wasn't psychiatry easy if you're the psychiatrist?

"I have so much shit on my plate, Jody. And Elsa, I'm. . ."

"Go on."

Scarlett had burned through half of her bowl, tamping and re-lighting several times. Lingering smoke rings and a haze engulfed the damaged sergeant. "Do I really have to say it? We're skating on thin ice. I've been working all the fucking time trying to crack this sicko. I have this awful feeling that. . ."

Jody's eyes and dimpled cheeks never moved from her patient's, absorbing her traumas and darkest fears. "It's about control, Sergeant. Control."

McNamara placed her pipe on the table next to her empty mug of joe. She leaned back and tightened her long, dark ponytail behind her head. "*Control?* That's all I'm going get out of you, doctor?"

Jody smiled like a mother would after watching her six-year-old daughter bring her breakfast in bed, although most of the burnt toast and oatmeal mixed with Skittles wound up in the carpet during transport. "You can't control everything, Scarlett. You certainly can't control others. Control is an illusion. None of us know what will unfold next. That's the beauty of life."

McNamara's legs began to quake, but she stopped it instantly. "That doesn't really help me as the lead detective on this case, Jody."

"That is a reasonable response, but it's sucking your brainpower. After all, you *did* come to our session today wearing your firearm."

McNamara sighed, a heavy outburst of carbon dioxide that melted her down into her patient's chair on the top floor of head case central. She looked up at the ceiling and raised her arms to grasp the back of her head. She interlocked her fingers and grabbed the base of her ponytail with both thumbs.

Her hands came down quickly, gently smacking both of her thighs.

"I almost wish I was back in the war, Jody. I can't believe I'm saying that. I almost died in that desert, but at least being a Marine was something I understood. I'm a soldier and always will be. War makes sense. At least it does to *me*. But this—this . . . *killer*. They're a ghost. The victims are random and they keep piling up. The only consistent piece of evidence is this cryptic calling card, some artistic symbol or drawing in the victims' blood. The team is fucking clueless! All I hear is 'it has to be a white male, ranging from twenty-seven to forty-five.' You know, the classic serial killer bullshit."

Jody swallowed the last sip of her now cold cup of coffee, taking in an inviting breath of McNamara's sweet Captain Black. "You don't agree with your colleagues?"

Scarlett got up and paced the room. "I'm a soldier, doc. That's how I think. The academy teaches you everything about being a cop, but when you graduate you fend for yourself. We studied Bundy and that freak Ed Gein, but that all seemed like fiction to me until now. Did you know that Gein had trophies around his house? He made furniture out of his victims' bones and had skull chandeliers."

"Fiction how?"

"I don't know. I'm showing you my ass in here. What I'm trying to say is I'm a Marine trapped in a sergeant's body. As a Marine, we had an enemy, a predestined one. Our job was to *kill* that enemy . . . plain and simple. There was no reasoning except to follow orders and kill or be killed. I guess what I'm saying is I'm the world's lousiest police officer."

Jody allowed Scarlett's monologue to linger with the pipe smoke, right up until the lengthy detective ceased her back-and-forth marching. "On the contrary, Sergeant. You and your killer appear to have several characteristics in common."

McNamara took one step toward Jody, placing her hands on her sides. "The fuck? I have nothing in common with this . . . *thing* out there!"

Jody put down her mug with a clink. "You're both killers."

Scarlett's cheeks turned rosy. "I killed one person in the desert before I came home. One! It was from long distance, and it wasn't even my fault. It was either them or us. Between that and the other shit, I couldn't cut it over there anymore."

"Please sit, Scarlett."

"I like standing."

"For me. Please."

Scarlett snatched her pipe from the table and went to the couch. She sprawled out like she usually did during their visits, resting her head on a yellow pillow. She was still facing the window of absolute gray.

"Do you remember what you said when I hypnotized you three years ago?"

She bit down on her pipe before answering. "I had nightmares every night and I still have them. Not like it was, but all this new stress is upping the frequency."

Jody brought her whole body forward in her seat, almost to the edge.

"Yes, but what else?"

"Why are you doing this to me, Jody?"

"Please answer the question, Sergeant."

She had already purged herself from it. Rehashing it still hurt, but she obeyed the order . . . like a good soldier.

"The guy . . . the bomber."

"*Yes?*"

"Under hypnosis, I said I was fascinated with his corpse after I realized I wasn't dead. How the bees swarmed to his exploded body in the desert heat, and I couldn't stop staring, that I carry a picture of him in my wallet that Hoyt took after the blast."

"And you remember what you told me as to why you still carry the picture?"

Scarlett wanted to throw her pipe through the window, but instead she gripped it by the bowl until her knuckles turned white. "A *souvenir.* A reminder that he tried to kill us, but he didn't."

There was a long pause before McNamara continued.

"None of it matters, Jody. The fact is, we'll either get lucky or this one will do something so impulsive it'll get her caught."

"*Her?*"

"What?"

"You said, 'it'll get *her* caught.'"

"I'm tired, Jody. I'm . . . tired."

Jody waited several seconds before responding. "Whether you like it or not, with luck or your own wisdom, you can relate to this fractured person. You've got a job to do. Get out there and do it."

70

I'm smoking a cigarette on a bench across from the loft Mick took me to.

You didn't think I forgot about him, did you, dear reader?

People are passing everywhere, like a sea of cockroaches scattering when the lights come on. I watch his German car pull into the garage, then I see him walk out of the main front door of his high-rise apartment. He's wearing a scrub suit, like the ones you see doctors and nurses wear in hospitals.

I need revenge. I know nothing substantial about him, except that he works as an undertaker.

No wonder you crossed paths.

I can't involve Snow. That would be too obvious.

Good thing I remember where he lives. Staking out a specific place in my city is the easiest thing. Why? Because nobody gives a fuck about anybody.

No one pays attention.

We're all trapped in our own cerebral islands in a cesspool such as this.

I've got this fucker. . .

71

A day has gone by since my stakeout. I'm enjoying some sun at a familiar place by the bridge, a grassy park next to the ocean. It's been a while since I killed the cabbie here.

What was his name?

"Saul?"

That's not it. . .

"Paul? . . . Pauly!"

Being close to this spot brings me satisfaction, like I can relive my art. It feels like having a good fuck and rehashing the details over and over. The park is practically empty, except for a straggler bum or two. I'm getting used to the color black since I've dyed my hair. Today is the first in several that it's not raining, so I've chosen black shorts and a tank to match. The tank says *NIN* on the front in big white letters. I bought it—not *stole*—from a record store on Van Ness. I've never heard of the band, but they are called Nine Inch Nails.

I listened to a demo while I was there. The dweeb at the front desk said they had a new album that I should check out. It was playing at a little station off to the side, like a desk with a pair of attached head-phones. Once I listened to their song "Wish" I was hooked!

It starts something like, "*This is the first day, of my last day*" and slays from start to finish.

I wasn't allowed to listen to anything like that when I was a little girl.

I braided my hair today and put on some red lipstick. The grass feels amazing on my skin. I'm white as a ghost, but I'm one of those chicks that fully embraces who she is. There's nothing worse than meeting someone who doesn't understand who or *what* they are. They stick out like sore thumbs, always apologizing and laughing, begging for acceptance.

Worst of all, trying to hide who they are.

Sure, I deceive people all day, but I have reasons—for survival and to continue my work.

I'm being consumed by the clear blue azure. I'm lying on my back in the grass, my hands and arms out like a dark angel. My wayfarers cut the glare and shield my eyes. Nobody bothers me. A single plane rides past in the cerulean sky space. It leaves a heavy trail in a straight line, as if leaking chemicals into the atmosphere. I pull a sucker from my pocket and get to work on it, resuming my trance.

I rest the candy against my cheek, allowing the liquid to take over my mouth. It tastes of strawberry and a hint of sweet chocolate. I swallow and smile, stretching and twisting my whole body in the warm green grass.

I blink. The plane disappears.

I blink again and it comes back.

The trail sputters, just for a moment, then resumes its course.

You know, I've heard people at work say there's a new thing the government is doing called 'chem trails.' The gist of the conspiracy is planes are armed with poisonous gas and fly over heavily populated cities and leak it all over, exposing the citizens to rancid toxicity.

That idea seems fantastical to me, but then again, I can see it being a thing.

I can see *everything* being a big ball of decay or a predestined simulation, one where nobody escapes.

I don't know . . . maybe this city is finally getting to me.

The biggest beef I have with a scheme like that is how chickenshit it is. If you're intent on manipulating or destroying a population, do it face-to-face, like *me*.

Cowards.

72

I need to study more about the mystery serum Mick uses to incapacitate his victims. I know he works in the medical field, which isn't a surprise. I think some of the worst people choose medicine as a profession. It's like playing God and *never* having to explain yourself. You get to control the most unhealthy and desperate people with no consequences.

My mother dabbled in the field when I was little. She wasn't a nurse or anything. I believe she was a medical assistant for a short while a couple years after I was born. Daddy's salary wasn't enough with his drink and other vices. She didn't last long because she was her own mess. She always said she quit because she wanted to focus on taking care of me.

That's a laugh.

She probably got canned for drinking on the job.

There's a library next to a cathedral in the city. It's not the same area where I ice picked that bitch lady, no. A different area. A section of the city called Russian Hill.

I've been coming here a lot, reading up on anything that can help me become a more efficient killer. A fantastic thing about coming to the library is that nobody asks questions. The main librarian is as old as time and blind as a bat. This timeless center for books is three stories high, flaunting the oldest and most beautiful texts I've ever seen.

I don't even remember the main librarian guy's name.

It's Patrick.

He talks like he's from a distant time, with a hint of trapped dust from the seventeenth century always lodged in his throat. The best thing about him is he's often upstairs playing chess with the fellow geriatrics.

The whole bottom floor usually belongs to me.

I don't have a library card because I can't have paper trails. Patrick leaves me alone and I never take anything from the book house besides handwritten notes. I did buy a sketchbook in cash from him, though. It's bound in old leather with a long strap that wraps around. The pages are thick and coarse, designed for pencil or finesse pen.

I draw my crimes in chunks of charcoal, doodling the blood and mayhem.

A skeleton here, a ripped-out liver there.

I must study a bit longer, then I can execute my plan. This will be the most calculated conquest of my career.

Nothing beats revenge.

～∞～

A storm rages as I enter the library. Rain falls sideways in sheets, dancing on the slick asphalt that is my carnival of chaos. I've forgotten what time of day it is, but the sky is a medium gray. A huge pool of water provides a mirror at the entrance door. I look down at it, finding my other half grinning up at me. I stop, then several drops from the ether come down and ripple her into oblivion.

I wanted to walk the whole nine blocks to get here, but it's too wet. I took a cab. There are some people inside the library, but they're all decades older than me.

But not me. . .

"How old are you, my queen?"

As old as the ocean breeze.

I don't see Patrick. Maybe he couldn't get his rickety ass out of bed. I'm wearing a dark hat and a sweatshirt with no hood. I'm not trying to disguise myself; this is just what comfortable felt like today.

I head toward the back of the place. The smell of old pages smacks me in the face. Nothing beats this smell, except *maybe* blood and the final gasps of a useless piece of trash. There are two computers on the main floor and they are usually occupied. Technology seems to be taking off in a big way, imprinting itself on everything.

I can only imagine what the year 2000 will be like.

It's not that far away, you know.

I don't get what all the fuss is about with these computers. I used one a few weeks ago just to see. I didn't search for anything incriminating because I wouldn't be surprised if they can track your history.

It is cool that you can go on some web page; I think the best one is called Yoo-hoo. You can type anything, like "how long does it take for a body to start decomposing" or "what's the record of murders for a serial killer in American history." I *really* wanted to search those things, but instead I typed in a few fashion questions.

I wouldn't be surprised if computers will be running it all in the next thirty or forty years.

That is, if people are still in the game.

I can totally see computers being able to eventually write books and paint paintings, all without the need for humans. A new breed of superior intelligence that humans foolheartedly create but never consider how powerful they could become.

Just watch . . . you'll see.

There isn't a specific medical section, so I must search a bit. I find several books on anatomy and dissection, texts that surgeons and medical professionals burn through before graduating.

I've learned that in some countries, formaldehyde is a drug that partiers lace in their cigarettes. The effects are nausea, delirium, and sometimes passing out.

Mick could've used *anything* on me.

He could've laced the weed we smoked that night.

He could've dropped something in my wine while I was trying to relax for once in my fucked-up existence.

It doesn't matter.

"It does to me. . ."

I know, angel.

What I do find is a real gem. It's in this old book about ancient medicines. There's a picture of a tree on the cover, a garden with mushrooms and plants all around. This intriguing thing, I later find out, is called *curare*.

Curare is a common name for various alkaloid arrow poisons originating from plant extracts. It was used as a paralyzing agent by indigenous peoples in Central and South America for hunting and therapeutic purposes.

Curare is prepared by boiling the bark of one of the dozens of plant sources, leaving a dark, heavy paste that can be applied to arrow or dart heads. In the art of medicine, curare has been used as a treatment for tetanus or strychnine poisoning, and as a paralyzing agent for surgical procedures.

Fascinating. . .

I think it's time to pay Mick a little visit.

73

I've been picking up some shifts but have mostly been obsessed with my mark. He takes his cadaver job seriously, working both swing and graveyard shifts. He does tend to falter in his routine, however.

I've been watching him for two solid weeks.

I've never seen him with Snow but have seen him with one other girl. I suppose she'll wind up like me, because he walked out of a bar in the Financial District with her. She looked drunk as shit, but not him. They disappeared into an alley a few blocks away from another bar called Schroeder's.

I followed but lost them, which angered me, but a light went on in a dingy apartment complex several hundred feet from where they disappeared. I assumed it was her place. She was in for *some* night with that little monster. I could've stopped it there, but I'm far too selfish for that.

I don't help anyone.

I act only for *us*.

74

The door swung open as Mick was just getting comfortable. He didn't look up from his dead plaything but shot up from his bent over position. "What?"

His new colleague clearly sensed his indignation as he ripped the Walkman headset from his bedhead of ashen curls. She didn't fully enter. "Sorry, Mick. Just letting you know I'm running for coffee. Want one?"

Mick exhaled and removed his lab coat. He circled around the metal slab for a table and huffed to a desk on the left side of the room, throwing the hospital garb over a chair next to his new computer. He didn't bother looking at her. "What was that, Gina?"

"It's *Mina*." She'd already been forced to work with him in Pathology for two months. As soon as her six months of training were up, she'd no doubt ask for a quick transfer.

"Vanilla latte with whole milk—large."

She gave him a salute and a half-assed smirk, then disappeared back out of the morgue.

Mick stood with his hands grasping the beginning stages of love handles. He wasn't fat or tall or skinny, but instead wholly average. Skinny fat, maybe. Was that a body type?

Once he was sure he was alone, he returned to his new prized possession. The body before him had been thrown from the back of a motorcycle, her boyfriend rider making off without a scratch. She'd hit her head in the perfect spot on the pavement, killing her instantly. Other than that, the corpse was in amazing shape.

He lifted the white sheet by her feet, removing his gloves to caress the top of her cold foot. There was still red nail polish on her toes, cracked and worn but pretty nonetheless.

Just for him.

"I think we're alone now," he said with a smile and began unbuckling his belt.

"She's pretty, *Mickey*."

Mick whipped around and hit his hip on the table, almost falling to the floor.

She entered his vision like a specter from the far corner of his office.

"*You* . . . how did *you* get in here?"

She was out of her hiding spot, the cadaver fridge in back providing a calm serenity only someone like *her* could adore.

"I've been keeping my eyes on you since our *wonderful* evening together."

Her voice was different, deeper, with a brooding intensity, but Mick didn't scare easily, especially by some cunt he'd already owned. She approached with a suffocating confidence, almost sliding across the squeaky-clean linoleum.

He was still in control. "I don't remember you being this tall."

"I don't remember you being this short, *Mickey*."

He swallowed but held his ground. She stopped a few feet from him. "What are you doing? I'm sure you're aware you're not allowed in here."

She performed a spin, throwing her arms out and twirling like a ballerina. "You like my outfit?"

Mick stared. She was dressed like a lab assistant or any other brand of humdrum hospital personnel. She even wore a name badge with a picture. No one would have stopped or questioned such a presentation.

The room grew cold in a way he didn't understand. The air became stale, and his breath turned heavy in his chest cavity. It suddenly felt as though a little person was sitting on his sternum. He spoke with all the remaining confidence he had left. "What do you want?"

She ceased her windmill dance. "Well, first off, a vanilla latte *isn't* coffee. I labeled you as more of a caramel frap with extra whip kind of guy."

Mick scowled, his cheeks heating. "You think this is funny?"

She removed her glasses and placed them gently in her lab coat pocket. She reached up and caressed her braided pigtails with both hands, giving them a twist. Her eyes went black, the blue washing away like sand in a rolling wave.

"I can call security right now."

She crossed her arms and tilted her head to the right, showing off a freakish display of flexibility in her long neck. "I see . . . and you'd tell them *what*? That you picked up a girl from a bar, drugged and raped her? Are we getting warmer? I don't know, *Mickey*. I don't think that'll look so good on your resume. Or *maybe* I can add that you were about to jerk off to your fresh lady friend over there."

Mick took a step forward. He'd never been demeaned by the opposite sex in such a way. He *always* had the upper hand.

Her eyes became blue again.

Mick blinked. He must be tired.

One of the lights above them began to flicker.

Just the hospital lights.

She reached for him, a hypnotic move he did not expect. Her hand touched his shoulder. It didn't feel like a squeeze, but the bizarre force made it so he couldn't move.

"Relax, Mickey. I've come to tell you that your little game is over. Maybe one day soon I'll go to the cops and tell them *exactly* what you are and what you've done."

She didn't allow him to answer; that wasn't part of her game.

She peeled off the stolen lab coat and badge, handing them over to him. Then she kissed him on the cheek and disappeared. He was left in the middle of the room, mouth open and eyes wide. He eventually turned around to face his tabled dead woman, her brown eyes open in a glazed eternal paradise.

Mick slammed his fist on the metal where she lay, narrowly avoiding her left arm and breast.

The coffee runner appeared in record time, offering up his vanilla sugar water.

"Throw it away. I don't want it anymore."

75

Tonight's the night.

I'll get this bitch.

I wasn't even reckless. She wasn't even a good lay.

She kept trying to wake up.

Can't she play dead like a good girl?

If she goes to the cops, I'm done. My job, my secrets, everything.

I've always wondered about killing. She'll do fine.

I knew there was something different about her from the moment I saw her in that bar. She looked like she didn't belong, like she was playing a part to fit in. When she got naked in that tank, she lit the place up. It was surreal.

She's probably just crazy.

The hard part was finding where she lived. All I know about her is she works at The Blue Lagoon.

I need to do this alone. I can involve no one, especially *Snow*. She's been getting on my damn nerves, anyway.

I should put her out of her misery next. Maybe I will.

I followed her one night from her bar job. It was foggy out and it sprinkled throughout my stalk of her.

She didn't look back once.

What an idiot.

She looked totally oblivious to my stalking. Classic dumb girl has no spatial awareness to anything around her. I watched her go inside some dive apartment complex. You don't have to card in or anything. I made sure she didn't see me and watched while she went up a single flight of stairs. Her apartment is to the right, just after the staircase.

<hr/>

I know she's home now because I can see her light on.

I've been standing out here in the cold for hours.

The fuck is she doing in there?

It's already well past midnight.

The covering of her window hinders me from tracking her movements. My backpack is heavy with all this shit in it. I've got my 9mm, a *huge* hunting knife and some rope. It might be tricky getting in the door, but I've prepared for that.

Hold on—the light just went out.

This is so exciting.

I'll wait a little longer, then go for it. She hasn't been to the cops yet. I just have a feeling.

It won't matter either way.

She's dead meat.

76

It's quiet around her shitty little complex. This is the type of place where someone comes to hide from the world or run away from something.

I press my ear to her door. I can't hear a thing.

This mermaid bitch won't know what hit her.

This door is taking forever.

Fuck.

I must be delicate, just like with my specimens at work. My loves, my dead vixens that please me the way I like.

Wait, yes . . . there's the click.

I'm in!

Fucking hell, what's that smell? It's as if she's been cooking alley cat.

I can't see shit, except for a grungy fish tank in the left corner of the room. It's bleeding a bluish-green light that accentuates the sludge. There's something weird in it.

It looks like a skull.

Who cares? Time to do this.

I don't see her.

The smell is getting worse, but I can tell she's been trying to hide it. It's being masked by incense and shit candle smell.

The fuck has she been up to?

I'm getting nervous. There's something off about this apartment. I'm usually indifferent to feelings, especially from others, but this feels wrong.

I have my knife at the ready, but I reach in and grab the 9-millimeter, too. Blade in my left, pow-pow in my right!

Now where are you, mermaid? Is that *you* with that smell?

I'm starting to like it. . .

I think I see her bedroom.

I've got her now.

The door creaks as I open it.

There's some light above her bed. It says 'hello there' in pink neon. Well . . . the 'o' has been damaged. It's dangling by a thread, fizzing on-and-off like it wants to come back to life but can't. The 't' is also compromised.

It says, 'hell here.'

There she is!

I can see her silhouette in bed. There's no frame, only a grungy mattress. It's small, not even a queen.

I'm right over her.

I'll just shoot her.

No—too much noise.

The knife will be fun. I should just start stabbing, but I *need* to see her. I'll pull back the sheet and surprise her so she knows it's *me* that did it. That I'm the one who ended her.

She brought this on herself. She fucked with the wrong guy.

Wait. She looks larger than I remember. She's leggy, but not like this.

It's probably just the lighting.

It's her. The little cunt.

I whip back the sheet. My left arm tenses and raises.

"What the. . ."

"Looking for *me*?"

I turn and see it. I say 'it' because it's something unspeakable. It's a mixture of her and something wretched. I don't want to scream, but it's all I can do.

Thwack.

77

"Rise and shine, *Mickey*."

He's not going anywhere. I've secured his hands and feet to the chair I've been working on. I've tied him round and round with the rope he brought in his little bag of tricks.

I throw water in his face. He jolts awake, just like that. I think he wants to scream again, but I've duct taped his mouth shut.

He moans like an animal for a while. He looks all around the room, not wanting to engage with me. He's squirming and shaking, trying to break free from his makeshift prison.

I slither close, right up to his face. I'm standing, so I contort down and in like a monster. The only lights I've allowed are from my fish tank.

I caress the silver lining of his mouth muzzle.

"Listen carefully, Mickey. If I remove this tape and you try something, you'll be dead before you hit the floor."

His eyes grow wide, making them look so animated and alive. It thrusts me back to my first victim.

When Wade bled out, his eyes were like this, like a cartoon character or Disney princess. It almost made me feel sorry for him.

Almost.

I want to pluck one from his head and eat it like a cherry. Savor and feel it pop and squish in my mouth, then swallow half his sight with sweet delight.

He nods, but I must be sure.

"Nice knife you've brought. It'll be in your ear if you make a sound."

Sweat pours from his head. I'm surprised he's not in worse shape. I whacked him good with that baseball bat. His body goes slack and his head slouches down, like it wants to unhinge and roll onto his lap. I grab him by the hair. His damp curls loosen from his scalp with my freakish effort.

I bring the tip of the knife to his left eyeball.

He doesn't shrink away from it, takes the intimidation like a man.

"*Understand?*"

He does.

I rip the tape away, along with some of his face stubble.

"Not the night you've envisioned, eh, Mick?"

He says nothing, just looks at me.

"What's the matter? Cat got your tongue?"

He pulls his head up and backward, a full reverse from a moment ago. His Adam's apple bulges from his veiny neck. "What did you h-hit me with, Ivy?"

"He speaks!"

"Do you *ever* stop fucking around?"

"Hmm, bold language for such a predicament you've landed your-self in."

He falls silent, and his body lowers even further in my bone chair. His head remains back with his face pointing toward the ceiling.

What a pathetic excuse for a man.

"A bat, Mickey. A wooden baseball bat. I was a tomboy when I was young. My daddy didn't like that, but he doesn't like anything *anymore*."

Something clicks in his head, as if an imaginary lightbulb is explaining what he saw in the dark a half hour ago. He pulls his head back to the center, glaring at me in absolute defeat. "What are you?"

"The direct approach! I do believe I've found a newfound respect for you, *Mickey*."

"You're a fucking murderer. That was a corpse in your bed."

I back away a couple steps. My raven hair blankets my face, so I push it back behind my left ear. My nude body glistens in the dank fish tank light. "Oh, him? He's mine . . . just like you. You're all *mine*."

He looks at the only light in the room. "Is that a skull in that fish tank?"

My queen smirks at him and massages her breasts.

Or is it me that's making the gesture?

"Let me go, Ivy. We both know things about each other. We can just go our separate ways."

"I'd love that, Mickey. I really would . . . but *she* won't let me."

"*Who* won't let you?"

"*Shut your fucking mouth!*"

He withers to nothing when she speaks. The life practically drains from him, straight down to my filthy apartment floor. Quaking, he says, "I've told people where I am."

"But you haven't."

"*Please!*"

I laugh and sit before him Indian style. My bare ass feels good on the cool hardwood. He's now looking down at me. I fold my hands and place them under my chin. "Have you ever heard of curare, Mickey?"

He wriggles in his seat, maybe out of confusion or piqued interest in the question. I'm surprised he hasn't noticed the leg bone I've attached to one of the legs. It really ties the chair together as a custom work of art.

"What?"

"Curare. I figure a dullard in your field of expertise would know what that is."

"My head hurts."

Pussy.

"That's quite the lump on your head. Lucky for you, you've got a thick skull. Now please answer the question."

He exhales, an intense one that deflates his ego to the point of non-existence. He shakes his head and clears his throat. "Curare is a type of ancient agent. The Indians used to use it. They'd lace their arrows and spears with it. It acts as a . . . a paralytic, I think."

I lean back and place my hands behind me on the floor, then straighten and cross my legs. I move my big toe along the fresh piece of bleached bone. I feel so powerful I'm bordering on frenzy. "I always knew you were a clever one, Mickey."

"What does that have to do with anything?"

"I thought you'd never ask."

"Go to hell, you psycho bitch."

I'm up and on him in an instant, smacking him square across the face. The sound rings true in my little house of death.

As he begins to scream, *she* reaches for his throat.

His squeal is stifled by *her* force, *her . . . supremacy.*

She's crushing him from the inside.

Gasps are replaced with gurgles.

Moments before he goes dark, *she* releases him.

He coughs up spit and drool. It splashes my tits and runs down my stomach. I drag my finger through some of it, bringing the mucus to my face to taste his warm fear.

"That's what I've done with you, Mick. I've given you a heavy dose of curare."

"Bull. That stuff needs to be placed on a wound to work."

"You should really check your head. That bump was accompanied by quite the gash. I stopped the bleeding, but you'll be out of luck very soon."

He writhes and tries to reach for his head. It's no use. "Just kill me. What the fuck are you doing?"

"*She's* not going to kill you, Mick. I am—*me*. I'm going to savor you. It'll be slow and agonizing."

His body begins to cave to my creativity.

The curare works like a charm.

His body is limp.

He can't move or speak, but his eyes show me *everything*.

78

You're probably wondering how I knew.

How I turned his little game against him.

Have you, my dearest reader, such little faith?

It wasn't hard. I forced his hand when I surprised him at the hospital. That was a huge risk for me, not to mention my future work. Once I made the bogus police threat, I *knew* he'd act.

Now you're asking, 'how did you know when he'd strike?'

I knew he was following me.

I pretended not to notice, but he gave himself away multiple times. All I needed to do was make him believe I was aloof.

You're right, though. I didn't know the exact night he'd come for me.

It took him seventy-two hours to act.

So, I waited . . . each night.

As far as the curare is concerned, I simply did a little homework. I shopped around China and Japantown for supplies. You'd be amazed what some of those smelly holes-in-the-wall can produce. The plants needed to be specific, extracted from the genus Strychnos family, including S. toxifera and S. castelnaea.

It sounds way more complicated than it was. After I got the plants, all I did was mash them up and mix them with water, then boil and strain the mixture until it became thick and syrupy.

Ta-da!

I wanted to test it on a dog or cat, but I didn't have the time.

The body in my bed is a dummy. It's stuffed with newspapers and big rocks. I threw some baggy clothes on it to make it look like a person sleeping. Remember the story at The Rock where three inmates pulled off an elaborate escape plan one night? It's the reason they shut down the prison before it became *my* prison. The escapees built dummy heads out of paper and plaster. They even went as far as painting them and stealing hair from the barber shop on site.

It was an intricate ploy to fool the guards, and it worked. Nobody knows what became of them. I think they all drowned—but not *me*.

We made that swim together.

Her and I . . . always.

That's how we survive.

79

I take my time with Mick. I'm not sure how long the curare will last, but I savor every second. He's very much alive. I throw him in the bathtub with his hands still secured. He can't move a muscle.

I cut him, bite him, suffocate him, then bring him back.

I rip off his fingernails one at a time.

I hang one of his limp hands over the rim of the tub, then whack it with a hammer. I'm careful not to make much noise. He tries to bellow and squeal, but I take his tongue. I grab it out with my fingers and take a chomp.

It's amazing that he can't move, but I know he can feel.

He feels everything.

His eyes water and he keeps making, 'mm, mmm' sounds.

I hit him more with the hammer.

It's crude and vicious.

I smash his balls and his knee, then he passes out.

I try waking him one last time, but it's too much for the puny prick to handle. He's still alive when I take both of his hands. I saw at them with a hacksaw I bought from an Ace Hardware on Hyde Street.

Do you have any idea how much force you must exude to saw through someone's body with a handsaw?

I lean on him with all my weight to make the jagged cuts. His blood spurts and flows, but I keep it mostly confined to the tub. He's still breathing after his hands are no longer his.

Even I can't believe that.

He convulses and starts to fizz at the mouth. His eyes roll back while his breathing turns into a heightened madness. He looks at me, begging me to stop with those eyes of horrified ice. He still wants to live, even after all this.

I don't care.

We smile down at him, enjoying our greatest conquest. I grab the knife that he brought to my party, bring it high above my head with both hands, and plunge it into his chest.

He's dead, but I keep stabbing.

His blood sprays my naked body, like a sprinkler head would a child on a summer day. I'm covered in the necrophiliac bastard's hot gore.

I continue my rage and begin working on his head. I saw at his neck, starting with two hands and finishing with one. With my left, I grab his hair and pull. His head finally gives way at the shoulders with some effort. I drop it in his lap and cease my killing.

I'm exhausted with satisfaction.

The room begins to spin and swirl. I already turned on the tub to help with the blood. The water is boiling hot. I try to reach over and turn it off, but can't. I give in to the sea of red and pass out in the steam.

80

I need to dispose of Mick. When I woke up, the tub was nearly full. I turn off the water and go to work. Up until now, I've never had to get rid of a body. The good news is I've contemplated and planned. There's no grand scheme to it, really. I have several black garbage bags under the sink. I grab his legs while he's still in the tub. I need him practically bloodless when I transport him in pieces, so after I chop off his arms and legs, I flip his torso over, thinking that will help drain the rest of him through the head region.

I don't care about the condition of my bathroom. I can clean it anytime, but maybe I won't. It's a masterpiece.

You can bathe in it, night after night.

I just need most of the chopped-up meat out of my sight. I dismember him the best I can, then toss parts and pieces into the garbage bags. I get ahead of myself with the cleanup and almost forget to take something.

Your trophy.

I want his brain.

Not the whole thing.

A little taste, then.

I don't know how to access it humanely, so I pulverize his mangled face with the hammer. He's expressionless, nothing more than a severed head on a pillow I used to brace the impact on the bathroom floor. I strike him numerous times until his brains are exposed. I scoop a handful off the floor and bring Mick's inner workings to my face. They feel like jelly and wet slime.

She wants to take a bite, but I intervene.

"Save them."

For later?

"Yes, my queen."

81

Once the heavy-handed things are taken care of, getting rid of the body is the easy part. I already lifted a suitcase from a bum camp near the freeway. I load a couple bags at a time, at all hours of the day. The trick to the apartment smell is to catch it early. I can refrigerate what I want, but room temperature flesh needs to be disposed of in a timely manner.

I use the incinerator in the basement of my apartment for some disposal, then carry him in bags to various locations in the city. It's fun walking by random pedestrians carrying chopped-up body parts.

I toss some of Mick in the ocean near the Golden Gate, a tidbit in an alley dumpster or two, and finally his head in Chinatown behind some donut shop.

I find a vat of something behind the place, a big barrel of what looks like thick sludge. I open the suitcase and take out the last plastic bag. I reach in and expose Mick's pulverized head.

I kiss him in the midnight dark.

The earth rumbles as a garbage truck judders by, leaving a waft of ripe stink in its wake. The sound is mixed with buzzing from an aging neon sign in front of the donut shop. It sounds like the lightbox wants to explode as I dunk Mick slowly into the chunky murk.

I read in a book once that revenge is a dish best served cold. I personally think I've dished mine out hot and heavy.

Now I'm in the mood for a good fuck.

82

I'm back in front of the cathedral where I've already had some fun. There's a memorial set up in the grass where I left the stinky vagrant.

How cute.

Come to think of it, I've misplaced my ice pick.

It'll turn up.

"I want to go inside."

What for?

"Please stop talking, just for a fucking minute."

It's your world, angel.

"Bless me, Father, for I have sinned."

"Of course, child. How long has it been since your last Confession?"

"Forever."

"Why so long?"

"I've been . . . away. I'm not from here."

"It matters not where you are or have been. You can *always* speak to the Lord."

I don't know why I came in here. It's late, and I've been out disposing of the last of Mick. The night's been long and unsatisfying. My mind continues to bend, night after night. Sometimes it feels like my head is stuck in a vice, and every moment increases the pressure.

I'm getting worse.

My bloodlust spills out into every waking moment.

Even when I sleep, I kill.

My dreams are overflowing with murderous rage.

I came in because my feet are tired. I'm a weary traveler in a huge city of bloody gold. This specific church isn't majestic or gaudy. It's small and unassuming, nestled in a quiet residential nook near the other bridge.

Remember, there's two leading in. This one is called the Bay Bridge. The wood fire smell and decorated windows of the church are what enticed me, and tonight I feel like talking. I'm not religious. Last time I was in church was in Kentucky, one year before Wade and Mama met their glorious fates.

I'm surprised the door is open at this hour. There's no one around, except for the priest. The wintery aroma is coming from here. It smells woodsy and rich, with hints of scented pinecones. It crackles and rises near the altar. Until now, I've never seen a church with a fireplace. Every church deserves one.

He grows uneasy that I've stopped talking.

I wanted to talk; I *really* did.

His body shifts behind the shielded barrier. I can't see him, but he seems caring.

Say something.

"Do you really believe that?"

"Believe what, child?"

"That God is *always* watching?"

"I do."

The air grows stuffy on my side of the talking box. It's quiet all around us. Incense burns close to the entrance, sending thin smoke vapors deep into the old church. The harsh smell tickles my nose, causing a sneeze. My black hair sneaks through my sweatshirt hood, nearly blinding my left eye. I tuck it back behind my ear and shove the rest of the spillage down through my collar.

"What have you come to confess, child?"

I think he senses the change in me. He moves again, sending his weight to the farthest corner away from me. We began close, the dark window screen providing feeble protection against a real devil in his holy house.

"She's awake."

An agonizing silence.

Are you awake?

I'm awake, child. You're my child . . . not his.

My eyes disappear upward and come back down black. My breathing becomes shallow, primed for my night's fill.

"I *can't* stop, Father."

"Stop what?"

His voice gives him away. Before it was gentle; now it owns waves of fear that choke him in his own house.

I tear through the flimsy partition in an instant.

He doesn't have time to scream as *she* grabs for his throat.

I don't have time to process his face. He's younger than I expect, but his overall shape is nothing but a cowering blur.

I tear him apart with my bare hands.

His last words are, "God forgives you."

83

"Quit breathing down my neck, rookie."

McNamara arrived last to the cathedral. Fleming and the rookie Ramirez had already interviewed the altar boy who had found the priest. It was early morning; McNamara hadn't even gotten a chance to get her coffee.

She was crouched next to the body.

"Look, if you keep stepping on shit, I'm gonna have to lock you up for the poor padre's murder. Just stand over there, will you?"

"Yes, sir. I mean *ma'am*."

Ramirez tiptoed over to the first pew, taking his place next to Fleming. McNamara finally joined them as the church bells rang out, signaling seven o'clock. She placed her hands on her hips. "What do you guys think?"

Fleming rubbed sleep from his eyes. "The altar kid found him. We interviewed him. He didn't see anyone enter or leave."

Ramirez frowned. "Here we are again. First the vagrant out front, now the priest. You think it's the same perpetrator, Sarge?"

"I do. She's returning to the scenes of her previous crimes."

Fleming yawned. "I think you need some coffee, Mac. The murder of the lady out front was calculated, cleaner. A straight puncture to the neck. A perfect kill stroke. This one looks like an animal came in and clawed him to death."

McNamara pulled her pipe from her overcoat. She held it in her left hand for comfort. "You're not wrong."

"And what's with the 'her' stuff again? Even if a woman did the lady, there's *no* way a woman did the priest. It's savagery. They took his eyes, for Christ's sake."

"It was mercy, partner. As if she didn't want him to see her for what she is. She even put him on his back after death. She folded his hands as if he were ready to be put in the ground. That's a feminine touch."

Fleming scoffed. "Removing a priest's eyes is a feminine touch? You need to see that shrink of yours more often, Mac."

She placed her smoking device back in her pocket and headed for the door. She spoke just before leaving the gaudy cathedral. "Maybe. Both of you keep looking. Don't call me unless you find something."

84

There's a hip donut shop close to my apartment. It's three blocks up, past a gas station and a liquor store called Royal Liquors. The sign also reads, 'I left my heart in Kentucky. Sorry SF.'

What are the odds of that?

This city humors me.

There's a booze house on every corner in almost all residential neighborhoods. It's as if the city officials demand their citizens be either drunk and incoherent or homeless and angry.

None of this matters to me.

I'm in my own private hell.

The shop is called All-Star Donuts, and they operate around the clock. They have a massive selection and I enjoy sitting in back at night, lost in thought. Sometimes after work I have an old-fashioned and a hot coffee here.

The city newspaper is usually scattered on tables or up at the counter. The sugar cakes *always* taste better when I read about another body turning up, or a headline about some "innocent" priest being ripped to shreds while his guts steam and rot at his precious altar.

Tonight is one of those nights.

I'm bored after last night's fun. I got off work at ten and came to All-Star. Obi made these special new shirts for us to wear while on-shift. The T-shirts are white and say 'The Blue Lagoon' in fancy cursive. The back flaunts a seductive-looking mermaid with two beer steins in each hand.

They're frothing and she's smiling.

I love it.

So here *we* are, having a chocolate donut and a steaming cup of black java.

The donut guy is cool and leaves me be. I'm cordial and I can tell he likes what he does. He always wears a Dallas Cowboys beanie and scurries around the place, eager to help a new customer. He smokes a lot. He's always taking small breaks, leaving his place unmanned for several minutes. I stare at him sometimes, watching while he puffs smoke rings and stares off into nothing.

I must admit that cigarette smoke, coffee, and maple donuts have an invigorating collective aroma.

I take a bite.

The priest is on page four.

What a load of shit.

I even carved my mark on his back with my nails. Can you comprehend how much force is required to break the skin across someone's back to draw blood?

I do—and it feels good.

I'm tired from the work night. I barely sleep at all anymore. *She* keeps me awake, nudging my brain and body, demanding more.

Three people walk in.

They don't see me sitting in back.

I take a sip of coffee and watch them.

The leader is no older than me. He's sloppily dressed, with a beanie hat and saggy jeans. His tighty-whities are showing. I don't understand that look on men. It looks like they shit in their pants. He's talking over both girls. It doesn't look like either of them is interested in the diarrhea spewing from his mouth, but they giggle and play along.

He asks the cashier about a specific donut behind the glass.

What's the cashier's name again?

He told me once, but I'm horrible with names. I'll call him Dallas, because he always wears a Cowboys hat.

The fucker asks Dallas if a specific donut is filled. He's asking if there's cream or some shit inside it. Dallas says no, then the guy asks if he can have it filled. Dallas looks at him, then gives an innocent excuse as to why he can't.

The jerk-off gives Dallas some lip, then pays for a drink and leaves. He's looking for approval from his female minions, but they refuse to play his game. I wait a minute after they leave, then get up.

An idea floods my brain as I head for the door.

I'll take one of his un-filled donuts and fill it with his own piss.

I'll watch him feast on it until I cut out his fucking tongue.

I'm salivating as two uniformed officers walk through the door. I abandon the idea of leaving, choosing to get a napkin from the counter and return to my seat.

I'm angry.

Relax; I can hardly control you.

I find myself responding to *her* more in my head than in words.

Our bond is growing stronger.

I watch the cops order coffee and donut holes. One of their radios sounds off. The voice comes from a small unit attached to the woman's chest. She's smallish and stocky with blonde hair. I can see it's tucked tightly underneath her patrolman's cap. The voice on the other end is also female, stern and purposeful sounding. There's a demand in her voice, one that the two officers jump at.

It sounds like the one from TV.

The blonde answers with her name. "Roger that, Sergeant McNamara."

Can't wait to meet her—little miss McNamara.

I'm going home for the night. Donut boy dodged a bullet.

85

Everyone's at The Blue Lagoon tonight, being that it's a busy week-end with a major sporting event going on uptown. I can't recall the actual day, but I think it's Saturday. Maverick offered me some ecstasy when I got to work. I pocketed the pill and have just swallowed it down.

A punk rock song bellows overhead, more like a whiny boy squealing about suicide and 'the kids aren't all right.' Delilah is just about ready to get in the tank for her show. I'm behind the bar with Maverick, pump-ing out everything from lite beer to perfectly calculated old fashions.

I've been on my feet for hours, so I take a quick break in the corner of the bar. The establishment is packed, but I'm off enough into the darkness to relax and allow the drugs to kick in.

My queen likes this feeling.

I can feel *her* caressing me from the inside, massaging my entire nervous system. My senses heighten and grow, causing me to sway in my seat.

Obi shuffles through the crowd and over to me.

"How is every'ting going tonight, Ivy?"

I shoot him a thumbs up. The music is loud, so he leans in and gets closer to *us*.

We don't mind.

His silk button-up shirt is damp, along with his forehead. Obi is the type of proprietor that doesn't sit around. He makes sure his team is taken care of and does all he can to help throughout the night.

His voice slows to a mellow comfort, probably due to the ecstasy kicking in. "I was t'inking . . . would you like to do anoth'a show tonight?"

I lift my head up toward him. My movements are slower, but I like it. "It's Delilah's night, Boss. See, there she goes."

She is already dunked in and is making her rounds.

The girl swims like a dying child.

I push my glasses up my nose and grin.

Obi stands tall and smiles back down at me. "Yes, but . . . I thought we'd change it up a bit. You can get in after her. I promise you don't have to do any'ting as crazy as you did 'da first time. Plus, it's another $100 for 'da night."

Just do it. I'll leave you to yourself. Go have fun.

"You're on, Boss."

<hr>

I'm at the last step up to the tank, staring down into the watery highlights of moving blue. I'm in uniform this time, playing mermaid dress-up. I almost forget to take my glasses off before scaling the ladder. Maverick taps me on the shoulder just in time. He's holding them until after my performance.

I'm desperate to check in with my queen, but she has done as she said and leaves me be.

It feels strange that she's so distant. I shake off the abandonment while the goldfish scatter, hugging themselves on either side corner of the tank. I slowly dip in with my fake tail and wig from the back office. I chose the Disney look, with a red wig and baby blue tail fin.

The water feels like ice. My goddess isn't here to shield me with her armor.

I go completely under as a mellow song hits the speakers. Everyone is watching at my feet with their drinks in hand. I do a few revolutions, slicing through the water with exotic grace from above. I do some slow flips and caress the tank with my hands, making eye contact with whatever patron I please.

My lung capacity is compromised without her, so I come up for air a couple times. I take a few breaths and taste some of the water, a salty treat for my heightened senses. I dip back down as my fake red mane drapes all around me.

The entire bar has stopped moving.

They can only stare at me.

I could've worn a glittery top to go with the outfit, but I chose not to. I'm nude above the waist. The drugs from Maverick are taking over, causing each new movement in the water to feel as if I've never touched her slick elegance until now. My nipples grow sensitive and rock hard. I swim closer to the front of the tank, grazing my breasts on the smooth glass.

I moan in the tank as my eyes roll up into my skull.

It's the single best night of my life.

86

At a pub called The Chieftain. I've been drinking Guinness for hours on a left corner bar stool. The pub coins itself as an authentic Irish delight. All the food on the menu looks great. They have it all—bangers and mash, fish and chips, and Irish nachos, which I've learned is steak fries instead of chips.

I'm not Irish, although I can pass for it with my natural mane of fire.

I miss that color.

The busy establishment is one big box, but it flaunts a serious type of class. I've never been to Ireland, but I can imagine walking through the lime green countryside and stumbling upon something like this after a long hike chasing rainbows.

The Chieftain is on the smaller side, but it prioritizes every square foot. Each wall decoration is perfectly situated and spaced out just right. The atmosphere lighting is dim and warm. Behind the bar, they have most everything, not just Irish drink.

I think the bartender is a real Irishman. He's small with tiny round glasses. He has the accent and is wearing a green Guinness shirt with a bird on it. The shirt is two sizes too small, but he's friendly and knows when to pass me another beer.

It looks like everybody knows each other in here, like they're sectioned off in their little groups. These insignificant meat bags come from all walks of life. Foreigners from everywhere come and go in this Golden City. They take pictures on every street corner, dying to cement their pathetic legacies in glorious 1999.

I'm the only solo explorer in here. These people are tightknit and disgustingly loud. I'm listening to three or four languages at the same time. The smell of fried fish and Guinness gravy mixes with my freshly shampooed hair, causing my tummy to growl and whine.

Who knows how many beers I've had.

6 . . . 7 . . . 12?

The Irish fuck keeps the Guinness coming because I'm a chick and can hold my booze. Speaking of Guinness, this beer may be the most well thought out of the entire brew family. Even while drinking, it looks like an inverted Guinness in the bottom of the glass. The flavorful froth is always present and remains rich and creamy. The blackness of the elixir is hypnotic, like the color of my eyes when I surrender all control.

The more I drink and judge these "people," the hungrier I become. They have no idea how average they are, how . . . insignificant. They are only as good as their world allows them to be. Most never dare to do something out of the ordinary, or work against the grain, or act out of pure impulse for their own evil pleasures.

I begin to feel queasy as a fire truck rolls by the front door. It's on the far side from where I'm sitting, but I have a bird's eye view of the whole place. The emergency lights flash red and white, pulsating into the cozy pub. The sirens aren't on, allowing it to roll by incognito. I'm the only one that noticed the truck. Everyone else is preoccupied with their shit conversations.

I need to get out of here.

I pay the Irishman in cash. He thanks me and calls me lass. I want to jump the counter and bust a bottle over his head, just to see if it will break.

My stomach is churning.

I make it to an outside alley and blow chunks. The taste is sour and the upchuck is black, a gelling of creamy Irish draught and sinister evil. There isn't a lot of light back here, but enough to show me my discharge. I'm shielded by a green dumpster and a big mural of the Stay Puft Marshmallow Man.

Once I finish puking, I turn toward the art wall. I look up at the doughy-looking giant and flip him the bird.

"Hey!"

The voice is right on top of me. I don't like being snuck up on.

"Are you all right, miss?"

I wasn't expecting a cop, but that's the predicament. I've already wiped my face clean, so hopefully he doesn't notice how sick I am.

I'm not drunk.

Maybe something you ate?

Could've been the liver I cooked.

It was a bit underdone.

I'm still mastering my art.

I believe he was expecting me to be startled, but that doesn't happen to *us*.

"Fine, sir. Thanks."

He shines his flashlight right in my eyes.

She doesn't like that. I bring my hand up in defense of my queen. "Do you *mind?*"

He keeps the thing on me, but he lowers it down around my stomach. "I'm just wondering what you're doing back here at such an hour. There's a killer on the loose, you know."

You don't say. . .

I straighten up and exhale. Hot steam escapes my mouth, showing the coldness of the night. "I don't think the Irish agree with me."

"Ma'am?"

"I had a drink at that pub across the way."

He chuckles and takes a step closer. His shiny black shoes make a scratch on the hard concrete of the dark alley. His radio begins gurgling, an incoherence of police dispatch jibber jabber. "Need a lift? My cruiser is right over here."

His skin almost matches his uniform. I can't tell if the threads are dark blue or jet black. He keeps his hat on, not possessing the courtesy to remove it while talking to the goddess that I am.

He's built like Wade.

"Sure. Thank you, officer. My place isn't far."

He turns and gestures with his hand, removing the flashlight from me.

He wasn't lying about his car. It appears right out from the alley entrance. The lights atop are on, bleeding a blue and red symphony. He opens the passenger door and I get in. He doesn't close it right away. He stares down and studies my body.

He must be a leg man.

My sable skirt rises a full inch as I cross my legs over myself.

He smirks and closes the door.

87

We don't talk much during the drive. I lie about where I live, of course. The occasional chatter of his blue blood colleagues hits the radio waves now and again, but it's a quiet night out here. It's cold in his car. My legs break out in gooseflesh as I tighten them to fight the frigid air.

I haven't looked over at him, but he does keep looking at me. He makes his head gestures obvious, soaking me in.

"You missed my stop."

"Sorry?"

He's being cute.

"I *said* you missed my stop."

He shifts in his seat and takes off his hat. He throws it in the backseat where criminals like me rot. "Oh, sorry about that, ma'am. I have a quick stop to make. Is that okay?"

My senses heighten and begin to explode from within. It feels like being awakened by a smack in the face from a deep sleep.

"*Whatever you say, officer.*"

88

He's done this before.

He doesn't admit it, but I know.

I *know* the cop type.

My chances increase as he chooses a desolate area to pull his car to a stop. The windows are beginning to fog. He's blasting the heat on purpose, trying to butter me up.

We're parked at one of the piers off Embarcadero. The popular one with the tourist attractions and gourmet chowder bowls is Pier 39. He has police access to Pier 27, which is down Embarcadero, moving closer toward the Bay Bridge.

We're in an empty parking garage with no cars in sight. I'm sure during the day this lot is packed with cars. I hear the ocean right next to us. It is straight out a few hundred yards. The bridge is to the right, a bright white silhouette in a sea of black nothing.

The police car remains running.

I don't move or say a thing, shut down for strategy.

He says something, but *we* disregard it. He leans over and tries to kiss me. As I pull away, he locks my door from his side. I try the handle, but he pulls some police magic to prevent me from fleeing.

It all happens so fast.

The night makes a slight transition on herself, and the ocean ahead slows to a glassy glaze. The wind stops breathing. He yanks my hair and slips a meaty hand up my skirt. The grip *she* gives while removing it from my pussy is incredible, slamming it into the resting shotgun mounted in the center console.

He pulls my hair harder, forcing me over and almost on top of him. I turn my head away, trying to reach the passenger door.

Then my head turns all the way around to face him.

Only my head. My body stays in the same opposite position.

I can't tell if it's me, or *her*, or *us* working as one.

It feels like a swirl of conjoining forces, all firing in unison from the inside.

His grip loosens and his eyes grow wide.

My arms remain facing away from him, so I use what I have in the moment. His neck is wide open for attack. I open my mouth and snarl, letting out a hiss that's part sea creature and something else.

I sink my teeth into him.

He tastes warm and sweet.

He tries to pull away, but it makes things worse for him. I grind down, sawing my jaw in a backward and forward motion.

I think he's reaching for his weapon.

He pulls with all his might, trying to release my bite of death. He gets free, but a heap of flesh dangles from my mouth. The wound sprays like a sprinkler, painting everything in its watery wake. The red stuff goes straight for my face and eyes. I moan as it shoots past me and drips down my inner thighs toward my cunt.

The blue blood gargles and tries to clasp his wound with his right hand. I grab his feeble effort with my scaly black hand, then wrench and break several of his fingers. It sounds like popcorn popping in a micro-wave. He can't scream, but he writhes and chokes in his seat until death.

I'm left panting, huffing *her* smooth breaths and my choppy ones.

His wound still gushes and leaks, occasionally squirting into the stale dead air. I carve my signature into his right arm with a dagger for a fingernail. Then I reach over and throw his dead weight against the driver side window. His head leans against it with one eye open and the other shut.

I don't know what to take, so I take his gun.

I'm not familiar with such a firearm. Wade always carried a revolver. This weapon is squarer with moving parts.

I shove it in my purse and kick out the passenger side window with my bare feet, then slither out like a gangly monster covered in blood.

I take a quick midnight dip in the ocean nearby. I keep my clothes on and swim down as far as I can go. When I reach the surface, I'm clean enough.

You killed another cop.

Things are getting interesting.

89

I can't fathom how much I've written since I've landed here. It all started as a childish manifesto, nothing more than angry handwritten blathering about *our* "so-called" crimes.

I've never fancied myself a writer. My art lies in my specimens, my keepsakes of flesh and bone. Who, if anyone, will read this? To be brutally honest, I couldn't care less if everything gets disintegrated down to ash.

I've toggled between pencil and pen along this journey. I realize that many pages will come off as incoherent, a sickening depiction of a fractured mind. However, I won't sympathize with you, my glorious reader. I've nearly given up trying to understand why I do what I do.

I'm covered in blood as this pen runs dry. I rarely wear clothes while in my lair.

Who did I just slaughter? Was it Mick? A hobo or cabbie?

My neck and shoulders scream while I'm on my belly in the middle of the floor.

It's nighttime.

I wrench my head and twist my long neck to one side, cracking the entire left side. I shut my eyes with delight. I've taken the sheet off the one window visible from the outside. I guess I'm that arrogant, not caring if someone tries to look in from the street. They won't see any-thing from their vantage point. I'm lucky the moon rests in the center of the window. It sits half-full, barely clearing an indistinct building on the other side of my street.

I can feel my world rolling toward the moon, or vice versa. I'm slip-ping down into the depths, the cold and icy chasms of sheer madness. It's painfully silent tonight. She's locked away inside me, hibernating after the slaughter we just committed.

It feels as though the more I take from this city, this . . . world, something happens. As if space and time are splitting away from my grasp. I'm incapable of feelings like love or fear, so in a way, it's inviting.

It feels like a simulation, not a concrete reality with any sort of meaning.

The last thing I want is understanding from anyone. The truest reason as to *why* someone like me exists isn't because we're traumatized, or beaten as a child, or angry at the world. Those things are true, but they have *never* shaped me.

I was born this way, you see.

That's what nobody with any "innocent" sense of humanity ever wants to discuss. It's nauseating to think that a human being can be born bad.

I'm telling you this is the case with *me*.

Even if I stayed in Kentucky with adoring parents and frolicked along the daisy fields of life in an Ivy League school and got a degree in business, you know what? I'd still be the same.

I am *her* and *she* is me.

She is my protector, my mother and father.

She is *everything*.

We kill for no reason at all.

Isn't that the most frightening? To do the abhorrent simply because. I can see you rolling your eyes while you flip through my mangled pages. You're saying, 'she does it because she gets off on it.'

You have no idea.

90

My favorite area in this hellscape is a district called the Tenderloin. It suits me because the people and layout match my tastes. It's grungy and despicable. There's more vagrancy here than anywhere else in the city.

I take a walk before work. The Tenderloin is a handful of blocks from the bar. My cup of coffee is smoldering. It burns my hand, but I continue to grasp it. The golden hour light is blinding, but soon it'll duck behind a tall skyscraper ahead of me.

I'm not hunting. This is more like scouting.

The Tenderloin also has the most crime. It's ten square blocks of deadbeats and criminals. Hippie-types and lifer residents are peppered herein, but I can spot them a mile away.

Tourists are *always* fun prey. They stick out like sore thumbs, their heads on swivels with a dumbfounded look on their faces, snapping pictures of street signs and cable cars.

The Tenderloin originally took its name from a New York neighborhood. The most logical reason, according to multiple reports I read at the library, is that the name stuck due to its "soft underbelly," with allusions to vice and corruption, *especially* with the police.

Another gory piece of intel is the Tenderloin police would receive hazard pay bonuses for working in such a violent area of the city. Also, the name could be a reference to the "loins" of prostitutes that still litter the streets today.

I like the name.

The meat looks good here.

The talking sheep and cattle look delicious.

We could kill them all right now.

They'd bow to us in horrified awe.

Right before I hit O'Farrell, I stumble on to something. I'm on the other side of the street where a small commotion has broken out. An old dude wearing all black with hair as white as a wedding dress is blasting a lady bum with a garden hose. She's just lying on the sidewalk minding her business. She crawls away and shields her eyes from the shooting water.

Oh, the irony of these blushing brides pretending they are virgins.

It's like me pretending I'm innocent.

"Beat it, lady! I told you to get off my property!"

She can't retort. She's dragging her grungy blanket behind her, a sopping mess of a thing. Water cascades down her and onto the concrete. I can smell the scene from over here. I remove my sunglasses and absorb everything that's happening. My coffee tastes better now that I've focused on one thing.

Satisfied, the man drops the hose and goes inside. It looks like an art gallery, Geffrey Fine Art and Frames. I'm confident he's the proprietor. I guess he's fed up with the forgotten people of the city squatting at his front door.

I haven't done damage here in a month, but I have to go to work.

You have a few hours.

My leather jacket conceals my work shirt. It's risky and I'm unprepared, but it's time to stake my claim.

91

I cross the street, narrowly avoiding becoming Swiss cheese by an on-coming cable car. The thing appeared as a blur with no one on board. I swear I looked both ways before crossing. I turn to hiss at the driver, but he looks soulless and stares me down. He has no face and wears an old cabbie hat. Worms and algae sludge are draped all over him. He smells of fresh sea water; that's how close he came to sending me to my maker.

Wait a minute.

He looks like the cabbie I suffocated out by the bridge.

What was his name?

Rob, Fred, Bob, gurgle pants shitter?

I wish I had some pills to suck down. Replacing a buffet of prescription drugs with booze and caffeine is a recipe for disaster.

Sometimes I wonder if I'm seeing things that aren't there.

It's as though my brain is slipping from inside my skull. There are times I want to cut myself open with a simple drill or crude instrument. Allow my brain to spill out all over the floor.

Maybe *that* will solve it.

I've lost several minutes and don't realize I've opened the door and gone inside the gallery. I can't tell you if the waterlogged bum is still outside. I peek through the window from the inside but don't see anything. She probably took up soggy residence at the Squarebucks a block over past Maple.

Christ . . . that coffee is shit.

These losers gulp it down like liquid gold.

"It's appointment *only.* Hey, didn't ya hear me?" The voice sounds Italian, rich and thick like spaghetti sauce.

I peel off my sunglasses and move toward the desk where he stands. The gallery lighting is cool and bright, causing a shooting pain to jolt between my eyes, as if I grabbed an ice pick and performed my own version of Doctor Jamison. "Is *that* how you treat your non-appointments?"

He shifts his weight to one side, throwing it all to his left. He's tall and middle-aged. He has a look on his face like he's seen some shit throughout the years. "How do ya mean?"

"The water sports broad out there. I saw that."

There's no shift in his facial expression. "Hmm. I assume someone did see that."

We stand there, waiting for him to elaborate.

"Truth is, I feel horrible about it. I really do. She's been warned countless times. My gallery is going to hell, and I can barely get anybody in the door. The city's decay makes it worse. You're not gonna call the coppuhs on me, are ya? It's just watuh . . . it's not like I blew her brains out or anything."

This guy's all right.

I move closer, almost sliding forward. He doesn't flinch. I don't care to check my surroundings; my focus is straight on him. I find my regular glasses in my pocket and put them on before responding. "Maybe you should have shot her in the face."

"You mean with the hose?"

I lick my lips. She's churning inside my stomach. She answers for me.

"*I don't know. . .*"

My face is to the floor, but only for a moment. Then I shoot a glare right into him. His eyes are a striking hazel, almost blinding. It's as if a dirty glacier is trapped inside his eye sockets, begging to be pierced, to let everything gush to the underworld.

He remains unflinching. His stature is strong and able, especially for a middle-aged person. Even with the benefit of surprise, he would not be easy to overpower. "That's clevuh. . . clevuh, indeed. But I don't think I'm *that* sick—am I?"

Clever?

Clev-uh, clev-uhh, clev-uhhh.

What a silly accent.

I want to go berserk on him.

"Like I said, I usually don't do walk-ins. But now that you're here, why don't ya have a look around. Everything ya see is mine. All my creations."

You should see *our* creations. . .

I do a quick scan, relaxing my obsession with him for a fractured moment.

I'm taken aback by the decor of the place. It's spacious and modern. The walls are painted black, and it pairs nicely with the elegant cool lighting he has going on. There are large lamps in the corners made from skulls and bones. They look like actual lamps painted black, gold, or silver. The shades are either red or black velvet material, with a rope that snakes down them.

The boiling rage inside me calms, almost sputtering to nonexistence. I run a hand through my raven mane and wriggle around, pulling my jeans up past my hips. "I think I will, thank you."

"My name's Max. Ya know, like the movies?"

I know what he's referring to, but I refuse to entertain the question.

"Anyway, I've got orders and paperwork to attend to. I'll be here when you finish your tour."

92

I don't know much about art, especially the traditional kind. I know *my* art, my work of dark delights.

I did read a book on the old masters, Picasso and Dali, but it was back in Kentucky. As far as drawing goes, I can't draw a straight line. I leafed through a large picture book about William Blake during my "stay" at The Rock. His moody dramatics were incredible for his time.

I don't expect much from my tour, but I'm wrong.

This old artist is some brand of hybrid theory. He's a photographer of landscapes and lands I've only dreamed about. There are these gigantic pictures on his walls. They look to be made from thin glass or shiny metal. I can't get over the rich details of the majestic mountains and trees. He photographs in a way where it feels as though I'm there, frozen in the stills of the wilderness with him.

That's how I want my art to be remembered.

The most fascinating things are his paintings. I've never seen a style quite like it. Some appear as portraits of people with no faces. There are hunks of different colors of paint slathered across a canvas with reckless abandonment, almost a maniacal sense of brazen craftsmanship.

Here's one titled 'Sea Creature.'

It looks like me.

Not with my current hair, but my natural hair of fire. The woman in the painting has pigtails and her face is gone, lost in a sea of different textures of chunky color.

My queen wants to rip it from the wall.

I want it, but the price is too much.

"This one is *quite* popular."

I barely hear him. I'm lost in his work. He says something else, an incoherence. I'm forced to answer.

"Sorry?"

He's left his desk and is standing next to me. Not too close, but a generous distance to where I won't strike. He shifts his posture and places his hands in his pockets, attempting to make himself smaller to meet my length. I'm tall for a goddess, but he's at least six-foot-five. "What do ya think?"

I can't take my eyes from her on his black wall. "Of what, sir?"

"Of this painting. I can see it speaks to you."

"I . . . I don't know art."

He smiles. His cologne wafts into my nose. It's a pleasant scent of man musk and trees. It reminds me of a freshly cut Christmas tree with a hint of something else, maybe tobacco. "I have many days where I also don't think I know art."

His painting loses its grip on me. I turn like a stiff ghost to face him head-on. "But you own an art gallery."

He walks by me, immersing himself in the bowels of his own artistic delights. He pulls off his spectacles and places them neatly in his left pants pocket, studying one of his creations, then moving to another. He responds while staring at a corner painting.

"Truth is, I don't know *what* I am. I've *nevuh* been someone who paints flowers and dogs and grandkids. I've *always* found that generic stuff to be quite boring. Trouble is, the average person seems to enjoy such formalities in the art world. The safe things, the vanilla junk. Not me. When *I* create, it's with everything I've got . . . especially while painting."

He has me intrigued, but I will not give him satisfaction.

Ask a question.

"Everything you have?"

He turns away from the bloody scene he whipped up, dating back to 1987. It's of a witch in a forest with horns bursting through her head. She's naked and voluptuous with large breasts. There's fire and death and blood *everywhere*.

It's as if she's fighting the whole world.

It claws at her back, trying to bring her to her knees.

He cuts off my infatuation with his other painting. "This may sound dumb, but my darkness channels my creativity. Hell, I'm almost ashamed to admit that."

My cheeks burn and my stomach does somersaults. My legs grow weak, but in a beautiful way. "I have to go."

Before he can respond, I'm gone.

93

Sergeant McNamara felt like the floor of a taxicab.

She hadn't planned on getting blitzed the night before.

She quaked in the restroom where she'd made her temporary escape. A group of reporters had followed her into the precinct. The silver lining was that the press conference was to be held on the top floor of her own stomping ground, not the courthouse uptown.

She still smelled of bourbon and rich tobacco. The dry-heaving session in the shower before breakfast hadn't done much for last night's actions. There wasn't even breakfast, except for half a cup of stale coffee she could barely put down.

There was no one in the bathroom, minus her beaten down reflection in the faucet mirror. She placed her slender hands on the sink while the water ran, allowing the rising steam to fog over her mirrored self. It was noisy out in the hallway. The conference was supposed to go live in fifteen minutes.

McNamara hated this side of herself. Her blatant human vulnerabilities.

That was partly the reason she'd quit the Corps. She was undeniably able and brave, but her mind tended to gain the upper hand under intense stress. The rawness of feverish empathy was no match for her conscious mind.

It felt like a war she could never win.

A piercing bang rang out from the hall. It made her flinch. It sounded like a grenade, one from the meaningless desert she'd spent two years fighting in. Her legs began to quake and her vision grew hazy.

"Pull yourself together, soldier."

The sound of her own voice provided comfort, but the one inside her head was much louder and more convincing. She arranged her necktie and smoothed her suit of black and charcoal stripes. The tie was blood red, a slender cloth that hung professionally from her long neck.

She pulled out her pipe and brought it to her mouth. She'd already smoked a whole bowl on the way over between sips of the gag-worthy thermos coffee. She wanted to light up again, but that would set off the fire alarm. She pocketed the Savinelli and accidentally nicked the butt of her revolver in the process. It sent pain to her hand and arm, but she disregarded it.

Her mind jumbled the more she tried to pull herself out of her own miserable abyss. Mitchell, the Captain, was usually the one who led the media circus. He was also a former Marine who had been on the Golden State's force for a thousand years.

He'd lost his athletic build over the decades but was doing all right after the heart scare. The politics were the worst part of the job, though. He loathed that side of it. Because of his decline in health, he had appointed McNamara to lead the briefing directly after the governor addressed the city with his political jargon. She wanted to decline, but the case had become unprecedented.

They were *all* feeling the heat.

It was as bad as anyone had ever seen.

A records intern stormed in and instantly noticed the lengthy sergeant. She voiced a few things, but it came off as mumbled nothingness to McNamara in her condition. The wily sergeant took a final look at herself and ran a wet hand through her slicked back hair to make sure the bun she'd made before leaving the house remained presentable.

Then McNamara sighed and turned toward the hazy figure, gave a hollow smile, and burst onto the scene of flashbulbs and chatter.

94

"Citizens of our great city, I must thank you, first and foremost, for tuning in with us today."

Mac hit her seat just in time, next to Captain Mitchell and Fleming. Her partner glanced at her in question, clearly sensing her struggles, but she forced a smile.

The press jumped right in, cutting off the governor.

"WHAT'S HAPPENING IN OUR STREETS? WHO'S DOING THIS?"

The governor took the outburst well. McNamara had met him once in passing, the day she'd been promoted to lead sergeant. His suit was well-tailored to his body. He looked like a doll, something almost too good to be true. His salt-and-pepper hair was slicked back, not a single follicle out of place.

He's a handsome fella, especially for his age.

A barrage of camera flashes sprayed the talking puppet, sending a stabbing pain through McNamara's head.

The governor raised both hands, palms facing the audience. "Please, ladies and gentlemen, please. I understand your anger and frustration, but let's hold all questions until the conclusion of our conference."

McNamara's right leg started to bounce. Her entire body was exposed to the rowdy crowd before them. She gripped her thigh with her left hand and massaged away her anxiety.

The questions and flashbulbs ceased.

The governor continued, "We have a *dire* situation in our great city. Crime has skyrocketed; however, our dedicated police force has met these heinous acts of evil head-on. They've worked tirelessly with no additional pay to catch this monstrous killer. We've added additional patrols surrounding our schools and neighborhoods. I have the utmost faith in our city officials and first responders. Most importantly, I have faith in *you*, the wonderful citizens of our beloved Golden State!"

The crowd grew restless. The cops could sense the air turn into a suffocating vortex of angst and fury.

"What about the killings? Nobody is safe walking across the street anymore! Things like this haven't happened here since the Zodiac!"

It was a collective jumbled shriek from all directions. Every person with a media badge was seething and chiming in, dying for their fifteen minutes of fame.

The governor in his pretty suit once again raised his vanilla hands.

Aren't they shiny and smooth, thought McNamara.

Another intrusion of *those hands probably do nothing but count money* swished through her depleted spirit.

"Allow me to hand things over to our police. Sergeant McNamara is leading the charge on these fiendish murders. I will give the floor to her. Sergeant?"

He turned to his left and smiled at her. His teeth even looked fake—too white and straight.

McNamara rose from her seat with a spinning head. She looked down at Captain Mitchell, who was seated on her left. Her partner,

Fleming, was on her right. Fleming knew she was hurting, but it was her duty. Marines were trained to elbow through shit at any cost.

Her world began to slant. It felt like Kuwait all over again. With every new flash of a camera, the onlooking faces became muted and indistinct. Some even looked like the enemy, all bloody and broken, with bulging eyes before being blown to bits.

The steely sergeant grabbed the pulpit with both hands, fighting for balance.

A barrage of questions, one after the other, so many that she couldn't decipher them.

"One at a time." Her voice was foreign and inaudible. She fought, gaining clarity within the press circus and her crumbling spirit. A rush of rage shot into her from an unknown force. "One at a time! And no more pictures. If I see one more flashbulb, I'm throwing you out!"

Everyone fell silent. You could hear a rat muffling his breathing in the corner of the precinct.

A brave reporter from the *Golden Gate Times* began the new order of questions. "Is it true there's a serial killer on the loose in our city?"

McNamara had a script on the pulpit, a written document of propaganda and canned responses she could go to in a pinch. Captain Mitchell had made her review it a day in advance. "We have concluded that several of the last two years' murders are connected, yes."

Her voice was back to her usual grit. She stood as tall as she could, using her length for dominance over the raucous crowd.

A different voice asked the next question. "How many murders in total?"

"Seventeen that we're aware of."

A new voice entered the ring. "Is the butchered family in Pleasantville included in that number? Is it true the baby was left crying with the bloody murder weapon in its crib?"

"That's out of our jurisdiction."

"How can you be certain it wasn't the same individual or individuals that slaughtered the family?"

"*Individual.*"

"Sorry?"

She brought her hand up to massage her temples. "This is the work of one . . . person . . . and *no*, we can't rule out the possibility that the same killer is not responsible for the family murders in P-town. In truth, *I* believe those murders are linked."

She was abandoning the script. She could feel Captain Mitchell burning a hole through her back.

"Is it true, then, there's some type of calling card? Words written in blood?"

"All true. The killer is signing their work. On the surface, the crimes come off as random with no solid MO. However, the signature has been more or less consistent."

She could no longer tell who was asking what. She no longer cared. She would be as transparent as possible.

"What does the signature look like? Is it words? . . . Lieutenant?"

"*Sergeant,*" she corrected. The room again fell silent before she continued. "It's a symbol—forged in blood. Sometimes it's written with the victim's bodily fluids. We've gathered it is an old aquatic symbol, pulled from ancient Greek mythology. It's the symbol of 'The Mermaid.'"

"'The *Mermaid*'? Are you saying, Sergeant, that a *woman* is responsible for these horrors?"

McNamara's world began to slosh again. She squeezed the bridge of her nose with her thumb and middle finger, staving off a blast of sickening tension. "I'm not saying that at all. What I'm saying is, it's a possibility we haven't ruled out."

The wily reporter from the *Times* again came forward. She was half Mac's size but loaded with spunk. "Yes, but—*certainly* these acts couldn't be carried out by a *woman*?"

"And why's that? You the detective now?"

Mac was on the verge of collapse. The stimulation was too much to control. She wanted to scream, but gathered her remaining stoicism to answer her own snarky question. "Keep your doors and windows locked. Watch your children closely and limit night travel in the city, *especially* if you're alone. On second thought . . . don't go out at all. You people don't know what you're up against. That's all. Thank you."

She barely made it off the makeshift stage. She again hurried to the bathroom and locked herself away in a stall, where she leaned over and put her face in her lap.

95

"Sarge?"

Computer keys were clinking, but she didn't hear her partner enter.

"Hey, Sarge?"

It took another few seconds. The typing didn't stop, and she didn't look away from her screen. "Hmm? What can I do for you, partner?"

He stood tall; his graying crew-cut gleamed off the precinct lights at his back. Her office was dark, always dark. Her computer screen supplied all the lighting she required.

"Another letter came in, handwritten, addressed to nobody. These love notes from every cop-hating poet in the city are piling up. Thought you should look first."

She didn't look up but did cease the keystrokes. "Leave it on my desk."

"You got it, Boss."

After her door closed, her phone rang. She answered and cradled the black receiver between her neck and shoulder so she could resume clicking away on her keyboard. "McNamara."

"We've got another one, Sarge. Could be the same MO. Too early to tell."

"Thinking all by yourself, now?"

McNamara tossed her raven-colored ponytail behind her head. It snuck up on her when she tilted her head to hold the phone to her ear. The rookie on the line breathed but said nothing.

"I'm on it, newbie."

She rose, scanning her tidy office in the half-dark to locate her sport coat. Her hazel eyes went to the letter on her desk. She picked it up, giving it a once-over. Icy cold ran through her body, a sudden flash of dread. A cop's sixth sense of something not quite right.

McNamara read the face of the envelope before sitting back down in her chair. She opened her desk drawer and found the letter opener, slicing it open with care. The front of the envelope read only, 'The Police.'

∽◌∾

Dear Sergeant McNamara,

You don't know me, but I know you. I've seen you. Do you think it was on TV, or in real life? You'll never know, because we'll always be ten steps ahead of you. Maybe I've seen you at home or in a café. Maybe I'm watching you right now as you open my letter.

Either way, I must clarify some things. . .

I don't appreciate the press reports about me. The lies, the blatant ignorance of my cause. There is no reason as to why I kill. I'm not like you, a mere mortal.

I'm something else.

Your cop friends say these "killings" are random and done by a disgruntled man. I find this funny.

I like your style and your face on TV. You have strong features and I like your raven hair. You exude a dominant femininity in your field, and I admire that.

Being that I know so much about you and you know nothing about me, consider this a warning.

Don't try to find me. Never try to catch me, lock me up, or cage me.

Allow me to continue my work, Detective. The world is diseased and must be purged. I'm doing you a service.

If you come for me, it won't end well for you.

All I ask in return for your life is that you stop the false reports and dense newspaper clippings.

I'm not a man. I'm not a woman. I'm more than both. I'm more than human. You'd better start understanding that.

Don't be surprised when another slab of useless meat turns up cold in an alleyway, or in another parked car out near Land's End. You'll know it was me, and you'll shudder. You'll bow at my kingdom, my playpen of a city you call the Golden State.

No one is safe, and no one can escape.

Not even you.

Regards,

THE MERMAID KILLER

96

McNamara looked up at the man standing in her doorway. "Ramirez?"

She was crushing the overtime, her obsession becoming borderline unstable. Elsa still wasn't answering her calls. She knew she'd fucked up, what with the binge drinking and the late-night fights, but it wasn't like Elsa to disappear for this long. McNamara was starting to worry.

She couldn't recall the last time she'd had a decent night's sleep. Lately, she lived either on the midnight streets or in her office, fueled by raunchy Chinese food from a dive next door and stale cop coffee. Her pipe hung from her mouth while she sifted through crime scene photos and other random bits of collected evidence.

"Sorry to disturb, Sarge. . ." The rookie's virgin lungs seized at the pipe smoke blanketing the office, and he started coughing.

"Out with it, Ramirez. Don't choke to death in my doorway."

Although Ramirez was standing, he looked pint-sized. McNamara towered over him even with no shoes on.

The choking continued, and she looked up from her computer, a rebel smoke ring escaping from her Italian pipe. "If you don't tell me what you've got, you're dismissed."

Ramirez persevered through his coughing fit. "We've got something. Video footage from one of the murders."

Mac perked up. She crossed her arms and legs, gripping her pipe in her slender left hand. "Close the door, rookie. You raised in a barn?"

Ramirez took a long inhale at the doorway, clearly hoping to get as much fresh oxygen as possible before entering McNamara's hive. He closed the door a bit sheepishly at her rebuke.

"Let's have it, Ramirez."

He handed her a VHS tape, and she slipped it into the player below a nearby TV. Uncomfortable silence fell between them as they waited for the video to play.

Ramirez assumed a standing position behind McNamara as she leaned closer to the screen, desperate for any clue they could use to catch this killer. "It's dark. What am I looking at?"

"It's a clip from next door to the sleaze joint on Broadway. The owner of the dry cleaner has some state-of-the-art camera equipment."

McNamara fast forwarded to the drunk man swaying in the alleyway in the dead of night. The reel was grainy and difficult to distinguish. It looked like he was talking with someone, gesturing and such, but the camera couldn't pick up who or what. The angle was off, only catching him in the frame.

The pipe dangled from her mouth as she spoke. "The fuck is he talking to?"

The reel glitched as a figure appeared on their knees before him.

"Why is it so hard to see, rookie?"

"It's 1999, Boss . . . not 2099."

She found that funny, but she'd never let him know it.

The file grew even more grainy, cutting and chopping across her screen. It looked like the victim was holding something in his hand, maybe a knife or pager.

Ramirez spoke with his hand covering his mouth. "Wait for it. . ."

The man went down, and the phantom was on top of him. It was all blurry and out of focus, dark and inconclusive. McNamara froze the frame where the guy went down and the thing had mounted him.

"It looks like . . . a man."

"Why would you say *that,* rookie?"

"Look . . . it's tall and bald. It's practically the size of the victim."

The footage was so butchered it allowed nothing but speculation. McNamara shot back, struggling to decipher anything from her seat, "Why would a huge bald man be blowing a *supposed* ladies' man in the back of a gentleman's club?"

Ramirez sighed and moved back to the front of her office. The over-powering smell of raisin and vanilla was beginning to clear. The footage ended with the victim on his back with no clear suspect in view. They could go back to the club and ask more questions, but they'd already done that. The victim was remembered and had frequented the estab-lishment before, but that was it.

Club owners of such places didn't like to get involved with the police, even when a patron was slaughtered like a pig in an outside alley. They'd gladly shut their faces and keep the rest of their shady antics to themselves.

"What are you saying, Sarge?"

McNamara chucked her dead pipe on her desk, scattering ash on the mahogany surface. She lifted her hands to her face and tried to wipe away her tired fury. "I don't know what I'm saying. It was nice work getting the footage. I'll send it out to Folsom to see if we can get it analyzed further."

Ramirez turned to leave, but McNamara spoke to his back.

"I'm just frustrated, Ramirez. This is the first solid evidence we've had on this thing. Now that we've got something, it's about as solid as a Taco Bell shit."

"I don't do Taco Bell shits like *that*, Sarge."

"Don't you just have guts of steel, Ramirez."

They held stony eyes for a fleeting moment before the rookie asked a burning question. "You don't see a man there, Sarge?"

"What if I said I didn't?"

"There's no way *that's* a woman."

McNamara leaned back as far as she could go in her leather chair, interlocking her hands behind her head. "You lead detective now, *rookie*?"

Red spawned to the surface of his olive skin. "No, ma'am. I mean . . . no, Sergeant."

"You're dismissed, Ramirez."

He was almost out before she spoke again.

"Anything back yet with the letter?"

He turned around. "Forensics analyzed five of them. Four had trace DNA. The authors all checked out. Just creative writers looking for their fifteen minutes."

"What about the one sent to me? With the cursive writing?"

"No trace DNA. It was completely clean."

The sergeant sighed and leaned, placing both elbows on her desk. "That's all, Ramirez."

The rookie closed the leading officer's door so gently it made no sound.

97

I throw myself back out into the night. I get dressed up, a little skirt with fishnets and a metal shirt. My lipstick is also black. I think about hailing a cab, but I can't be that close to a living person right now.

I scored some pills from Maverick at the bar. He told me what they are, but I wasn't listening. I haven't taken prescription medication since my island imprisonment. I take two different pills before leaving my apartment. One is rough textured and red, the other a smooth blue.

I caress Mick's freshly bleached skull before I leave. I retrieved it from the alleyway sludge vat.

I just couldn't let it go.

I've been using it for a cereal bowl. There's a generous gap in the left side of the skull from all my hammering. Some Gorilla Glue and duct tape have taken care of that.

I make sure the pills work before I head out. These aren't like Jamison's concoctions; they're milder but evoke a sense of mild hysteria and paranoia. It feels as though I'm at constant war with myself, hyper-aware of my dreadful thought patterns.

I like the feeling.

Living on the edge is where I do my best work.

I cut through the city until my feet hurt. I'm wearing heels, but they are thicker and more comfortable for my lengthy frame. I'm an easy six-footer while wearing them.

The sky tonight is purple and orange and baby blue. Clouds are scattered all over but remain thin and transparent like floating specters. They perform a glowing dance with the stunning sunset.

I pass by the baseball field near the water. I think the team that plays here is called The Little Giants. The other bridge, not my favorite one of golden fire, is here next to me. I've never cared for professional sports, but these city fucks *love* it. They wear the garb like it's a literal part of them. They holler when they win and shut their faces when they lose.

Wastes of oxygen.

The air becomes more chilled as night approaches. I have no jacket but welcome the cold. I'm starved and can't remember the last time I've eaten anything substantial.

What about your skull cereal?

Was that yesterday or the day before?

It was this morning, love.

"Thank you, angel."

My bloodthirst is at a minimum; however, I need some food. A guy lumbers by after I pass the field to my right. He bumps into me while carrying a goopy sandwich.

My voice raises three octaves. "Watch it, you fuck!"

He says nothing, and I don't turn around. My vision shifts and tilts, as if I'm underwater. I can't hear anything. Car horns go silent as the soothing sound of the ocean to my right goes dead.

"Miss? Do you know a good restaurant around?"

I find another dullard on a bench. She's young and wears workout clothes. Her legs are crossed, and you can barely see that she has pants on at all; that's how short her shorts are. She's blabbing to someone in the middle of the street. They're screaming at each other, but I can't hear *anything*.

"Can't you hear me?"

Her mouth moves frantically while she stares straight through me.

I'm right in front of her!

Her animated eyes remain fixated on my chest.

"The fuck is wrong with you? Answer me!"

I tear off away from everything. People are peppered around, moseying in their own worlds. Cars pass by; buses come and go. Streetlamps turn on as the day melts away, transforming into the satisfying dark. I stop on the sidewalk and sink my head in my hands. It takes an agonizing minute—but the sounds of the world return. They rush back in an awesome wave of heightened sensitivity.

I can hear again.

Someone bumps me and says, "Oh, excuse me, love."

I catch a wave of food smell. It creeps into my nostrils and mixes with the sea. I lift my head and stare at a long pier. It goes for miles. My eyes start to strain, but I see no distinguishable end. The light-up sign has just kicked on. It's enormous and shaped like a rainbow.

It reads, "Golden State Carnival–come one, come all!"

"Don't mind if *we* do. . ."

98

Who goes to a carnival by themselves?

You do. That's who.

You should know by now that I'm never alone.

I have *her*, my goddess of death.

As soon as I pass the ticket booth, I'm thrust into another dimension. There're people all over; the night air grows warm as the girls are dolled up with their guys in thin tees and sandals. Twinkling amusement park lights claw at my eyes in all directions. The ordeal swallows me in an instant. The laughing meat sleeves carry various things—stuffed animals, beer, hot dogs, mini meat sleeves. Nobody knows who I am or what I've done. They're clueless, trapped inside their own trivial existences.

I'm no different.

However, I've come to accept my nihilism long ago.

My head starts to swim again, but an invigorating smell breaks me free from it. I look up and see a giant sign that reads, 'Outlaw Burger' and next to that, 'Jumbo Corn Dog.' Smoke billows from the cooking apparatuses behind the elaborate booths. I can smell a dozen different aromas at once—deep-fried Oreos, cotton candy, giant turkey legs, and French fry platters oozing with nacho cheese sauce and jalapenos.

342   THE MERMAID KILLER - JOSEPH MIGUEL

The last time I ate a corn dog was back in Kentucky. It was those frozen ones that you toss in the microwave. I order a jumbo from a pimply-faced kid that looks like he's thirteen. My order comes out quick and I sit down at a nearby bench for a few bites.

It tastes so good it hurts.

Mick's brain tastes better.

The corn dog is crispy and golden brown. The meat itself is juicy, and each bite causes steam to rise from the thin wooden stick. I lose myself in it before wanting a drink to wash the rest down. I go to the other stand at the opposite end of the makeshift food court. I point at the beer I want while still gnawing at my delicious corn dog.

I'm back at my bench with my legs crossed, enjoying how I look and feel. Tonight's carnival is like the one each year in Kentucky, but on steroids. Bowling Green had two food stands—well, just one, really. The other was strictly for beer. The cheeseburgers were handmade each year by our local pharmacist, Chuck. The burgers were pretty good. I remember Chuck priding himself in his perfectly prepared cow patties. They weren't hockey pucks and still had pink in the middle. I could never get a straight answer to what seasoning he used.

I even tried my special charms on him.

I sit here and eat, alone in my fluctuating world of mostly pain. I scowl at the "happy" families going by, the girlfriends and boyfriends holding hands while swapping spit and cotton candy. I get up several more times for more beer. The booze is pricy, but I have plenty of cash. The skies become delightfully dark before I realize I've been here on this bench for over an hour. My bare legs are sweaty as I peel them off to stand.

I continue farther into the extravaganza.

They tout all the main attractions: a Ferris wheel and merry-go-round, and that one game where you shoot water into a clown's mouth to see if your balloon can pop first. I swivel my head as I walk, attempting to soak up all that I can.

"Step right up, missy! Nobody leaves a loser!"

He's old, one of those authentic carney types. I count two teeth in his stew hole, even from my cool distance. His schtick is to throw a softball at a stack of heavy white bottles. No one is at his booth, and his perfectly stacked gimmicks beg for a sucker.

The bottles are cemented to that little table there.

"Probably."

If you nail that pyramid just right, the softball might bounce back and wind up in somebody's skull.

My eyes grow wide as my mouth turns from a solid purse to a vivid row of teeth. I go past him, a haunted house, then a ride called 'The Whizzer.' The haunted house is micro but has some wicked art painted on its black walls. There's Dracula, looking fierce with blood oozing from his mouth, a werewolf that's half wolfed-out, and finally a siren.

She's blonde and voluptuous, nothing like me at all. She rests on a rock with a wave crashing behind her. A lighthouse in the distance beams its brightness on her sultry face. Several seamen fall at her feet while she licks her lips, exposing her slithery tongue.

I briefly run into a palm reader. He grabs my hand and runs his dirty finger over the lines. He wears a red hat with a sash on top and sports a handlebar mustache that completely covers his lips.

He looks deep into my eyes. "Look here, little lady. This line; this one here. My, you're already dead!"

I get away from him and come upon a caramel corn stand that is built like an oversized popcorn machine. I can't help myself—the smell is too intoxicating.

Do you know that smell, the overpowering waft of carnival pop-corn, glazed in caramel and cooked to perfection?

I buy the smallest bag they offer and head back toward the Ferris wheel. I marvel at its beauty, watching the multicolored lights dance and play at their own pace while riders laugh and carry on, huddling together in a single seat.

I want to go for a ride, but for some reason I hesitate.

"Who rides a Ferris wheel by themselves?"

"We do, sweetheart."

Wait. That voice isn't hers . . . it's *not* my queen.

I spin around and see her. She's long and pale like me, but her hair is white as a chilled December.

Snow.

We wait for her to speak again.

"My God—*Ivy*, right? What are the odds?"

She's dressed down but looks even more striking than the first time I saw her in the candlelit rape pad. Her chocolate eyes twinkle with the frantic neon that envelops all of us. A seabird lands nearby and gives an ugly squawk. The dirty thing waddles over and steals a French fry from the asphalt near the haunted mansion.

This is strange and foreign to me.

I *want* to see her, but not.

You haven't responded to her. . .

She's patient and waits until I'm ready.

"I just had to know. These carnivals are neat, yeah?"

She perks up. "I know, right? Tonight's the last night; then it packs up and moves to Southern California. I haven't been until tonight.

I usually come with friends, but thought I'd just come alone. *Weird, right?*"

I shove a single piece of caramel corn into my mouth. I swirl it around with my tongue before taking a bite. The sugary sweet shell collides with my tastebuds and forces a wince of unabashed overindulgence.

I'm still chewing as I answer. "Not as weird . . . as you might think."

"You're alone, *too*? Ready for the year 2000? It's right around the corner!"

You're never alone, angel.

I smirk and make a weird affirmative sound.

She leans in and touches my arm. It's a gentle graze, one that only Snow can execute with perfect precision. It sends shivers up my spine. The baby hairs on my neck stiffen with delight. It almost catapults me back to cuddling with her while she worked her ASMR magic.

Snow wants to ride the Ferris wheel.

So do I, if I'm being honest.

My goddess isn't interested, so I override her.

I bet, my delightful reader, that you didn't know I could do that. We can disagree, but at the end of it all we are *always* in conjunction. *Her* or *it* or whatever you think *she* is has been integrated with me.

We are inseparable.

The huge carnival wheel creaks and takes its time in the night while we smile and chat. I feel normal, whatever the fuck *that* means, if only for ten minutes as we go up and around. She mentions Mick and how he's gone missing.

She almost seems relieved that he's gone.

At least that's the impression I get.

She apologizes to me while crying. She stresses that she's aware Mick is capable of hurting people, especially women.

Was capable.

She pleaded with him to stop in the past, even threatening to go to the authorities herself. I pretend to feel something, some . . . real connection. She caresses my face with her hand, and it makes my eyes close as my head falls into her.

I want to tell her that her brother has been stopped.

I want to say I've been drinking beer from his pulverized skull and have chopped him up into thirty-five pieces.

I crave for her to thank me and tell me I'm unique and original.

However, those wants fade quickly if you're me.

Nobody will *ever* understand, least of all Snow. She can try to grasp what I am, but it's unfathomable.

We finish off the night with a kiss at the entrance to the dying carnival in The Golden State. Her breath smells of beer and her smooth tongue is cold and tastes of strawberry ice cream.

Let me have her.

I will not.

She calls a cab and wants to share the ride. I decline and watch her go, the taillights smudging in the midnight air. I finally take off my heels and disappear into the bleeding twilight.

99

I'm still reeling from leaving Snow. I can still taste her cotton-candied breath on my tongue, a lingering reminder of something painfully sweet. I don't know where I'm walking. I want to go home, but my mind is too active.

The city is something to behold during the witching hour. Tonight's sky is black but flaunts a delightful magenta glow. I crane my neck to see a domineering skyscraper sitting in the airspace, partially blanketed by thick fog. The fog appears to glow a purplish haze that creeps throughout the land. It smells like rain, but the world can't seem to commit to the start of a storm.

I saunter, alone in the night, like so many other nights before. I'm not hungry and neither is my goddess. She hasn't stirred for most of the night.

The wind swirls and cuts through my clothes without mercy. I walked inland for several blocks, but I think I've gone toward the water again. I'm now in front of this huge dome-like structure. It looks regal, with giant sloped walls as high as the eye can see. It's like an outside museum with gaudy statues cut from marble and stone and encased in mighty pillars.

There's a lit pond in the middle of the yard with real fish, brightly colored and moving in the dead of night. I look down into the gentle

THE MERMAID KILLER - JOSEPH MIGUEL

water. *Her* reflection stares up at me, my underwater muse. The fish grow anxious and disappear. They can sense their own inferiority; I know it.

I'm about to turn back when a large statue catches my eye. It's godly, like the ones you read about in Greek mythology books or in scripture. He's muscular with long and wavy hair. A beard consumes half of his face, cascading down to a chiseled chest. He holds a trident with a strong right hand of rock. I look into his eyes, large white semicircles cut to perfection. My raven hair blows in the wind as I inhale a giant breath of fresh, damp air. It smells of the sea and the fleeting remnants of Snow's perfume.

I hear waves crashing in the distance.

He's judging me, this hairy god of a distant past.

"What are you staring at?"

I want to go home more than ever. I turn around and catch a figure in the corner of my eye. I haven't seen anyone for blocks, including inside this Palace of Fine Arts. It's a silhouette, a micro one at that, jogging toward me.

No time to think.

I duck behind a wall with an inscription on it. It's written in some other language.

It's Latin.

I leave everything up to fate. She can run in another direction. If she does, I won't give chase. But if she runs past me, it'll be the last thing she ever does.

She's coming. . .

She jogs by.

I lunge from my hiding spot and grab her from behind. She's so small I have to bend down a bit to corral her. I tower over her and outweigh her by fifty pounds. I stop her dead, flinging her backward into the wall I've just jumped from.

She bashes her face into the brick, a glorious sound of skull meeting rock formation.

I'm all over her.

I am surprised she hasn't screamed, though.

She kind of exhales and offers me a grunting noise. I go for her neck, slipping both my arms under her chin to settle into a chokehold. She grinds her teeth and gags, spewing something at me in another language.

Chinese, maybe?

She doesn't try to fight my grip, which I find odd. Blood from her nose drips down to my bare arms of slender superiority. The feeling makes me break out in goosebumps all over.

Something clicks.

I break my grip and let her go as she turns and swings her blade in a swift motion. I dodge; it barely misses my face.

I open my mouth to laugh because I'm certain she doesn't know how to use it. She will probably hold it like a fireplace poker, flinging it in front of herself like a crazed idiot.

She does none of this.

Instead, she turns her body a bit to the side, as if protecting her vital organs. She gets lower to the ground with knees bent in a sturdy defense. She pulls the blade up to her face, turning it outward and away, then grips it with the cutting part facing away from her.

This one knows how to fight.

I crave the challenge.

My eyes go black as I grow another three inches.

She's awake and with me, my alluring teammate.

The scrappy runner springs first, stabbing her weapon toward my chest. I catch her arm at the wrist, stopping the attempt in an instant.

Time slows to a crawl. Seconds turn into minutes.

She doesn't say a word, bringing her other hand over and slugging me square in the throat.

It's a perfect shot.

I fall to the ground, still holding her arm with the weapon in it. We both go down together. The knife skitters away from us.

We wrestle for I don't know how long. I can't understand how strong she is for such a tiny thing.

I wind up on top, but just for a second. When I go to bring my hand down on her in a hammering motion, she dodges my brutish attempt. She slips out from under me and gets around to my back, wrapping her little arms around my neck. I duck my chin, not allowing a smooth wrench around my throat.

"Unhand me!"

It's not me talking . . . it's the *other* me.

I'm certain my victim notices my change. She says something else in her native tongue. It sounds crazed and terrified. I manage to shimmy my head down and get my mouth close to her dainty arm. She's wearing a thin jacket, but I can still smell her fear. I bite into her forearm, a victorious chomp from my jagged grinders. I saw back and forth, creating a gaping hole.

She releases me with a grunt, her breaths coming in frenetic bursts.

I'm calm. My heart remains in a smooth rhythm and my breathing never heightens.

This is what you're designed to do.

She starts to freak out as we square up again.

I'm taller than *ever*.

My scaly skin of sickening black swallows her up, smothering the artistic lighting that casts a warm hue behind us from the god statue. Her eyes grow wide as she looks around for her lost knife. She goes right, but I've got her. I have her by the throat as I smash her face into the wall.

A second time; now a third.

She whimpers and her body goes slack.

I can feel her life giving up.

Do you pitiful ingrates know this feeling?

It's indescribable.

I release her, and she crumbles to the pavement. She looks even smaller, a shriveled ball of splattered nothing.

I lost one of my heels in the fight. I bring that foot down on the back of her head. It's a solid strike, causing her body to gyrate and quiver. I kick her again but do not receive the pleasure of a seizing response.

I'm about to turn her over and carve my signature when I hear the drunks coming. It's about two and all the bars in the city have booted the frat douches into the streets.

They're coming fast.

We don't care how many there are.

We'll kill them *all* for the disruption.

I suddenly feel strange and lightheaded. I look down and spot my victim's knife. It's protruding from my thigh, right around the halfway mark to where it meets my quadricep.

You need to go.

It remains in me while I run. I finally pull it out when I'm good and clear.

It doesn't hurt.

I'm surprised by the amount of fight in such a petite woman.

I've dressed the wound and I'm keeping the knife. Another keepsake from my dead unfortunates. Now here *we* are, cleaned up in our bedchamber, with nothing but *us* and the pink neon after another spontaneous kill.

What if she's not dead?

"Then I'll find her and kill her."

Good girl.

We fall asleep together, just *her* and I, while I click the bloody blade open then closed like a gory hypnotist.

I wake up thirty-six hours later.

100

How do I explain to you, my humble and innocent reader, as to *exactly* who I am?

I've pondered this throughout my manifesto, wondering if it's all for naught. I don't expect you to understand. The best way I can describe my convictions is like that of an animal.

Take a lion or tiger, for example. These predators eat when they are hungry, sleep when they are tired, and hunt when the need arises. They don't get lost in future or past misfortunes of mind. They act purely on instinct. Their conscience doesn't get in the way of what they are going after. They kill to survive, but more importantly, because they *can*.

Just like me.

However crazy or mad or insane you presume me to be, always remember that deep down in *you,* there's a little bit of *me.*

You know what *real* crazy looks like?

I cringe at what things will become in twenty years. These fleeting years of the 1990s are wild enough, especially with *me* running around. All the new talks of radically advancing technologies, chat rooms, and theories that one day people will have pocket phones that will track their every movement is *insane.*

What'll be next?

A self-learning computer that can think and improvise all on its own? I bet in thirty years there'll be a computer that can write a novel all by itself. It'll be heartless and hollow, but I doubt anybody will think twice.

Can you fathom that witchcraft?

Now who's crazy . . .

101

"Dr. Lisicki, please report to the OR, stat."

The city hospital was busy. The whole population remained in frenzied panic. Every cop and politician could feel the tension building.

McNamara's head felt as though it were swimming on her shoulders. She was trying to attack hundreds of details all at once.

No suspects or solid leads. Every news station in hotel lobbies and bars ran the same loop:

KILLER ON THE LOOSE | LEAVES A GRIZZLY CALLING CARD INKED IN BLOOD | MERMAID KILLER STRIKES AGAIN!

"Dr. Lisicki, report to the operating room, STAT!"

McNamara answered for the doctor, quietly and to herself. "Yeah, Lisicki. Move your ass."

She slouched in the uncomfortable chair at the foot of the hospital bed. Her lengthy body sprawled halfway across the room. She'd rallied her clothes as best she could, hurrying to the ICU from a choppy slumber. She hadn't washed her hair in days, but it still looked presentable in her tight ponytail.

The rain started right after she arrived. She'd already been there for four solid hours.

Fleming came to the doorway. "Sarge?"

"Hiya, partner." McNamara's eyes trailed off into nothing. The room was dimly lit with a small warm light surrounding the bedridden patient.

Fleming swallowed a bite of a Snickers bar before speaking. "The whitecoats say she's in a coma. Christ, she looks beaten half to death. They said she was barely alive when they brought her in."

McNamara listened, but she already knew the situation. She'd been briefed by the neurologist on call. She fixated on the unconscious victim, with tubes sticking out every which way. Her head was wrapped in a thick gauze and her right arm was heavily bandaged.

Fleming remained in his place at the door. His silver crewcut sparkled in the hallway light.

The outside rain intensified and started to whack the fourth-floor window at the edge of the gloomy room.

Fleming spoke again. "The surgeon who did the emergency operation said she may never come out of it. You think this is our guy?"

McNamara pulled her Savinelli from her breast pocket. There was no tobacco in it. She brought it close to her mouth and sniffed the bowl for comfort. "I do."

"How long have you been here, Mac?"

"A couple hours."

Fleming entered. "If you slouch down any more in that chair, *Marine*, I'm going to have to pick your ass up off the deck."

McNamara rolled her eyes. "I could use some coffee."

"We don't have to stay, Mac. The doctors will notify us if she wakes up."

"I'm staying."

Fleming paced the room, taking a closer look at the tiny woman who had just gone to war with the devil herself. He stopped near the window. "Well, what should I do?"

"Go interview the drunks that brought her in. I doubt they saw anything, but it needs to be done."

He released a long exhale that deflated his chest in his tight polo shirt.

"And bring me that coffee before you go."

102

Two full days went by. Nothing came back from the partiers that had stumbled upon the mutilated jogger.

McNamara didn't leave the hospital. She couldn't, and she didn't know why.

She'd changed once during that time. She had gone down and retrieved another work shirt from her car. There were seventeen total murders being investigated up until that point, all spanning a short window of eight months. The steely sergeant thought about going to the press with the newest victim but thought better of it.

She owned the element of surprise.

The killer had been interrupted, unable to finish their gory intentions. There was no signature or calling card, things that were all unprecedented thus far in the spree.

This woman needed to wake up.

She was the only victim left breathing.

103

It grew late on the second night. McNamara dozed in her stiff chair next to the victim. She had never worn her firearm for so many hours in her career. The weighty revolver dangled under her left arm.

The entire city was on high alert. For all she knew, her ravenous killer had figured out what went wrong and would pop out any second to finish the job.

The team of doctors monitoring the victim had believed they needed to do another emergency surgery to release more swelling to her brain; however, her condition had improved, then declined again. Her family was in Japan. The parents had been notified, with the father flying out first thing in the morning. McNamara had needed a Japanese interpreter to speak with them on the phone. They stated that their daughter knew little to no English.

Mac's eyes throbbed. The lights were out in the quiet hospital room. The TV was off and there had been no overhead pages or codes for hours. It was eerily quiet for a Friday night. She went to grab one of the three Styrofoam cups at her left, but they were all bone-dry.

"Fucking fuck," she muttered.

She pulled herself out of the faded pink chair that had become another enemy to her tired body in the last forty-eight hours and whacked her arm on the butt of her gun for good measure. She reached for the sky in a stretch, twisting her body before speaking to the unresponsive patient.

"I'm going for more coffee. You want anything, sweetheart?"

She thought she was talking to herself, but when she heard the scratchy sound of a woman's voice at her back, she almost lost it.

"Miss Fujima?"

The woman's head remained wrapped, and she'd been placed in a neck brace after the initial surgery. Her voice was weak and delightfully foreign, her natural language sounding elegant to the American officer.

"I'll get a doctor."

Fujima kept talking, reaching out to her lean guardian angel.

McNamara took her small hand in both of hers, swallowing it up and massaging it. "I can't understand what you're saying. I need a translator."

She wouldn't be able to get one until morning. She tried to get help, but the patient wouldn't let her.

"Okay, I'm here."

Mac reached into her other pocket on the opposite side of her hand cannon. She always carried her little tape recorder, just in case she needed a voice statement on the fly. She pulled it out and fired it up, placing it on the bed between them.

"I'm recording us, okay? Tell me what you remember."

Fujima remained stoic. She spoke like she hadn't been near death for days. It sounded as if she were telling a simple story, recalling an event from her foggy memory bank, though she struggled to speak English. "At-tack, f-f-from . . . behind."

"I understand, Miss Fujima. Tell me about your attacker."

She began again, the foreign words pouring from her mouth in waves. Her right eye was swollen shut, the left one barely open. She looked into McNamara's eyes, pleading for assurance the ravaged sergeant didn't know how to give.

The tiny woman began to paw at the tubes and wires that were stuck in her with a free hand. She muttered a word, then said it again. Her one good eye grew as large as a golf ball. Her breathing intensified and her blood pressure spiked.

"It's all right. You're safe."

The woman's brain was stuck on a loop, repeating the word over and over again. She thrashed in her bed.

McNamara got to her feet and pushed the Code Blue button on the other side of the bed. She ran out of the room and threw up her hands. "Doctor! We need a doctor! Get the fuck in here!"

The hospital operator received the alarm after McNamara hit the panic button. A booming voice came overhead.

"CODE BLUE, SECOND FLOOR, INTENSIVE CARE UNIT!"

A team rushed in moments later. McNamara went in after them, but a supervisor stopped her.

"Please don't interfere, officer. Let them do their jobs."

She complied, peering in the doorway until the last possible moment.

Miss Fujima continued talking right up until her body went completely slack in her bed. The word she couldn't stop saying was "KAIBUTSU."

104

"What did she say, Kato? Tell me *everything.*"

McNamara had gone straight to the precinct. The sun rose hypnotically out in the distance during her gloomy drive over. The fog was beginning to burn off already. It looked like it would be a mild and clear morning in her city of blood and pain.

She arrived before eight, stopping at her favorite donut shop and ordering a chocolate twist and a maple old-fashioned, paired with a large cup of black hazelnut coffee. She usually took a splash of cream with her java, but not today.

She removed her heavy leather shoulder strap, releasing what felt like forty pounds of insufferable bulk. Her feet were up on her desk, crossed at the ankle. She smoked, sipped coffee, and ate breakfast in the confines of her office nook.

The Japanese translator was brand new to the force. Even the rookie Ramirez had more clout. He had been working traffic for several months, hoping to one day have the opportunity to work narcotics. He stood at her doorway, dressed in full uniform. He had been headed out to work his usual intersection when McNamara had dropped the tape recorder in his lap. It had taken him ten minutes to work the translation and arrive at her office.

"It's jumbled and bizarre, Sergeant, but I have the gist of it."

"Enlighten me." Mac spoke with her mouth full of maple donut and smoky Captain Black. She swallowed and blew out the remaining steam through her nose like an angry bull.

It was the first time the two had formally met. Officer Kato had never been called to a supervisor's office for such a crucial piece of evidence before.

McNamara took her feet off the desk and sat up straight in her leather chair. "Come on, man, what does the recording say? Out with it—and take off your hat. It's bad luck to be so proper in here."

"Uh, yes, ma'am. Yes . . . *Sergeant*." Kato had her recorder in his hand, along with a piece of paper. He handed the typed document to her.

"Thanks for the transcript copy, but I want *you* to tell me what she said."

He went through it in detail, stating that Miss Fujima said she had gone for her usual late-night jog. She was attacked from behind but managed to fight her attacker from the beginning. She mentioned martial arts training and thought she had the upper hand, even though the attacker was much larger than her.

"What did she say about the attacker?"

Kato lifted his naked head toward her, gripping his patrolman's hat with both hands. "That's where it gets fuzzy, Sergeant. She thought she recognized the suspect from somewhere, maybe a bar or club. She was starting to slur and repeat at this point, but she vaguely described a woman in a tank of water, like a live mermaid show?"

McNamara put down the Savinelli and rested it on a clean napkin from the donut shop. Pipe smoke twirled in the space between them. "The Blue Lagoon does shows like that. I've never been in there, but I know the place. It's not too classy, but also not a dive. Keep talking."

"Well, she mentioned the show, that she was there one night. Her cognitive ability began to sink, and she didn't authentically say that she recognized her attacker from a specific bar."

McNamara began reading the translation report. "Go on."

"Well, Sarge, she didn't come out and say it, but I think she was trying to say that her attacker was a woman . . . at first."

"At *first*?" She took another bite of the chocolate twist on her desk. "My patience is wearing thin, Kato."

"The demeanor in her dialect had shifted, transitioning from somewhat coherent to jumbled and frightened. She says she fought and maybe injured the assailant, but it had been very dark. She did say she could distinctly smell the ocean right up until she blacked out."

Halfway through the translation reading, McNamara threw the paper down on her mahogany slab. "What was the word she kept saying until she died, Kato?"

The traffic cop shuffled his feet. "Well, it's like I said. She may have been rambling due to her dire condition. She died shortly after your conversation?"

McNamara sighed, but not from annoyance. It was an overwhelm of fatigue and shell shock. "Right after."

Kato nodded. "Right up until the repeating word, she started to describe something else. She said it was large, and she mentioned scales. It didn't make sense, to be honest."

"The *word*, Kato. What does '*kaibutsu*' mean in Japanese?"

"Monster."

105

I must keep up my silly façade at the bar. My apartment won't pay for itself, although ripping off an occasional corpse or lifting something from a department store is much easier and time efficient. If I get better at stealing, perhaps I can quit bartending and strictly focus on killing.

Murder is all I can imagine.

No matter how many I do, it's not enough.

I eat, sleep, walk, and drink death.

It is ever constant and all around. My dark art is as present as each passing second. The only difference is the time changes, flowing from one unpredictable moment to the next. I'm stuck on a loop, salivating over what I've already done and will do again. The only time I authentically feel is when I'm in the act. I doubt my perception of feeling matches yours, but then again—maybe it does.

I'm sure you've thought about it, once or twice, in your perfect little world. That one boss who constantly gives you shit, or the boyfriend who cheats on you with a smile on his face.

It's crossed your mind—you'd be lying to yourself otherwise.

I'm infuriated that I didn't get to finish with that jogger slut, and she managed to stick her knife in me. It hurts, but I can't show it. I'll check the newspaper to see if there are any updates.

You're slipping.

"I am not. Leave me alone."

106

The bar is dead tonight. Maverick and Obi are both out with the flu. I've laid low, trying to heal my knife wound and get a slight hold over myself. I've stopped drinking and have laid off the stolen pills. My mind is bent, and my sea creature pesters me nonstop. Her voice can get ugly at times. I sometimes wonder which one of us is the true voice of reason.

She's my strength, but what am I?

You're everything else, angel.

"Mm."

The evening rush hasn't started. Delilah walks in and heads to the back to get dressed. I must be daydreaming. I'm cleaning a beer glass when I hear a voice from behind. I don't know what they say, but when I turn, my knife wound screams at me. It forces me to wince.

"Everything all right, miss?"

The cop.

The woman cop.

The one who hunts me.

I don't understand.

How? It's not possible.

Say something. Act natural.

"Perfect, thanks. What can I get you?"

She must love that pipe. Each time I've seen her, she's been sucking it like it's her last meal.

Maybe I should make that happen.

Easy. . .

She reminds me of a female Dirty Harry. She dresses the same and has a similar build. I will admit she looks more striking up close.

She stares at me dead in the eyes. "You sure? It looks like you're in pain."

"Not me! Just happy to see you. What'll it be?"

Careful. . .

I can tell by looking at her face she's been beaten to the bone. She's grasping at nothing, alone in the pitiful dark.

Turn up the heat. . .

I turn my back to her and grab a fresh beer glass. I pour her the darkest one we have. She looks like a stout gal. We have an Irish elixir that I've learned to pour like perfection. It takes a few extra moments for it to settle just right before I whip around and place it in front of her. "On the house."

She doesn't even look at it. "What for?"

"Looks like you need it." I pour a shot of bourbon for me and raise it in front of her.

What she does next surprises me. She grabs her glass and slings back half the beer in three huge gulps. She then clinks me, and her glass is empty by the time my shot creeps down my throat.

107

Miss Priss Delilah has returned from the back office, ready for the water. She's such an actress, a costume princess playing mermaid.

She is darling, though. I wonder what her insides taste like. . .

"Delilah, could you man the bar for a bit? The police are here."

The pipe smoking pig doesn't seem surprised that I've already sniffed her out. After all, her face is on the news day and night. She *always* says the same garbage. 'We're trying this' and 'that's classified' that. 'Lock your doors and bolt your windows.'

Like that'll stop me. . .

It's all so comical I can hardly stand it.

We take a small table in the back. A few regulars pay and go, leaving no one around but workers.

I want this conversation.

She's obviously struggling.

I mean, look at her. . .

The lady comes off like she hasn't slept in weeks. The fact that I have her little girlfriend all to myself is just *too* good. My left foot begins to shake underneath the table, but I catch it quick.

"What brings you in, officer?"

She gets right to it. "Were you working Sunday night?"

"I can hardly remember my name half the time, if I'm being honest. I'm Ivory . . . Ivory Blake."

Don't put your hand out.

Don't tell me what to do.

I shove my right hand toward her chest. She doesn't take it, instead choosing to pocket away her pipe.

"McNamara. Homicide."

"*Homicide*? Hey, wait a minute—I've seen you on TV."

She leans in uncomfortably close to my face. Her eyes pierce right through me, straight into *us*. She's not scared. "Answer my question."

I bite my lip and cross my legs. She can't see that.

Can't she?

"Let me think. U*h* . . . Sunday, yeah, I did. I've been working a lot these days."

"We have evidence that a patron here was targeted by The Mermaid Killer."

She's lying, fishing for anything. I don't have to entertain any of this. I dodge some more rudimentary questions, small talk bullshit. She asks about Delilah and Obi. She wants reports on who worked on specific days.

"I'm not the boss. He's out sick. I can give you his number."

"I'll get it from downtown."

She gets up to leave as abruptly as I noticed her when she snuck up behind me. She drops a five on the table, paying for the dark beer I said was on the house. She's not all the way turned around before I test her.

"Targeted *how*? Should we be worried?"

I rise, and we square up with each other. I'm surprised at how tall she is. She may have me by an inch or two. I think she's wearing shoes with a slight heel. I'm wearing Chuck Taylors and black shorts. Who cares if it's late December?

She pulls the pipe into view, gripping it in her left hand by the bowl with her thumb and index finger. "*You* . . . worried? Not at all."

I'm certain she discloses what she says next because she has some dumb cop instinct. She's not your average gumshoe.

"A woman was attacked while jogging, out by the Palace of Fine Arts."

Attacked? We slaughtered the little bitch.

"That's awful."

Our noses are practically touching. I enjoy her smoky breath mixed with the Irish beer. I sniff in her intoxicating aroma. She smiles before her next tidbit, a full array of healthy teeth filling a slender face of rugged beauty.

I almost envy her. The *audacity*.

She doesn't wear makeup and still looks good. I want to yank out some of those mouth bones, make her squirm until she begs me to kill her.

"She fought back and survived."

Liar.

"She . . . *survived*?"

"Long enough to make a statement."

"Oh, wow."

She pulls her smoking device to her face, nibbling on the tip. "Yeah— oh, wow. Here's my card. Tell your boss to call me when he gets in."

"Sure thing, officer."

"*Sergeant*. Sergeant McNamara."

She comes off as military trained, perhaps in a previous life before settling down in this hellscape of a city. There's a bravado underneath her classical exterior.

Wade had none of these qualities. He was a sloppy cop, and a bad one at that.

"Sergeant, yes. Thank you."

She heads for the door. "Catch you later, Miss *Blake*."

We can't wait. . .

Everything has changed.

108

McNamara was at her wits' end. The unsolicited interview of Ivory Blake at The Blue Lagoon had been another panicked attempt to gain any sort of traction in the case. Ivory hadn't bent, but Mac had her suspicions.

She was outside the precinct the following day, having lunch by her car. Javier made the best street meat hotdogs in the city. All the cops knew his routine. Each day around one, he'd roll up the sidewalk with his little cart, wafting steam and delicious aromas that would make any mouth water.

Nobody cared that he didn't have a permit to sell his grub.

McNamara hadn't yet eaten, but she'd guzzled a gallon of coffee before craving real sustenance. Javier knew Mac's order. All she had to do was greet him and put up one lanky finger.

"Si, si, Miss Scarlett."

Then he'd get to work, loading the sizzling hotdog with peppers, onions, and jalapenos. Then came the ketchup and extra mayonnaise. He'd pile it up just the way she liked it, wrapping it neatly in two pieces of tinfoil.

She was alone on the sidewalk while she ate, leaning against her Firebird. Her dark aviator sunglasses shielded her eyes from the cloudless, sunny day.

She replayed the Blake interview in her head, searching for anything suspect. Something wasn't right with that girl.

"Excuse me, ma'am?" a male voice asked. He had walked over from the opposite side of the street.

She turned to him with a mouth full of food. "I'm a little busy, pal."

The man remained. His jeans and tight polo shirt gave away his slender frame. "Oh, uh, sorry. It's just . . . I may have something for you about the killer."

The sergeant swallowed hard. She postured up with him feet from the precinct double doors. "Who are you?"

He ran a hand over his forehead. "Can we go inside? I'd rather do this properly."

McNamara looked him over, studying every inch. "Come with me."

~~~~~

They went straight to her office, exchanging formalities along the way.

"What have you got, Mr. Hagerty?"

He sat across from her, his gray eyes almost matching his ponytailed mane of silver ice. "Please, call me Marv."

"Marv, yes."

McNamara eyed his quaking legs. He was nervous.

"Your office has a distinct smell to it. Pipe tobacco?"

"Guilty as charged." McNamara smiled with all her teeth, twirling a pencil in her right hand. "Do you mind?"

The slender man ceased his shaking. He straightened. "No, I think it's lovely. My grandad used to smoke a pipe around the holidays when I was a boy. The smell always reminds me of more pleasant times."

She nodded, allowing him to continue.

"The reason I'm here is . . . I used to work out at Alcatraz Island."

McNamara put down her pencil and folded her hands over her desk. A religious zealot would think she was about to pray. "Used to?"

"I quit two months ago. I was an orderly for ten years."

"May I ask why?"

His face shifted, a subtle angst that the detective zeroed in on. "Let's just say I didn't agree with the facility's recurring practices."

McNamara leaned forward, closing the distance between them. "You island folk have always been hush-hush out there at The Rock. Your lead psychiatrist was murdered."

Marv tilted his head to the floor. "We were told Dr. Jamison passed unexpectedly at home, but the details were never disclosed."

"I see. What else?"

"We had an escaped patient back in July of 1997."

"I thought The Rock was impenetrable. No one has ever escaped and been found alive."

"Correct, ma'am. If you're aware of our practices, you can imagine something of that nature would need to be buried."

"Just like the murder of your head psychiatrist." McNamara found her pipe in her drawer, but she didn't pull it out. Instead, she placed a piece of notepaper in front of her. Marv had said nothing, so she asked, "Who was the escapee?"

"Her name was Holly. Holly St. James."

"Why was she in such a facility?"

Marv began biting his nails. "Records are sealed. Being that we are a psychiatric facility, such sensitive material is difficult to access unless there is solid reason to do so."

"Tell me more about Holly."

"I believe she was shipped to us from another state. I was one of many orderlies for her lengthy stay. She had no criminal record, at least not to my knowledge. I always found her to be reserved and intellectual, like she was constantly reading the room. She received some of the most extreme treatments."

"Why?"

"There was something between her and Dr. Jamison. I never found out what, but they were enemies. He was constantly trying to break her, to push her to show him something he wanted to see."

"I'm not a psychiatrist, Mr. Hagerty. What does this St. James look like?"

"Tall, pretty, fire red hair, and blue eyes. I believe she has a slight accent, but she hid it to near perfection. She also wears prescription glasses."

"How did she escape?"

Marv leaned back, his gaze darting to the floor. "That's the thing, officer. We don't know. There was a security breach, and we think she made it to the roof."

"Did you search the waters out there?"

"Discreetly, but we found nothing but her jumpsuit by our shore. If she braved the waters, the cold would have killed her."

McNamara stopped writing and looked up, staring directly into Marv's soul. "Then she's dead?"

"I may sound insane, but . . ." Marv wrung his hands. "Something tells me she made it off that rock."

"That's pure speculation, Mr. Hagerty. The odds were not in her favor. Do you have a photograph of her? Can I access her files on the island?"

"Unlikely. It was never supposed to get out that she escaped. It would look terrible for the facility's reputation."

"Hmm. I think we're done here, then."

"Yes, ma'am. Thank you for your time."

He stood, but McNamara stopped him. "One last thing, Mr. Hagerty. I could get fired for showing you this, but . . . does this note look like your gal?"

Marv took it with a hesitant hand. It was laminated and had just come back from the lab. Another dead end. "You think the actual killer wrote this to you?"

She worked around his question. "Do you think *she* wrote it? Holly?"

His gray eyes looked over the document, studying its crazed elegance. "Whenever Holly wrote, she used all capital block letters. She was also left-handed. This note is written in cursive and has a slant. Almost looks like a righty did it."

McNamara stood and placed both hands on her hips. "Clever observation, Mr. Hagerty. You might have made a good cop in your day."

"I don't know about that, but I hope you find who's doing this." Marv sighed, as if a small stone from a huge remaining boulder had been lifted off his shoulders. "Thank you for listening to me."

"My pleasure."

McNamara knew The Rock wouldn't disclose any details about their escaped patient, or their murdered shrink. There was something about Marv, though, like he knew he'd made a mistake and was trying to correct it.

It was a long shot, but it seemed she was getting closer to the truth.

109

They've found me.

I don't know how, but they've found me.

The streets have been like a ghost town at night. The moronic cops are desperate. All I see on television is news about my deeds. People are afraid to leave their homes and apartments after dark. The city has toyed with setting a curfew, but it hasn't happened.

I'm not angry that they'll come for me.

In my line of work, this sort of thing is inevitable.

I'm in my lair, finishing an overdue project. A masterpiece, if you will, that has taken a bit longer than expected. I hope they find it, or at least some of it.

I knew this day would come. I've been as careful as someone like *us* can be. I've also been reckless, and I admit that.

I hear sirens in the distance. They could be gunning for somebody else, another shot in the dark to solve the case of the century.

It's just that I've done so much. My body count has become absurd, and each new conquest sets my course for another.

She is *never* satisfied and *never* will be.

My workdays are mundane filler to keep payments on the apartment. The luxury of a safe space to run to fuels my nights of what you people call terrorizing.

Did Marv rat me out?

Good old Marv.

How would he know if I made it off The Rock?

It can't be him.

The bitch that got away, the one at the Palace of Fine Arts, where I was a little too drunk and careless after Snow. Did she figure out who we are? No measly human can identify my queen. She has no fingerprints or traceable data.

Ivory and Holly do.

They took my blood many times while I was imprisoned at The Rock. I don't remember leaving blood or evidence during my ravaging, but I can't be certain.

Fingerprints don't matter, either. *She* has none and disguises mine when we become one.

It's no use trying to figure it out. The fact remains that it's time.

Time to abandon my hive of artful wickedness.

I'll escape.

I always do.

I hear the screeching of tires, radio chatter filling the afternoon air. The tension builds in every cell of *our* body. The sound of flat feet making their way up the single flight to my door grows deafening.

I must go. . .

110

"Five minutes out, Sarge."

McNamara pulled her revolver from her armpit, releasing the lever to expose her loaded six-gun, then smacked the assembly back together. She holstered it and raised both hands to the back of her head, tightening her ponytail until it hurt. "Less talking, more driving."

Fleming did as he was told. Silence ensued, but he soon broke it. "But seriously, partner. How are you so sure this is the one?"

"It's the first woman suspect. It's more than a hunch, Robert." She rarely, if ever, called him by his first name. "Everything the victim from the Palace said. How it was a woman but changed into some other . . . *thing*. Not to mention Hagerty's report on St. James. It's the same girl."

Fleming was trying, but he had to play devil's advocate. "Listen to yourself, Mac. The poor kid in the hospital was dying. We had to get an interpreter to fill her gaps. She couldn't speak a word of English. And about Hagerty . . . the girl drowned. Nobody has *ever* escaped The Rock. That swim is impossible."

"What if she really is a mermaid?"

"Huh?"

"You heard me. Are you getting to a point, Fleming? Don't you remember the surveillance footage from the smut joint on Broadway, or the letter addressed to me that we studied for weeks?"

They were both fighting the car's siren.

He revved up his voice. "You can't honestly believe any of this. That recording didn't show anything. The footage was pixelated and chopped to death. We're wasting our time—*again*. Talks of shapeshifting poetic women and ghouls and goblins. I know you've been through it trying to solve this fucking riddle, boss. We *all* have, but . . . it's a *man*. A big, ugly *man*. No woman is capable of such savagery."

"You *really* don't know women, do you, Robert?"

"Cute, Sarge. Real cute."

"It's her, Robert. It's St. James. Her hair was a different color, and her eyes were somehow darker, but the woman I met in that bar was her."

"Okay, but you tailed her for several days. She wasn't evading or hiding. She basically let you follow her around."

"Just do your job, Fleming."

They were almost there.

III

"Sierra-19, stand by until I give the order."

The morning clouds had nearly burned off, giving way to a cerulean blue. They were in the shit part of the city. The apartment complex had succumbed to homelessness and drug crime.

The perfect cover for a serial killer.

McNamara pulled on her bulletproof vest while standing near the open trunk. The black armor and her white buttoned shirt gave off an impressive contrast.

"You wearing your vest this time?"

Fleming lifted his shirt. "Who needs it? I'm bulletproof."

McNamara reached into the black-and-white, pulling out another vest. "Put it on. That's an order."

Fleming shuffled and rolled his eyes, removing his dark aviator sunglasses. "*Yes, ma'am.*"

There were four cars total on scene. Fleming and McNamara had arrived in the squad car, while two others were loaded with three SWAT officers apiece. The rookie had driven in alone.

"I still can't believe the DA issued this fuck show warrant. Your evidence is as thin as your frame, Mac."

McNamara moved to the opposite side of the car, shielding herself from the main entrance to the beaten down housing complex in her city of tainted gold. They weren't trying to hide. They had rolled right onto the scene with sirens and flashing lights for added confidence.

"Don't make me knock you on your ass, partner. We scored the warrant because we finally have something solid. Hagerty's report gave us a person of interest. Plus, I'm a persuasive bitch."

"You said a mouthful, Marine."

They grinned at each other from opposite sides of the car.

"Be careful, partner."

Fleming drew his Beretta 9mm from his back. He pulled the slide, exposing a fresh hollow point, then winked at his colleague and headed for the door.

112

They all entered except for McNamara. She remained on the outside giving orders via radio. The group of SWAT commandoes entered first, followed by Ramirez and Fleming.

The name Ivory Blake had always come back with nothing. Holly St. James, however, had a face and a history. Only the DA and McNamara's team knew those fresh and crucial details. She was presumed dead after her escape, but the sergeant knew better.

The landlord of the complex was as old as time. All he gave was a young woman lived alone in the apartment one floor up in his land of degenerates. He said nothing about her, stating she paid rent in cash and kept to herself.

"Oscar-14, report."

The rookie's channel. There was garble and a sound of heavy footfalls. "Oscar-14. We're at the front door."

"Police! Open your door!"

Knocking could be heard as Ramirez clicked off his radio signal.

"Alpha-7, report."

She remained out front, using her car as a shield. Her job was to make sure the perp didn't flee. The only way out besides the front door entrance was a small bedroom window. It was a ten-foot drop down to an alleyway.

"Speak, Alpha-7."

Fleming entered her ear. "She's either not coming to the door or nobody's home. I smell something ripe, like old fish or hot garbage. I can't tell—"

"Break it down."

McNamara couldn't stand the tension. Sweat had broken out underneath her arms and now dripped down her sides. A small crowd of onlookers had formed by the clustered police cars. Traffic was heavy in this section of the city. Everything from hobos, tourists, and walking suits and ties were littered all over. The flow of cars was moderate, but not a standstill. A packed cable car lumbered by, followed by a city bus. The number on the bus was 2525.

"Alpha-7, report."

Nothing.

"Oscar-14?"

The rookie responded. His voice was frantic and high-pitched. "Sarge, there's *bodies*—and *bones!* The smell. . . I think I'm going to be sick. I think she's in the—"

McNamara sprinted from her position. She nearly barreled over an old woman crossing in front of the dilapidated apartments. Right as she entered, a shockwave rocked the foundation. There was a mini sonic boom, throwing the sergeant off her feet and onto her face. Smoke billowed and crept down the staircase to her immediate right. The small apartment window shattered, glass cascading down to the street.

As her face smashed into the floor, she was catapulted back to the desert.

113

'1991'

"McNamara!"

Mac stopped eating her chow. She'd landed in Iraq two days ago. She was the newest recruit in the Operation Desert Storm unit, squeezed fresh from the Marine Corps grinder. Her commander had startled her, almost causing her to choke on her peas.

She swallowed and got to her boots. "Sir!"

"We're heading out. It'll be simple intel and translation. We'll have four HMVs in tow. You'll be crammed in the second vehicle. Now's your chance to see the real Kuwait, freshman. Get your ass back to your bunk and grab your gear. We leave at 0800."

McNamara saluted. "Sir, yes sir!"

The ride was gritty, the air stifling. The crew inside the vehicle was McNamara, her commander Spencer, an Afghani translator in American fatigues, and another Marine named Hoyt.

"Hoyt! Hey, Hoyt!"

He looked through Spencer, not paying attention. He had his earphones in, jamming out to some heavy metal garbage. They were packed like sardines in the rugged tank, but the soldiers had made their proper adjustments for the assignment.

McNamara leaned over and whacked Hoyt's leg.

"Christ. Relax, rookie!"

"Address your commanding officer, Lieutenant."

Hoyt didn't even have his helmet on. He looked around for it in the bumpy tank car. He didn't bother to look at her, but he did rub his leg and wince. "I'm *also* your commanding officer, Mac. *Fuck*, you hit like a goddamn guy!"

Spencer stopped the stupidity. "Cool it, both of you. McNamara's right. Ditch the music for five seconds of your life, Hoyt."

Hoyt squished his blonde hair inside the helmet he'd finally found. "Come on, Spence. It's not like we're about to see any action. It's all paperwork and translation on this shit mission."

"Either way, listen up. We'll be in town in thirty minutes. Samir needs to translate some information with a leader or two. We've got new intel about some heavy shit potentially going down soon. The CIA will be assisting him via telecom."

Mac smiled. "That's why we're lined up in this fancy conga line all the way to town, eh?"

"Affirm, Mac. We'll take all the help we can get, even on a strict intel mission."

Spencer's radio alerted him. "Commander, a rogue motorcycle approaching from the west."

The road was narrow with nowhere to go, surrounded by high and jagged rocks on each side.

Another squawk rang out from his chest radio. "He's strapped with explosives. He's a fucking suicide—"

BOOM!!!

The explosion sent the heavy tank skyward, flipping it onto its side. The sound fractured the tiny airspace from inside, causing one of the doors to fly completely off its hinges. Everyone went careening into each other, smashing into metal and their fellow soldiers.

Samir was nearly thrown from the vehicle, but he hit his head on the roof, which saved him from being tossed into the sunny desert.

Everything went silent.

Dead silent.

114

'1999'

McNamara shook her head free and fought back to the chaotic present. She got to her feet with a heaving breath.

The world slowed almost to death, as if each passing second was being strangled to its breaking point. Screams and yelling came from all directions, inside and outside the building. She looked back toward the front door. The old woman was down on her face, not moving.

Her partner. Her team.

Mac's head swam as if a rickety fishing boat had suddenly entered choppy waters. She was bleeding but didn't know from where. She wiped the dripping crimson from her face, but it merely smeared and burned in her right eye.

Her radio lay a few feet away in the smoke and dust. It had taken damage. It must've hit a wall after being flung from her hand.

She grabbed it anyway. "Alpha-7 . . . Alpha-7, report!"

The device made a flatline beeping sound.

She tried again.

It sputtered with discontent.

She shook it and threw it into the smoky abyss.

"FUCK!"

The battered sergeant pulled her revolver from her left armpit and staggered up the exploded staircase.

115

There were ten steps in all. Each one seemed like a fresh slab of quicksand. Mac's left knee throbbed, a reminder that adrenaline was spiking and dipping at a nauseating speed. She could see only thick white smoke ravaging the tiny airspace. She covered her mouth with her right hand—the same hand in which she held her heavy gun. On the seventh step, she choked, the dust and debris stifling her already damaged smoker's lungs.

There was more space when she finally reached the top of the staircase. The smoke thinned some, offering a mediocre view of the hallway ahead. As she turned, she tripped on something heavy, causing her to nearly face-plant again. She looked down with her gun pointing at the ceiling.

It was one of her SWAT team. He was down, not moving.

A fresh pool of blood had settled beneath the center of his body. He was laid out on his stomach while the red poured from his midsection. His helmet was on, and his dark clothes and gloves remained intact.

She kicked his leg, but he offered nothing.

Glancing forward, Mac saw another commando down. He was in front of what used to be the suspect's front door. He was on his butt with his back to the adjacent wall. The sturdy barrier was smashed and caved in, as if he weighed a thousand pounds. He was helmetless, his head slouched down to the right.

He looked as though he was merely taking a nap.

In fact, he was dead.

"Fleming! Ramirez!"

Nothing but the incessant whirring of fire alarms responded. They kicked on late from several apartments down the hall. One was a constant whine; another did an on-off howl. The competing sounds pierced her already fragile skull. Blood trickled down her face and nose, making its way to the destroyed floor beneath her.

"Partner! Answer *me*!" Her voice cracked and lost its pitch, giving away her crumbling spirit.

It suddenly smelled of rot and decay. She'd always had a strong stomach, but this stench was unlike anything she'd ever experienced. She swallowed down vomit and inched toward what remained of the apartment's front door.

Another explosion would blow her limb from limb.

Her past had come back to haunt her. The pointless desert war had risen from the grave to finish her off, to cement its bidding.

She longed to run. To dash outside and regroup. Get to a phone and call for help.

What if Fleming is still alive? What if Ramirez needs me? What if this bastard killer is still in there, waiting to kill us all?

A door flung open from down the hall. A hefty figure entered the hallway in a blur.

"What the holy hell is going on out here?"

She could barely see, but the voice was undoubtedly male. "Back inside! Call the police!"

He hesitated and stood there, an unbelieving skull with eyeballs in a silk bathrobe. His eyes went to the lanky officer with her gun and her downed colleague. "Y-yes, ma'am!"

The door slammed.

Mac brought her left hand up and gripped her handgun with both hands. She cocked the hammer and disappeared alone inside the apartment of death.

116

The apartment door was blown clean off its hinges, while the burning stink had become unbearable. She knew what rot smelled like. Her convoy in Desert Storm had come upon a mass grave during a hot day in July.

She doubled over only a few steps inside. A fresh pool of vomit splashed the floor at her feet. McNamara wretched several times as her eyes filled with water and her stomach contracted. Snot and barf dangled in ropes down her chin.

She gripped her gun so tightly her hands shook, as if the world was getting ready to crack open and sink everything into oblivion. Her senses were on planet infinity, dying to take over due to her ugly concussion.

The fire alarms ceased, giving way to a deathly silence.

"Fleming! Ramirez!"

She made the first corner that entered the living room. She hugged the wall and threw her gun out into the void. The kitchen was attached, separated by a flimsy open wall designed to be a small bar. A fire roared and crackled from the kitchen. It was contained, but it raged with sickening delight.

McNamara inched toward the flame ball. Before she reached the kitchen, she caught half a body lying on the far end. It was only the lower half. The rest of the unfortunate soul was no longer attached.

It looked to be the rookie Ramirez.

She found the rest of him near the initial blast zone near the microwave. He had been standing right next to it when it blew. The upper portion of the freshman officer was unrecognizable. Some of him was charred black, other parts a bloody pulp. His intestines were strewn about the area, scattered here and there. Some of him dangled from a trash can in the kitchen corner, while other organs were littered around.

She wiped sweat from her brow and backtracked, her attention drawn to a chair in the middle of the room. It was a maniacal construction held together with human bones and glossy flesh.

She couldn't believe what she was seeing. The air remained suffocating, as if being in the general vicinity of such mayhem was enough to kill.

She stopped in the middle of the room and noticed a dinner plate in another corner. Maggots and roaches covered it, making squishing noises in their own morbid dance routine. The unfinished meal looked like half of a human brain. A butter knife stuck straight up from it, as if someone had stabbed it there just to see if it would stick.

"*FLEMING!*"

A gurgle filled the air. She could barely zero in on it.

"M-Mac."

The bedroom door remained in perfect condition. It was slightly ajar. McNamara kicked it in.

It was her partner.

He was down on his side a few feet inside. Pieces of floppy cardboard and a heavy sheet covered the window, making it dark although it was afternoon.

She was greeted by the cursive pink neon above the bed:

'hell here'

She was so concerned with Fleming that she hardly noticed the figure in the bed. She wanted to unload her revolver but did not. Her finger massaged the cold trigger, but she did not squeeze.

"POLICE! Show me your hands!"

No movement.

The mass was covered with a thick blanket of ragged sable. She went right for it, nearly stumbling over her own two feet. She ripped the sheet away, revealing a sight that wasn't designed to be seen by a rational human person.

She heaved again, but there was nothing left to throw up.

It was a torso, undeniably male. The arms and legs had been severed. A huge incision had been made from sternum to groin, opening to all the slimy contents that made up humanity.

The bed was soaked with blood.

A whiff of fresh shit filled her nose.

McNamara turned away and ran to Fleming. She dropped to a knee and set her revolver on the floor. It hit the hardwood with a solid thud. Her partner was in one piece, but he did *not* look good. Most of his face was covered in ash and blood. Several fingers on his left hand were missing. A trail of vermilion had followed him into the bedroom. He had crawled inside after the explosion.

Fleming choked and tried to talk. His silver crew cut caught a reflection in the chilling pink neon.

"Easy, partner. I'm here." McNamara checked his vitals. His heart rate was weak and fluttering. He was bleeding from somewhere, but she couldn't tell where.

He managed a whisper. "S-She was . . . here."

"How do you know, Robert?"

His eyes were closed, but he opened them and looked at her. "A h-hunch. G-Guess you and I aren't s-so . . . different."

"I *need* to get you help, Robert."

His entire body constricted, followed by a choke and a frightening wheeze. He was being suffocated by his own blood. "Forget all that. You n-need to go."

She looked for his radio but couldn't find it. "Don't move, partner. I'm going for help."

His gaze pierced through her soul as he shook his head. Then he closed his eyes and mumbled, "You were right, Mac. You were . . . *right.*"

Fleming's head dropped back to the wooden floor. His chest made one last surrendering heave.

And McNamara's partner of four years died in her arms.

117

McNamara's team was dead.

She was alone, almost murdered herself by the sadistic Mermaid Killer. She placed a blood-soaked hand over her partner's forehead, hoping to ease his journey to the netherworld.

As she rose and turned to go, her eyes met a closet on the other side of the room. The sliding doors were closed, and the paint was chipped in the corners. It had once been white, but the undercoat of dark brown was showing through. Newspaper clippings and polaroid pictures were mounted on the double doors. They appeared to have been nailed on in a haphazard type of shrine. Many clippings were of the various un-solved city murders, while some of the taken pictures depicted mutilated bodies and chopped-up parts. Most of the photos looked to have been shot inside the apartment.

McNamara continued studying and settled her defeated eyes on a paper clipping of herself. The city had done a spread on her right after she was assigned lead detective on the case. She hadn't wanted to do the piece, but it had been Captain's orders.

The Marine sergeant moved in and placed her hand on the right-side edge of the closet door. There was no handle, but instead an ugly gold bar that protruded outward to assist in opening and closing.

Her gun remained down by her side.

She pulled the door open and almost dropped her weapon.

"Oh, *Elsa*. . ."

It was her.

Her lovely Elsa.

She had disappeared one night without a trace.

Elsa had been transformed into a doll. She was frozen, Indian-style and naked, stuffed into the small confines like a trophy piece. She was sitting on a tiny stool. Thick candles that had burned out or were on the verge surrounded her.

They were red and smelled of cinnamon gum.

Elsa didn't look real. She looked like a wax figurine, as perfect as the ones a tourist would see at the Rainforest Café near Pier 93. She was sewn together at various sections of her body. Her killer had taken their time, going as far as covering her entire body with a thick glaze-like substance.

McNamara sobbed as she touched her girlfriend's face. It was hard and smooth, a sickening display of gruesome savagery. Elsa's eyes had been removed, replaced with what were presumably big white marbles. They'd been painted in meticulous fashion, nearly resembling her real eyes of warm amber.

She wanted to embrace her lover and carry her away from the devil's lair. She tried moving her, but she was heavy and glued to the stool. Maybe she would stay there and never leave, fall away into hell with her darling. But she merely cried, crouched down while caressing the body of wax.

A note was affixed to her chest, stabbed clean through the heart with a screwdriver.

McNamara plucked the note away. She was gentle, not wanting to harm her partner any further. She brought the faded white paper to her face.

'YOU'VE FAILED, PIG. SHE'S ALL MINE.'

The all-caps message felt like a bullet to the heart.

It was scrawled in blood.

Elsa's blood.

The note was signed 'MK' with the familiar symbol of the mermaid that had destroyed her city.

McNamara crumpled up the evil art and gave Elsa a final goodbye kiss. Then she rose and relaxed the hammer on her cocked weapon, pulling herself together before she made her way back through the carnage and stumbled out onto the swarming street.

118

Would you like to know how easy it is to make a homemade bomb? With the power of the revolutionary internet, it's never been simpler!

I made two, one with explosive chemicals that I placed in the microwave on a timer. I tried to make another one out of a pressure cooker. That one took some doing, but I rigged them as best I could. I also added several canisters of gasoline in the kitchen, hoping for maximum damage.

The only real obstacle was timing.

I had to be sure they were coming for me.

I was still inside my apartment as the cops banged at my door.

We could smell them.

Yes, but they were also loud and sloppy.

One of their radios chirped right before they tried the door. I was out the bathroom window before the explosion hit. It was *so* loud and amazing I was laughing as I hit the pavement in the vacant alleyway. The drop down was significant, but I landed on my feet.

The lady cop had been following me for a week, shortly after our conversation at The Blue Lagoon. The tails were pathetic, and *we* could see her from a mile off. I allowed her to follow me home one night. I knew she didn't have any substantial evidence against me. Even the media had said the jogger bitch was dead. Nothing she claimed about that night had made the news.

I hope she enjoys what *we've* done with the place!

119

"*D*rive—or I'll kill you."

It's minutes after the explosion as pandemonium breaks out on the street. A car accident has blocked the whole way down Geary Street. A delivery truck and a small rice rocket have collided after my glorious BANG!

People are down on their faces in the street. A mob of pedestrians is on the other side by a disgusting Chinese food restaurant.

The cabbie doesn't respond, even with the gun in his face. He nods, and I sneak in the backseat.

"Wah?"

He's asking 'where.'

"The fire bridge. Go."

We make it a few blocks. The only sirens I hear are moving away from us. They're responding to my funhouse. A firetruck rolls by, lights going and whistles blaring, with a woman firefighter holding on at the back.

I take the pistol I scored off that rapist piggy and jam it into my driver's temple.

His head leans against the grain, but he doesn't say a thing.

"Don't you want to know who I am?"

He shakes his head, like a child refusing a shot at a doctor's office.

I take offense to that.

I push my glasses up with my free hand. "I'm the one all over the TV. The one your shit city can't stop talking about."

No response. Either he doesn't want to know, or he can't understand.

"You speak English or *what*?"

A red light approaches, along with a thick blanket of fog in the near distance.

"Don't stop."

We blow through the light, narrowly avoiding a red pickup with off-road tires. I don't have a plan except to get over the bridge and out of the city. I can regroup once I'm gone. We're speeding straight for the fog; it will assist with my escape. I sit back and try to relax.

I hear the siren. This one isn't moving away.

I fling my head around to look out the back window. My hair is down, tucked messily into a black sweatshirt. Some of it sweeps over into my line of vision.

The motorcycle appears like a rumbling specter. I watch it lurch out from Ashbury and pull hard right. It nearly collides with a car, but it doesn't stop. The engine revs to a squeal as it gets closer and closer. I turn my body all the way around to face it, staring out the back window.

"No."

No. . .

She's survived and is all over *us*.

It's just her, her dark hair whipping in the afternoon air. She wears no helmet and flaunts a look that I almost envy. She gains fast right up until the fog bank. We pierce through it and are transported into another realm. The scattered sunlight gives way to gray and drizzle.

That's how this city works. One block can be sunshine and rainbows, the next shadows and bums and living corpses shooting heroin in the gutters.

I whip back to my driver as the lady cop enters our world of gray haze. It doesn't seem to faze her, the police lights glowing red and white in the eerie murk.

I go to hit my mute driver in the back of the head to make him go faster, but he slams on the brakes. My body flies into his seat, nearly smacking our heads together. I peer over the console and see a huge traffic jam. We're on a one-way street, a single block away from my intended target. I can barely see her golden silhouette hovering like a gorgeous menace on the outskirts of my city of blood.

I must go.

I *also* need to test out this gun.

"Thanks for the lift!"

I pull the trigger.

The bullet goes straight through the back of his head and out the front windshield, shattering it. He goes limp and slouches down onto the steering wheel, causing the horn to honk. His blood sprays all over me, splattering throughout the tight space as if a sloppy abstract painter flung red paint all over the car.

All this excitement makes me giggle.

I open the door and get out in time to watch the lady cop lay down her motorcycle. The fog is so dense that visibility is near impossible. She somehow jumps from it as the bike crashes to the asphalt on its left side.

I wish she was going faster.

I raise my gun toward her as she tumbles in the street. She disappears for a moment, smacking her body into the rough pavement. I have a good shot, but a big white truck pulls up and shields her from harm.

It looks as though it ran her over.

Let's hope so.

I lower my weapon and run.

120

The traffic thins. My lungs scream while I heave breaths of moist coastal air. The driver asshole's blood is everywhere!

It feels so good.

I wipe some of him away with my right hand, causing the firearm in my grip to make a metallic clicking sound. The bridge is right here. She glows as her pillars stretch into the cloudy heavens. They disappear with the thickness of the dark, eating huge sections all around me.

I flee until I need to walk, using the bridge's sidewalk to my immediate right. It's a long path for bikers and joggers to traverse the bridge, providing a golden opportunity to jump cities.

Almost there, angel.

I'm livid that everything has boiled down to this. The answer to how I've been found will always evade me. I've made mistakes and have been impulsive, allowing my compulsions to rule me to the point of utter madness.

I regret *nothing*, even while I run for my life.

The air is chilled, but there is no wind. The fog hangs around like a ravenous blanket, ready to hide anything in its gothic wake. No cars approach in my intended direction. I still can't see far in front of me, but I know I'm almost all the way across. I lumber like a madman by cyclists and tourists, causing them to gasp when they realize I'm covered in blood and waving a gun.

A sick grin contorts *our* face as I notice the flashing lights ahead. They're faint but grow to horrific intensity. These aren't headlights, but a red and blue symphony blocking my escape. Police cars from the neighboring city have been tipped off, boxing me in.

I have no choice but to turn back.

I'm so tired from all the running I could just lie down and give up.

We don't give up.

The light rain grows heavier back the way I've come. I must be near the halfway mark on this bridge of fire. I run by a lady walking with her son. They didn't see me because they were heading back in the same direction as me.

Here comes that sound—that . . . motorcycle sound.

Her.

The lonely headlamp approaches in the thick mist. It gets clearer until she emerges from the wet haze. She slams on the brakes and dismounts the bike.

I only have a second to react. I turn back to the mom and kid I just ran by. I grab the little fuck by his arm and drag him away from her.

"My God! What are you doing?"

I point the gun at her. She drops to her knees and sobs like a dog.

"*Mommy*?!"

I want to silence her forever, but I need the bullets. I stare down at the boy. He's no more than ten or eleven. I think he looks right into *us* because his eyes get big and he screams. I press my gun to his sandy blond hair that dangles into his face above his eyebrows. The barrel presses squarely between his eyes.

"Don't give us any shit!"

He's easy to manipulate because he goes slack after looking into *our* eyes. I wrench him by the arm and pull him back to where the king shit cop is waiting. She stands in the middle lane of the wide bridge of red, her huge revolver outstretched in both hands.

I yank the kid closer to me, backing up to the very edge of the railing. I look down, then behind me, to nothing but a murky abyss, a watery descent into the unknown. A far-out ship makes a sound that ships make. A flock of seabirds fly overhead and squawk. The wind seems to suddenly stand still, as if time wants to quit its insufferable tick.

I lock my eyes on her.

She takes a limping step toward us.

We pick the kid up like a rag doll.

He sort of squeaks as he's lifted, not comprehending *our* strength. He's become my shield, my pint-sized meat puppet to protect *us* from the blue blood in *our* way, attempting to crumble *our* empire of damnation. I wrench my gun into him, in the crease on the left side of his neck. His entire body is being handled by *our* other arm.

He smells yummy.

I lick his face, all the way up his jawline to his temple. He tastes of damp fear and salty tears, an orgasmic combination of innocent dread. He has completely given up in my arms.

I scowl back at her, this thorn in my side that will *not* stop.

A rogue angel up against the epitome of evil.

It's just *us*—and her.

121

"Release the boy."

We're close enough for shouting to become unnecessary. She could have, but we've shattered her spirit to pieces.

"Did you like my funhouse . . . *Sergeant?*"

Her grip remains steady on her firearm. It's zeroed right on me, an unflinching menace fit to explode. She disregards my question along with my smile of death.

I loathe being ignored.

"Drop your weapon and step away from the ledge. Let the boy go."

"You're not very bright, are you, *cop?*"

I shift my squirming pet from my center mass to other vital parts of my body, providing the aiming officer nothing to fire at.

She cocks the hammer of her gun.

The sound alone can be heard for miles, as the mechanical click echoes down to the choppy grave water below. It's hundreds of feet down, proving practical suicide.

My eyes roll over black as I hiss at her, a roar of utmost superiority.

I don't understand her response. *We* simply can't believe it.

The battered officer in her long coat that's been ravaged by asphalt raises her head and stares into *us*.

I don't know what's happening. It's as if she sees us both. *All* of us.

She's not horrified and does not shrink away. Her eyes begin to glow, as if her warm hazel orbs are trying to match my pitiful black. She shifts her weight like she wants to take another step forward.

"*Don't*! One more step and I'll send this kid straight to hell!"

She stops advancing with a wince, indicating she's been badly injured during all our fun. She lowers her weapon, releasing the double-fisted aggression. The gun dangles limply at her right side. She gently raises her free hand, attempting to comfort the kid. "You're all right, son. I'm with the police."

How cute.

"You have no idea what you're up against, do you, *Sergeant?*"

Her messy ponytail dangles over the same shoulder as her resting gun. The hammer remains cocked. "Point the gun at me, Ivory. Point it at me."

"Ha! Is *that* my name?"

"That's what you told me when we met."

"Stupendous work, Sarge!"

Her arm flinches as I whip the gun out toward her. She doesn't move.

"That was a mistake . . . *Mac*."

"You seem to know a lot about me."

"I know you've been chasing something you can't comprehend."

She smiles at *us*, but it's not out of spite. I don't know how I know that, but I do. "I'll give it a go, once you're put away forever."

I hear more sirens. They're now on both sides of the bridge, but the fog is so thick I can't see. It doesn't sound like they're advancing.

We'll kill them all!

"You've got me all wrong, cop. I'm *never* going back in a box to rot. I'm so much more than that. I mean—look at all we've done in such a short time!"

She wants to crumble before us, to abandon the bravado and realize she's already lost. I've taken her lover and played until she couldn't take any more.

She was so much fun to own.

McNamara responds, an unflinching pillar in a thicket of gray, "You've destroyed my city. I have nothing left to lose."

I have a good shot at her. Her gun is down, and she looks ready to die right here on the bridge.

Now.

"Don't do this, *Holly*."

Do it.

"I think I'll kill you both!"

I have her dead.

The fog becomes denser than ever.

A bellow of thunder cracks above, readying to give way to a skyward deluge. I move to squeeze the trigger as the lady cop swings her gun back up toward *us*. The kid sees it because he tries to wrench himself free from our grip. We fire simultaneously as lightning bolts zigzag behind her, causing a hazy flash of yellow blur.

The cop falls backward and strikes her head on the concrete. Her gun goes flying.

I hear her moan like she's been hit, but my world has turned completely upside down.

Her bullet misses the kid and rips through my right shoulder, spinning me around as the molten lead exits my back. I still hold the gun and the kid, but it's too late for me. The ledge is short as I start to go over. The kid breaks free, but I throw my hand out and corral him.

I grab the hood on his little red sweatshirt.

He squeals as we both go over together.

I make no sound—there's nothing left to say.

The gunshot wound to my shoulder doesn't hurt.

Everything happens so fast.

I see the kid in blurry flashes while we tumble—down, down, down.

Down into a watery grave.

I lose my grip on him and desperately try to raise my gun to shoot him before we hit the water. I unload several shots, but I think I've hit nothing. I land face first, as if I've been crushed by an oncoming freight train.

It all goes black.

122

"Lie back, Sarge. You're going to be all right."

McNamara felt like she'd been forced to drink hot lava. The bullet went just under her vest and lodged inside her steaming guts. She writhed on the cold ground at the feet of the Bridge of Fire. Her smoking revolver lay just out of reach.

A talking figure in street clothes kneeled over her, dangling a gleaming badge, nearly hypnotizing her to death.

"K-*Kato*."

"I'm here, Sarge. EMS is two minutes out."

She was sprawled on her side but shifted to her back, howling in agony. She tried to sit up and reach for her water-speckled revolver.

Her freshman colleague grabbed her hand, stopping her.

"The . . . boy?"

"He went over with your mermaid. We're combing the sea for the bodies. I'm . . . sorry."

123

'2030'

"Nanuk cua natook."

"Tuk tuk slagoot?"

I cannot comprehend the sound of these voices; however, within my mind, I understand.

I can't see anything. I think my eyes are closed.

The last thing I remember is. . .

"Tuk tuk slagoot!"

My eyes open, as if opening them for the very first time. I'm hovering above a slab, strapped in midair by glowing restraints. I can move my head, but that's it. The first thing I notice is all my hair has turned gray.

The things standing over me are unbelievable. They fill me with a feeling that's nothing short of dreadful. They appear as giant squids, these slimy organisms that dominate the metallic undertow.

I look for my bullet wound, but it is no longer there.

Where are *you*, my goddess?

They pierce into my brain, knocking down the heavy door that is my skull. They speak gibberish, but my mind hurts with their forced clarity.

Do you understand?

You're inside my head.

Do you . . . understand!?

My mouth is dry. I look down at my naked self. I can tell I've aged some years, but with grace.

"What is this?"

An invisible dagger pierces me between the eyes. A loud slap and the slither of tentacles smack my breast and run down my leg. I don't fight.

Where is *she?*

You're missing the point.

What is the point? Send me back.

We cannot. We can only replay what you've done.

Is this my death?

This is a construct, an in-between. Your world no longer exists.

Why would I care?

Your actions spawned many after you, helping the inevitable destruction of your kind.

What day is it?

Your question holds no relevance.

I don't understand.

This is your final chance . . . to repent.

Never.

It feels like I'm being surgically cut, but with no instruments. My hideous captors are doing it with their elaborate minds. My body turns rigid as I thrash in my restraints of electricity.

"Stop!"

We have allowed you to see; to re-construct what you've done. The choice is now yours.

I feel nothing.

The second creature wraps itself around my neck. The slimy appendage pulsates and lights up. I hallucinate and am thrown back to one of my "crimes." I begin to feel—to feel so much pain and remorse I can't stand it, watching myself murder and maim.

"It hurts!"

This is what human empathy feels like. You must repent, or you will be thrown into a realm with nothing but pain.

"Good!"

We cannot send you back. Your world is no more. The ones like you have destroyed it. We are unbothered by your plight. Your oceans remain—that's where we have survived.

"*Unhand me!*"

My queen, *you're* here.

We thrash together, combining our strengths to release the chokehold.

They're laughing—laughing at *me*!

I look down and see *her*.

My body hardens, a scaly armor that bends the restraints. My eyes blacken, throwing a red glow over my alien prison. My mermaid tail whips, causing the foreign current to short and spark. I scream and use all *our* strength, destroying the last strap.

I rise. My legs come back under me, and the aquatic things shrink away. I face them transformed, puffing steaming breaths with jagged razors for teeth. My hands outstretch, flaunting long, thick knives for nails.

The sea belongs to *me*.

Kill them all.

Epilogue

Sergeant Scarlett McNamara received a medal and promotion, ringing in the year 2000 with the golden key to the city. She recovered from her wounds; however, the psychological scars of war, along with the worst day of her life, would always remain.

There was no closure for her efforts that day.

Perhaps those feel-good stories aren't designed for soldiers or officers.

The headlines gloated that a lone wolf sergeant with nerves of steel single-handedly hunted and killed the most notorious serial murderer in American history. The boy was recovered a week later. Sharks and other sea creatures had done a number on his bloated little body.

The city police called for federal and state assistance for the additional search of unpredictable waters surrounding the infamous Golden State. They searched for months, racking up millions in extra labor costs and state funding debt.

The city could finally sleep better at night, at least for a short while.

People roamed the streets like before, and businesses eased back into staying open late. They did so out of certainty that no human being could have survived such a fall.

It was suicide; plus, she'd been shot.

Her blood had been found on the bridge railing. Efforts with new DNA methods attempted to concretely identify the elusive madwoman, although her identity remained a mystery. The blood was contaminated, a medical anomaly that experts could not scientifically understand.

Any raw evidence left by Holly St. James was nonexistent.

No fibers, hairs, nothing.

Her written manifesto was buried away in her fiery apartment floorboards, just like her father's diary before her. The text was studied and marveled at right up until the skies fell and the cities crumbled and descended into the oceans. The whole of humanity was extinguished by either God or Mother Nature's wrath in the year 2029. The world became ruled by water, endless miles of watery deep.

Up until that fateful year, copycats sprang to life, racking up monumental human destruction after Y2K. With the combination of remaining missing persons and other bodies found after the infamous bridge incident, The Mermaid Killer's body count was never authenticated.

The experts guessed 47 people had been murdered in the short two-and-a-half-year spree.

The Mermaid Killer's body was never recovered.

THE END